Praise for S

"*Finding Destiny* unfolds a gripping story of intertwining lives that will inspire the reader to tears of anguish, tears of joy and ultimately, revelation. Lessons are learned in forgiving the past and forging the future with the inner strength that comes from trusting one's self and one's destiny. The novel's complex characters are fully fleshed out until they come alive, and Sinor's exquisite writing style paints pictures in poetic prose that lingers in the mind to be savored again and again. We witness the heroines overcome guilt, fear, and glimpse at how the Universe can work for one's highest good and growth. When the novel's journey has wound to an end, it leaves the reader wanting more—I am looking forward to a sequel!"

~Paula B. Slater, M.A., Paula Slater Sculpture, author
Beyond Words: A Lexicon of Metaphysical Thought

"*Finding Destiny* mesmerizes as it wraps itself around your heart. Two women—each on opposite spectrums of the journey of self-discovery–find their lives intertwined in a most unusual way. The entertaining storyline prompts the reader to delve into the depths of their own consciousness. *Finding Destiny* contains all the elements of a heartwarming novel with rich characters and plot, synchronicities, and a healthy dose of a mesmerizing sea. "

~Trisha Faye, author
A Second Chance and *My Wildest Dream*

"*Finding Destiny* invites us to find inspiration and to remember the interconnectedness of all things. One question asks the reader, 'When we fall in love, where does the love come from?' This in itself is a great starting point for a reading group; I would love to discuss this question with the author straight away. *Finding Destiny* addresses the reader's self-awareness, and Sinor nudges us gently to continue our journey of finding our own personal destiny. Reading the book felt like watching a movie; nail-biting moments, tears, and goosebumps—all the ingredients a good Hollywood movie needs!"

~Barbara Patterson, *Soul Matters* Radio, Germany

"Finding Destiny goes beneath the skin, down to the internal turmoil and sacrifices of two women a half century and oceans apart as they, with their best conscience, make life changing and altering decisions. Reader's will enjoy Sinor's unique gift of sharing these stories, without bias, as the women discover the long term effects of the paths chosen."

~Mary Catherine O'Heart, RN, RScP

"Finding Destiny is the story of two strong, fiercely-determined women living a world apart but inextricably linked by love. Their compelling journeys inspire faith in the power of women to overcome and triumph over the worst of life's societal blows."

~Lin Waterhouse, author
West Plains Dance Hall Explosion

"Finding Destiny opens readers' minds to the reality that no matter our age or location, we are all walking toward our true destiny. Sinor's book gives us permission to overcome challenges, fight for what we want, and live on purpose."

~Robin Marvel, author
Life Check: 7 Steps to Balance Your Life!

"Finding Destiny is an engaging book, exploring connections of people separated by time and space. As a woman who has experienced unplanned pregnancy, I was especially appreciative of the exploration of themes regarding how these women dealt with their decisions about an unexpected pregnancy, and how those decisions affected their lives. *Finding Destiny* is a positive book, filled with insights and stories of growth and adventure."

~Juanita Emery, M.A., Health Practitioner

BARBARA SINOR PhD

Marvelous Spirit Press

Ann Arbor • London • Sydney

2nd Printing January 2017

Library of Congress Cataloging-in-Publication Data

Names: Sinor, Barbara, 1945- author.
Title: Finding destiny / Barbara Sinor.
Description: Ann Arbor : Marvelous Spirit Press, 2016.
Identifiers: LCCN 2016013263| ISBN 9781615992997 (pbk. :
alk. paper) | ISBN
   9781615993000 (hardcover : alk. paper)
Subjects: | GSAFD: Occult fiction | Love stories
Classification: LCC PS3619.I57625 F56 2016 | DDC 813/.6--
dc23
LC record available at https://lccn.loc.gov/2016013263

Distributed by Ingram (USA/CAN/AUS), Bertram's Books
(UK/EU)

Published by Marvelous Spirit Press, an imprint of
Loving Healing Press
5145 Pontiac Trail
Ann Arbor, MI 48105

Tollfree 888-761-6268 (USA/CAN   FAX 734-663-6861
www.MarvelousSpirit.com
info@MarvelousSpirit.com

    Permission to use text from *Ships and Havens* by Henry Van
Dyke is gratefully acknowledged.
    Cover photo by Tracey Clark. Used with permission.
    All other referenced text is used with permission under the
"Fair Use" requirements with grateful acknowledgement.

Dedication

The storyline within *Finding Destiny* can be found in every culture. The hardships women face regarding rape and/or an unplanned pregnancy can be traced from generation to generation throughout time. Women face their destiny regarding sexuality, rape, pregnancy, and motherhood with fearlessness and sometimes regrettable choices. It is time in this Twenty-first Century to support all women and their unrelenting journey for acceptance.

I dedicate this book to those women who have experienced any of the struggles found within these pages. You are the true heroines of your destiny.

Also by Barbara Sinor, Ph.D.

Beyond Words: A Lexicon of Metaphysical Thought

Gifts from the Child Within

An Inspirational Guide for the Recovering Soul

Addiction: What's Really Going On?

Tales of Addiction and Inspiration for Recovery

The Pact: Messages from the Other Side

One

The young woman touched her belly as an unfamiliar sensation moved like a bubble floating to the top of a flute. She was aware of the intruder that was making its presence known, but would rather discount the movement to a touch of gas finding its way through her digestive tract. After all, she did not ask to become a fetal-carrier like some animal in the woods. She did not ask to be mounted like a breeding mare with her private parts spread for the taking. The woman, barely so at seventeen, was unprepared for the harrowing experience of an unjust, unloving act that left her womb inhabited with a life she could not acknowledge.

Her mind was racing like a bullet train riding the rails to its next destination determined to stop only long enough to allow its occupants a hastened exit. What should she do? Where should she go to hide the cumbersome entanglement? She knew the final deed must be completed with closure, absent of drugs and little aftercare. It must be done quickly, leaving any establishment as if she were never a resident but only leaving a piece of baggage by the door. Her childlike mind was firm; she would travel to a faraway land inhabited only by monks or nuns. She would ask for entrance with tearful begging, unveiling her belly to secure the pact. After the task had been completed, she would smile in gratitude and be on her way.

For several months, a flurry of internal questions unrelentingly haunted her days. Will there be remorse for her actions? Will she weaken her stance and change her plans? Will there be a moment when she might be tempted to touch the cheek of the interloper to submit the truth of her plight? Realizing there was no time for retreat, or to dally with the thoughts jetting through her mind, she chose to continue her subversion and travel the distance alone.

The Tele, firmly mounted on the wall to assure its safety from thieves, blared its alarm, "A Teen Runaway!" Her finger touched a button to silence the obtrusive bloke. She rolled over on her side just far enough to accomplish a position of comfort without the acknowledgement of her belly's obstruction. The bland room had been her refuge for the last few months as she sequestered herself to allow the intruder its gestation. The corner deli provided her needs for nourishment, the Tele her entertainment. She was well aware of the time sequence involved; she had marked an "x" on the calendar tucked in her pocketbook. Her hibernation must end in two weeks; and then, she will hitch to the manor discovered in a mixture of crazy panic and intellectual calm.

The young woman was an avid theorist who wrote in journals to capture her thoughts before they flew from her mind like a drove of honey bees. Glancing at an entry several pages hence, her eyes spied two words: "Why me?" Then she addressed herself aloud, "Why not me?" Rethinking her question written so blatantly it could not be mistaken for another, she began to pen her thoughts:

> Why not me? If there is a God, He (or is it She?) could pick any lonely girl to be a toy for an adolescent Neanderthal's pleasure, and then discarded as if used equipment. If there are human trials for all of us to undergo, why not this one for me? If there is a God and humans have been given the capacity to overcome—to heal and regenerate—then why not experience this malady head on? Do I even have a choice to ignore the encroacher within me which sits like an atom bomb that will eventually explode? I think not.
>
> At this moment, as only a humble human surfacing to breathe, I feel as though I have no right to ask questions. I feel as if I have no right to dream, or even to envision a normal life filled with laughter and love...I feel like a prisoner locked away by my own body.

The girl lowered the cherished journal while considering her thoughts. She adjusted her body again to an upright position on the too-soft mattress. The bed reeked of vinegar stains, a vague attempt to nullify the odor coming from the spots that dotted the coverlet. Folding the bed clothing in-half exposed a grey-tinged sheet abused so often it displayed fraying edges. Reluctant to sleep, she flipped the journal pages again, curious to reread her previous entry:

> What a trick! My eyes closed to the probabilities of the night, I made my way to the bash being held to entice the young people of the college. I flagged a motorcar and jumped in not caring if the driver was a lady or gent. It was a gent, rather droll, about forty, who wanted company on his journey to the next casino. His eyes were obsidian black and his hair straight as straw poking unevenly from beneath his trilby. After signaling that my destination was near, he pulled the motorcar to the side, politely smiling a grin of lust.

She closed her journal and tried to remember each step taken while walking to the party that dark October night in 1975. Had she been nervous? Did she have even a hint that her life would be so misdirected in ways too unperceivable to imagine? Not wanting to actually visualize the event for the millionth time, she quickly changed her thinking to impose a random thought to her present expanded awareness: *What if I somehow created that night? What if subconsciously, I had a role in my own undoing?* She surmised the interesting theory and opened her brown eyes wide to grasp the unconventional concept that suddenly tempted her consciousness. *Could I actually entertain this bizarre concept?* she silently asked herself. *But, if God gives humans freewill, why would we create pain and suffering? Perhaps, He/She isn't on our side after all.* Rethinking her position, she said aloud, "Perhaps, He/She is a prankster poking fun at our plights while waiting for us to choose mediocre roles of self-sabotage and destruction, just to laugh at our plays!"

The woman-child closed her eyes to finally allow the dregs of night to bring a morsel of rest to her brain. Alas! Her dreams were of no release as the squatter flayed inside her. The semi-conscious dreamstate took her to depths of sorrow and a longing for a life she felt was rightfully hers to create. Lately, her dreams contained a theme of infants floating to her side, and images of her parents' faces forced with frowns of disgust. She would often jerk herself awake at the slightest vision of her parents, and lay frozen with fear gnawing at the pit of her stomach. It was then that she would grab her pen and write out the dream to capture its essence. *Will you ever forgive me, Mum?* she thought, as she lay awake, afraid to enter another damning dream. *Will you ever understand why I fled from your hearth without a mention of retreat? Your useless words hang in my mind like used garments left for rags in a damp closet. I am sorry…I am so very sorry.*

Marking out on her calendar the last few days of the three month siege, she felt a surge of emotion well up from deep inside and lost control of the tears she had shut away so tightly. There were no tears after her attacker finished his deed. There were no tears as she made her way home dabbing with a cocktail napkin the blood running down her leg. She allowed no tears to smudge her makeup two months later when the urine test edged its way into visibility, divulging the trespasser's presence. *Tears are for children,* her thoughts proclaimed. *I am no longer a child. I must remove my burden alone, without the knowledge of another whose eyes would trade the secret to anyone searching. No, no tears. Tears are meant for tots who fall from swings, wet their knickers and scratch their knees, not for young women who know a bit of life and its pitfalls.* She wiped her eyes with the back of one hand, attesting that her current circumstance was only a reflection of the casualties she had endured.

She had always envisioned her parents as uptight Brits with the emotion of turtles wavering on a piece of wood deciding whether to continue the climb or relent and back away from the challenge. They were nice enough, even caring at times; but, her childhood was fraught with "what-will-the-family-or-others-think" kind of dilemmas. Over and over during her younger years, she heard the neverending questions, "Will the nanny think we are too lenient?" "Will Mum approve of your dress?" "Does your father know you are reading *that* book?" "What will your teachers think of us if you are late for class?" Most of her young years trod by without an awareness of her parents' mutterings. Then, one day she suddenly felt free from their words that hovered in her brain like vultures eyeing their prey. At that exact moment, her life became her own.

The woman-child had no trouble hiding her current encumbered condition from her parents. After she dealt them her silent solitary hand, their interest in her dashed out the window with the frilly curtains sailing in the breeze. Her anonymity was also not difficult during this necessary respite. It was a bit like playing "Hide the Mouse," carefully omitting a name to her persona. When she needed to sign the hotel register, she used a mysterious name to invoke a curious look from the bint behind the counter. It worked perfectly. As she took the room key, she laughed out loud as she recalled the time she had faked her identification to get into a pub with the name, Candy Duncan. The bouncer knew the candy brand and offered a donkey-laugh while pretending to eat her arm! No, there was no problem in keeping herself unnoticed and unfound.

On the final day, she stepped from the grimy shower bath only to catch her reflection in the thin rusty mirror behind the door. She stared at the girl's face looking back at her. A common face with wide brown eyebrows that matched shoulder length hair, full natural lips sheltering imperfect ivory teeth, and high cheek bones smoothed by creamy skin inherited from her mum. Her eyes were normally brown, but turned hazel when the sun was high and shone directly upon her face. She reluctantly glanced downward and gazed un-approvingly at the limp frame standing before her. Trying to avoid viewing the large bump spreading across her middle, she turned sideways only to feel her eyes riveted to the grotesque swelling. She could not look away; her eyes were glued to the mirror in a transfixed glaze. How did this happen? It felt like an atrocity, a moment in time turned inward on itself producing a calamity of injustice. Grabbing the one scrawny towel provided the room, she covered herself only to have it gape wide to once again display the telltale deformity. *Disgusting*, she thought. Quickly, she began throwing on the loose-fitting clothing she had found in the rubbish bin a few months prior.

Checking out of the hotel, the girl inquired about the nearest bus station to the maid who was thoroughly surveying the room to make sure nothing had been removed. She walked to the station, which helped stretch her calves that had been latently waiting for release. She paced herself, knowing there may be another short hike to her final destination. Boarding the shuttle, she sat alone, taking two seats to discourage another from placing their body next to hers. The young woman closed her eyes to hopefully relieve their aching, and released a slight sigh of relief.

One rap, then two upon the entry door brought a doughty woman with a sluggish smirk who spoke with an unfamiliar accent, "Who's there then?"

"My name is Destiny. I have come to bear my child and leave as I came," the girl announced dramatically, pulling back her wrap to reveal her condition just as she had envisioned the scene.

"Come in young lady. You be far along then?" the matron asked as she viewed the girl from all sides.

"Yes, ma'am. The event is forthcoming. I wish to stay only as long as necessary to rid myself of this...this freeloader," she replied with directness of tongue even she surmised, after-the-fact, to be too stern.

"Oh, ye wants nothing to do with the wee one then?" the matron inquired.

"No, nothing," she answered flatly.

"Aye, deary, we'll take good care ye sure enough," the woman said, leading the newcomer down a long hallway within the antiquated manor.

Destiny surveyed the room with white painted walls and white curtains draped over one small window. Pulling the curtains to one side, she viewed a waist high deteriorating garden wall made of grey stone. The bed was narrow, but adequate for one. She placed her satchel on the oak chair crouched in a corner looking afraid to speak its name. There was no clothes wardrobe.

"Surely this will suffice for the few days that remain," Destiny softly voiced her approval.

"Come now, supper's on the table for the get'n," the lady ordered.

"Yes, thank you. I am hungry," Destiny spoke, trying to sound proper.

The dining room was large, seating at least a dozen women, obviously all weighed with child. Some of the residents glanced up as Destiny entered and took her seat; others not bothering to invite a connection, kept their faces close to a plate filled with chips and fish. Destiny smiled to those who caught her glance, and then proceeded to eat in silence as the other diners were portraying so admirably. The evening ended quickly, and after everyone finished their meal, they vanished into individual rooms to wait for signs of their impending event.

The following morning in the shared lavatory glistening in white shadows falling on a perfect oval sink, Destiny approached a shower bath to find a frail girl exiting. She noticed the petite girl was burdened with an oversized midriff that tilted her body forward, mimicking the famous Italian tower. When their eyes met, a moment of kindness shone as if each knew the plight of the other. They shared a silent smile and nudged bellies to complete their opposite destinations. Destiny hoped the girl would be available when she finished her shower, eager to make a connection with someone who might tell her a bit about the manor that would be her temporary residence. However, when she returned from her bath, the skinny girl had left. Destiny dressed and arrived at the forenoon meal just in time to eat a banger and scone. She spied the skinny girl at the far end of the table, and regained eye contact as they both drank their sweet juice that was provided in abundance.

Leaving the dining room, the two girls walked silently to the sitting area intent on a verbal exchange.

"What's your name?" Destiny asked the skinny girl with the big belly.

"I am Tina. Did you just arrive?" Tina inquired.

"Yes, last evening. I am Destiny. I know this isn't the place to make real friends, since we will be leaving soon; but, I would like to know more about this place. Have you been here long?" Destiny tried to sound friendly, but at the same time distant enough not to warrant a close friendship.

"Yes. Actually, I have been here for several months because I had nowhere else to go. The attendants seem nice enough, although they don't talk much to any of us," Tina said in her soft-toned voice that danced in the air.

"I felt they were rather cold, but then so am I at this point." Destiny smiled, then continued, "You look too young to be...with child."

"I am a full fourteen, but *this* was not my decision or desire," Tina said, pointing to her belly that sat on its own pillow as if detached from its owner.

"Well, I will not pry. I do not wish to tell others my life story either. But, we could tell each other of news and information we might hear. Would you be willing?" asked Destiny.

"Oh, yes, I am happy to tell you anything you wish, Destiny. I do know that the East Hall is where the birthing takes place. I have witnessed several women wheeled down that hallway, but have not ventured to talk to any of them when they returned to their room," Tina shared her information freely.

"That's good to know, Tina. May I ask...are you afraid?" Destiny inquired without hesitation.

"Oh, yes!" Tina exclaimed, then lowered her voice and covered her mouth with her hand. "I am really scared, but the attendants keep reassuring me. They claim it will be over in a few hours. Then afterward, I will be free to leave with my baby within a few days."

"Oh, Tina, you are keeping it?" Destiny said with an air of surprise that rudely displayed her opinion.

"Oh, yes, of course. I could not give up a child to another when I have grown to love it dearly for so many months," Tina replied, stroking her belly with one hand and then the other.

"Oh, I am sorry, Tina, if I sounded so surprised. It's just that I cannot think of this...this leech inside me, as a *baby*. It was spawn from an involuntary event that certainly has ruined my life. You must have experienced a different conception, one in which you both were in love I imagine," Destiny stated, trailing her assumption with a caring gesture by placing a hand upon Tina's belly.

"Well, I do love the father of my baby...but," Tina leaned in toward Destiny's ear, "he is also *my* dad."

Destiny jerked her hand away not believing the words whispered in her ear by her new friend, the skinny girl with the big belly. "Oh, my God! Is this really true? Oh, Tina, I am so sorry for you! Has he been arrested?" Destiny questioned in a whisper.

The tears began to form in Tina's eyes until she blinked and sent them dripping down her cheeks. "I am okay...and no, my dad was not arrested. My mum did not believe me when I shared the news of my situation and who was responsible. She sent me here before my condition was apparent. I have accepted my fate. I am actually looking forward to having a baby to keep me company. I will never go back to my parents' home," Tina said with confidence.

The two continued their revealing conversation for a few minutes longer, and then one of the attendants entered the room to announce that Destiny had to go to the medical wing. She motioned for Destiny to follow her and turned abruptly to lead the way. As they walked to the end of the corridor, the doors along the hallway were closed with no hint of life on the other side. When they arrived at the last remaining door, the attendant signaled for Destiny to enter and sit in one of the chairs that faced an old oak desk scrolled with spirals on the front panel. Just as Destiny finished making circular motions with her eyes that followed the carved spiral patterns, a large buxom woman entered and took the high-backed chair situated behind the ornate desk.

Two

Luana closed her new book. She placed the blue beaded marker she'd made last year deep into the book's spine. When she was reading a good novel, time seemed to dash past her consciousness like a wisp of fresh air seeping through a crack in a wooden window pane. A friend had suggested she read the book, telling her it was about a young woman filled with the eternal questions of love, life, and death. After reading only the first chapter, Luana knew the book was meant for her to consume like her favorite fruit in springtime. She gathered her cup of tea to deposit in the sink to wash at a later time, knowing she must quickly return to her new treasure.

Luana's time was her own since retirement had encroached upon her years, which left only memories of guiding others on their journey toward fulfillment of a life they had once dreamt. She had been a good mentor, a competent counselor to those who sought a woman with empathy and the patience to listen for hours to their tales of tattered lives. Now, it was time for Luana to enjoy her time to play the piano, write poetry and read enticing novels of life, love, and lust. She chose to sit outside, thinking the mild autumn sun would feel warm on her cold feet and be perfect to enlighten each word. Sitting in the lounge chair, Luana propped-up her feet to absorb the warm rays. Fingering her beaded bookmark, she hesitated a moment to reflect on the words in the first chapter she had just read. Questions roamed her mind as she recalled the two young women waiting for their labor to commence; she intuited their lives would change forever.

"Are you Destiny? What is your last name, dear?" asked the unknown woman facing Destiny on the opposite side of the oak desk.

"No need to know my last name…doctor?" Destiny re-
torted.

"Oh, I am sorry. I dare say, I thought you were told who I
was…my name is Dr. Ellsworth. I am the head obstetrician here
at The Charter Manor for Women. There are two medical
doctors on staff and four nurses to assist you during your time
here," the doctor stated matter-of-factly. "Now, I do need your
full name."

Destiny took a long breath inward, then released her first
inspirational thought, "Lovelost…Destiny Lovelost."

"Oh, I see. Well, Miss Lovelost, we are happy to assist you
in your current situation. I was informed that you do not wish
to keep your baby, is this correct?"

"Correct," replied Destiny, with a solid tone that assured the
meaning of her response.

"I will have the nurse give you the proper papers to fill out,
and then tomorrow we will go over them after I give you an
examination," the doctor instructed, rose from her perch and
vanished.

Destiny blindly noticed the nurse standing on her right trying
to shove a stack of papers into her hand. She told Destiny they
were to be completed by the time she returned the following
day. The nurse left the undecorated room as swiftly as the
doctor, leaving her to find her way back to the residents' wing
unassisted. As she passed the dining area, she was able to
retrace the route back to her private room. Needing to pee
terribly, Destiny made her way to the lavatory just in time to
relinquish a deep sigh as the urine flowed from her body.
"What did you expect?" she asked herself aloud, without
considering if anyone else was in the loo. Settling back in her
room with its little window and shy chair, she lay on the bed to
process her thoughts.

Destiny realized she had dozed off when her nap was
abruptly interrupted by a piercing scream. She sat upright and
strained to hear the whispers down the hallway. The words
were not audible, but the scream sounded a second time and
brought her to her feet. She placed her ear to the old door that
smelled of lemon oil, but nothing more was heard. Her mind
was racing again with thoughts and questions that stung her

temples. She grabbed her satchel to find her loyal journal, sat on the edge of the bed, and began to write:

> Again, why me? I know…why not me. My life has little to offer, so why not trade one life filled with dreams and desires for one of trauma and grief? One life isn't more valuable than another, I shan't think. But where is the Divine Being that is supposed to harbor those in pain and suffering? Where is the God that is supposed to wrap children in love and assure their path is a productive and creative venture?
>
> I think I am creative; I know I am creative. I enjoy seeing and offering new ways of imagining the world, though most have been met with deaf ears and blind eyes. Do I not deserve to relish in a proper vision like anyone else?
>
> I come from a rightful family line that should ensure its lineage be directed to realizing their dreams. What has happened to my path? Enough! Enough sulking and projecting the pain of the other women staying here. I shall receive my rightful heritage of a life filled with productive abilities, and hopefully even love.

Destiny closed her journal, determined not to dream this night of floating babies or her parents.

When Destiny was about ten years old, she asked her mum why she had been named Destiny. At the time, her mum shrugged her bony shoulders only revealing, "In hopes that you would find your right path." She took the answer without inquisition, knowing her mum well enough to understand she did not want to talk about the subject. Her parents had been a bit overly protective of her, until she closed them out of her life during her experimental teen years. She would purposefully leave home late at night, well-knowing her parents could hear her exiting the stately manor. Once in 1971, when Destiny was returning from a bash given by an older friend whose parents were traveling abroad for the summer, her parents confronted her tactics by standing firmly in the hall blocking passage to her bedroom.

"Why must you put us through this kind of charade, Destiny? Do you not care about how we will look to our friends if they found out you had been gallivanting around all hours of the night?" her mum asked, displaying what looked like real tears pooling in the corners of her eyes.

"Oh, Mum, you worry too much," Destiny replied, edging her way past the pair who stood stiff in their cotton night clothes.

Turning to witness Destiny's bum stride down the hallway, her father shouted, "We shan't have any more of this, young lady, or it's off to boarding school!"

Destiny did not curb her pubescent behavior that year, and was sent the following to attend the all girls Charlton School in Telford. However, she was not upset about the transfer to a boarding school; actually, her life became less complicated. She continued her pranks and was put on report several times, but managed to graduate with little effort. Destiny was a brilliant student and she knew it. The school afforded her the time and space to study alone, a place to sleep, and optimal opportunity to sneak out to the many parties hosted by nearby college students. She was an only child, fated to learn about boys through individual exploitation—usually theirs, not hers. She fancied herself as an independent thinker with good genes, not a stunner.

Prior to this current setback, Destiny had experienced the drama of falling in lust with a boy her own age, only to tire of his inept capabilities of pursuit. The courtship ended in its third month of floundering hands and lips missing their mark. There was passion in her body, that was not the issue. Soon, the boy became a whim to display like the chessmen she used in games to challenge her professors—she always won. After this vague attempt to be with a boy her own age, Destiny preferred older college boys.

Since Charlton was less than ten miles from her parents' home in Wellington, they visited often. Destiny was expected to appear before them when they arrived to check on her progress. The headmistress would politely walk them through the halls pointing out the classrooms their daughter was attending, ready to attest to her above average marks. Most times, they needed to wait several minutes in the large receiving area until Destiny would finally arrive, only to kiss them on the cheek and tell them she was fine but had to leave for class. She figured, why take the time to pretend she cared enough to chat like old people over a cup of tea who only wish to hear the latest gossip of the village. Destiny felt she had received little affection as a child, so thought, why submit to niceties at this age just to appease her parents?

Many times, for the three and a half year span at Charlton, Destiny would not even bother to return home to spend bank holidays. She would relish the fact that she had the entire school to herself without the usual dormitory hallways resounding muffled giggles and high-pitched screams. She cherished her time alone and often faked illness during school breaks, just to secure her hiatus of seclusion.

Dressed and ready for the appointment with Dr. Ellsworth, Destiny again felt the bubble of life within her belly. To distract this awareness, she sought out Tina to ask if there had been a delivery last evening when the screams echoed through the halls. Spying Tina in the lounge area, Destiny slowly approached not wishing to interrupt, or join, Tina's conversation with another woman sitting on the couch next to her. She judged the woman to be older, probably even in her late twenties. Obviously in her third trimester, the woman sat upright with a stiff frame, as if to signify she would need to rotate her entire body to view the space around her. Destiny stood a distance away, trying to look like she had business in the room other than to spy on the pair sitting on the couch.

After a few minutes, the woman rose from her sitting position, seemingly without bending, to stand nearly six feet tall. She left the room, leaving the pillow vacant for Destiny to roost beside Tina.

"Good morning, Tina," Destiny offered, "Are you well?"

"Oh, yes, Destiny. I feel very well this morning, better than many days," Tina replied, adjusting her big belly to face Destiny.

"Who was that woman, do you know her well?" asked Destiny.

"Her name is Iris. Isn't she a stunner? She is so tall and regal!" Tina reported with her light blue eyes shining in the rays of the morning sun.

"Yes, she certainly is, though a bit older than I would expect to see here. It's a bit off-putting."

"Well, one never knows…her dilemma is one many women experience who have found themselves pregnant at a time in their lives that isn't suitable for various reasons. How are you feeling?" Tina inquired, changing the topic of discussion.

"Oh, I am fine. I am always fine. Do not worry about me, Tina. Did you hear that terrible scream last evening? I jumped out of my skin!" Destiny said, widening her brown eyes.

"Oh, yes! I certainly did! It was not the first scream I have heard here. Mind you, I have been here for many months and have seen many girls come and go," Tina explained, as if to remind Destiny what she had said the day before.

"Well, is that the common thing? To scream like an animal?" asked Destiny with surprise etched across her pale complexion.

"Yes, I am afraid it can be. I guess if labour starts without warning, one would be taken off-guard to its pain," Tina offered. "I have been reading the books in the library here and they claim the pain is bearable if taught how to breathe correctly. The attendant named Mary is working with me now to ensure I know how to command my breath during my labour."

"Well, another good-to-know fact. I have my first exam this morning with Dr. Ellsworth, so better push off. Do you have any insight to share with me about pelvic exams?" asked Destiny.

"Have you not had one?" Tina countered, sounding surprised.

"No, but it cannot be all that bad, right?" Destiny asked, expecting to hear Tina say, "No."

"Well, I have been getting them regularly during my stay here. But if it's your first one…well, just try to relax." Tina placed her hands on Destiny's shoulders, pressing down to adjust their stressful stance.

"Thanks, Tina. I will try…chat later." Destiny rose from the couch, which took a bit more effort than usual. She waved her hand to Tina as she rounded the corner to walk down the long white hall for a second time.

Destiny entered the doctor's office, sat in the chair facing the oak desk, and began her compulsive spiral eye-patterning to pass the time. The nurse appeared right on cue and Destiny held up the papers she'd filled out. They were placed directly on the desktop to politely wait their turn to be reviewed, and then the nurse vanished. When Destiny was finished with her second round of eye-tracing, Dr. Ellsworth bounced into the room.

"Hello, Destiny. How are you feeling today?" the doctor inquired, displaying a bit more compassion than the day before.

"Oh, I am fine. The papers are filled out. The nurse put them on your desk, there." Destiny pointed to the small stack that lay inertly to await its discovery.

"Yes, I see. Thank you for getting these back to me so quickly. Many young ladies don't complete their paperwork for days, even weeks." Her long fingers grasped the papers that were ready to be thumbed through to reveal Destiny's current circumstances.

"Now, I see here that you have not received any medical care whatsoever, is this correct?" asked the doctor while placing the papers on the opposite end of the desk.

"Yes. I have not been seen by anyone but the clinic technician who gave me the e.p.t. pregnancy test," Destiny replied, and then twisted her position to relieve the twinge in her lower left groin area.

"Well, then, it is a good thing you have arrived a bit early so we can take a look at your status, and get your blood workup completed," the doctor told Destiny with a look of concern. "I'll go through your paperwork later. Right now, if you will please follow me to the examination room?" The doctor stood and motioned for Destiny to follow.

Once settled inside the exam room, Destiny felt a cold draft of air creep up the thin paper gown reaching the bare tissue exposed to the doctor. She was not modest; she never had a reason to be, but this foreign pose was certainly a challenge. She tried to hold her knees together for a slip of privacy, only to have the nurse instruct her to part them and scoot her bum to the edge of the table. Destiny obeyed, and then immediately felt like a slab of meat being butchered while still attached to its owner. "Ouch!" she yelped, without realizing the sound was her own.

"I am sorry, dear, but now I have to press on your tummy at the same time that I feel your uterus to determine how far along you are," the doctor said, as she held most of one hand inside Destiny, and pushed her other firmly on the incumbent belly that had been neglected until this moment.

Destiny bit down on her lower lip to stifle another exclamation of discomfort. *No wonder Tina didn't want to tell me the truth about these exams!* she thought, as she pushed back up to the middle of the exam table as instructed.

"You can get dressed now and meet me back in my office," the doctor told Destiny.

"Okay," Destiny managed to say as she jumped off the hard table. She waited for the doctor to exit before removing the gown now drenched with a gooey paste that reeked of fish-odor and blood.

Destiny appeared in front of the old oak desk to find the doctor's attention consumed with the stack of papers that had patiently waited their turn. No words were spoken for a full two minutes, until the doctor tucked the papers inside a hard manila folder with a tab marked, "Lovelost, Destiny." "Destiny, I am going to be frank with you; but first, I need to ask a few more questions. You wrote that you do not know the name of the father of your baby, correct?" asked Dr. Ellsworth.

"Yes, that is correct." Destiny replied curtly, not wishing to divulge any information that didn't need to be revealed.

"So, if you leave your baby with us to be put up for adoption, the father will not be opposed to the decision?" the doctor asked, trying to open Destiny's vault.

"Yes, that is correct," Destiny replied.

"And your parents, Destiny? Where do they live? You didn't give any information listing them, or anyone to contact in case of an emergency," the doctor asked tilting her head, displaying a hint of worry that deepened the lines in her forehead.

"My parents are no longer living. I live alone and have no relatives to contact. My new friend, Tina, who is staying here is the closest friend I have," Destiny lied as if her tongue knew the familiar journey of deceit.

"I see," the doctor said, "are you completely positive you'll be giving your baby up for adoption, Destiny?"

"Yes,"Destiny said with a firmness the doctor could not challenge.

"All right, Destiny. When your baby is born, it will be taken directly to another facility where it will be taken care of until a suitable couple is matched for its adoption. There will be more paperwork for you to fill out. You should be delivering your baby within the next few weeks. In the meantime, you have developed a vaginal infection and you will need to use the medication I am going to prescribe. The directions are on the label, but if you have any questions just ask one of your attendants. Have you met any of the attendants?"

"No, I have not," she replied.

"Well, all right, Destiny. I will check on you in five days to see how you are progressing. You seem to have your course of action established; but if you have any questions, please know I'll be glad to answer them." The doctor stood and offered a hug in a gesture of comfort, but Destiny quickly left the room to find the nearest lavatory.

Three

The sun was setting behind the barren cottonwood, throwing intermittent rays of light upon the book's pages. At half-past six, Luana lifted her awareness from reading to her current environment near a private pond. Her home was nestled on a hillside along the California coastline. The sun signaled dim light turning to night and she lamented having to close her newest pastime to prepare a meal for one. Luckily, she realized there were leftovers from the previous evening that would ensure a limited time away from her new novel. Luana gently set the beaded marker tight at the inside spine. She placed the precious gem on her dining room table next to her iPhone, which had not summoned her in several days.

Living alone had its rewards for sure, but there were those days when Luana yearned for a bit of conversation, if only to use her vocal cords to clear her throat. She understood Destiny's philosophy of independence, having her own streak of Capricorn individuality. Luana turned from the stove to admire the colorful artwork displayed on her new book's cover, or was it a photograph?

Luana felt herself quite artistic, having dabbled in many of the creative arts as far back as the 1960s when she was a mere teen. Her rough paintings, completed in her early twenties, had kept her artistic juices flowing. In this same period of time, she'd learned to play the rote head games of follow-the-leader in college to massage her professors' egos. Studying came easily to Luana, probably because she loved to read. All the rooms in her beach cottage were filled with the hundreds of recommended college texts stacked like sentinels attesting to her accomplishments. Since her retirement, she had learned to indulge in the pleasures of causal novels, and *Finding Destiny* was succeeding in gratifying her literary thirst. She settled in her chair to eat the small meal of reheated baked potato with a mound of crisp asparagus, when a gusty breeze flipped the book open to a page yet unread. Acknowledging a synchronistic gift when it presented itself, Luana began to read the paragraph that tempted her curiosity:

> Journal—Aug. 1981: What the hell am I doing? I don't even like this chap! Why must I always choose such wankers that cheat their way into my heart? I am twenty-three years old, where is the fellow who is supposed to be my soulmate everyone is raving about? Soulmate, what a crock! From now on, I am going to lay off gents altogether.
>
> Aren't I supposed to have real love in my life? Is there such a thing as real love? I see through all the happy marriages that find dark halls to play illicit games of lust and deceit, it turns my stomach like a bitter lemon drink. Never again will I allow a bloke to enter my private seclusion. Why did I drink so many pints? I think it must be poison to my brain. I can't believe I allowed myself to get so wrapped up with a chap like that. I don't even know his full name! I pray he stays away from me when I don't show up at the pub tomorrow. Maybe I won't go back, ever...

Luana quickly closed the temptress, not wanting to unjustly form a new tale in her mind before the plot rightfully unfolds. While eating her dinner, she thought back to her own youth, admitting to herself that she was still a virgin in the early 1970s when she was twenty-six. What was it that kept her from experimenting sexually while all her college friends were casually sharing joints and giving blowjobs? What held her back from a firsthand experience of pursuing the Sixties in all its Beatlemania and sexual revolution? Even now, with her unspoken questions lingering in midair, Luana's face reacted with its usual flush that stained her cheeks in crimson patches of inhibition. Settling in her reading chair, complete with its own modern lamp to ensure her books were well-lit late into the night, Luana stretched the cover of her new book to reopen Destiny's saga.

After returning from the lavatory, Destiny went to the lounge in search of Tina and found her sitting on the same couch, reading a book. "Tina! I would rather sit for tea with my parents than go through that again! I tried to relax, but it really hurt!" Destiny exclaimed, trying to muffle her remarks with her hand.

"Oh, Destiny…I am sorry it was hurtful for you. It does take a few of those exams to get used to the intrusion," Tina agreed and closed her book. "What did the doctor tell you?"

"Well, the event will happen in a few weeks…and I have an infection *down there*. I have this cream I am supposed to use," Destiny said, displaying the little white prescription bag. "I'm a bit fogged, so I better open this up to figure it out."

"Just ask Mary, if you have questions. She is a spot-on attendant. Oh, Destiny, you will be having your baby about the same time as me!" Tina said with excitement.

"Tina…pleasezz don't say it that way," Destiny begged while looking down at her bulging middle. Trying not to sound hurtful, she explained, "This is not a baby to me. It is just something I need to deal with to get on with my life."

"Oh, yea, I forgot. I am sorry. It is so difficult for me to think of anyone not wanting to keep their own baby. I shan't bring it up again," whispered Tina.

"Well, I *will* share…I was raped. I was a virgin and barely knew the bloke who was an older college student. The whole experience is a fuzzy blur that I do not want to remember. So, now you must understand," Destiny said, revealing her secret to the first person to hear her tragic story.

"Oh, no! I am so sorry…I don't know what else to say," Tina offered and reached over her big belly to hug Destiny.

"I am fine. I am always fine. I have dealt with it, and cannot wait for this to be over," Destiny reported. "I am going to go back to my room to check how this medication works. I hope it makes *things* feel better."

"Okay, I will see you later at dinner then," Tina said, trying to erase the image of her new friend being raped. Tina settled back into the soft pillows and closed her eyes to mentally rewind her own visions locked tight in her mind.

Tina had not shared her entire story with anyone. She felt there was some unwritten rule she had to follow about not causing disdain to her parents. Her story began to play in her mind like an old silent film, presenting actors on a screen whose mouths were moving without words to hear. She loved her parents. They had been the center of her young life, and certainly provided well for her. The love shared between the three was visible to all their relatives and friends, but little did those loved ones know of Tina's family secrets.

Tina's dad was old enough to be her grandfather. At fifty-nine years old, he was a distinguished Englishman with proper employment. He managed an establishment of character in the southwest borough of Cheltenham. He and Tina's mum had experienced the Blitz of 1940. She had been a mere seventeen, and he was twenty-two years old when they first met. She was seriously injured while running down the stairs of the nearby bomb shelter. Her right leg had been severely damaged and was amputated above the knee. As Tina understood the story, the pair fell in love at the worst moment in their lives, and then became each other's steadfast companion at a time when all of England thought the world would surely end.

Tina's mum once revealed to her that she could not become pregnant, but a miracle happened. Tina was conceived as a menopausal baby. She knew there must be more to her mum's story, but knew better than to pry into her parents' privacy. Tina also kept the secret of her dad's nightly drinking ritual that often found him passed out on the parlor floor. Her mum seemed to be unaware of her husband's condition. She would retire early to her separate bedroom, leaving Tina the task of getting him to his. Many times, during these nights, her father would share his stories of lament with her.

His eyes filled with brandy-tears, he would confide with Tina that he had only been allowed to love her mother intimately but a few times. Barely a preteen, Tina would listen without completely understanding her father's discussion. She continued to ask questions that eventually led to more explicit explanations, including a bit of intimacy between the two. After many close father-daughter chats, Tina found herself in her current condition and totally oblivious to its implications. When her mum discovered the pregnancy, Tina tried to explain the circumstances but her father denied any wrongdoing. This, of course, exacerbated the situation and in a hysterical rage, Tina's mum told her to leave and never return.

How strange life is, Tina thought to herself. *My situation is no worse or better than Destiny's, yet we seem to be unwinding the same shreds of hope for a happy life. She will be without anyone to comfort her...and me? Well, I will have my dear sweet baby to ensure I will never be alone.* Tina opened her eyes to see a burst of sunshine enveloping the far side of the garden spilling its warm colours upon the thirsty shrubbery. The summer had been the hottest ever experienced the Tele had declared, bringing with it a drought to England unseen before. The news chap also mentioned that Cheltenham had experienced one of the hottest days on record, at just over 96F degrees. *Poor Mum and Dad,* she thought. Just viewing the barren garden encouraged Tina to go find the water pitcher provided the residents. On her way to the dining room, she ran into Iris who was also searching for the pitcher.

"Hello, Iris," Tina said, as she poured the clear liquid into a large glass.

"Hi, Tina. The doctor just told me I will need to be admitted to the hospital in a few days. I need to have a caesarean birth. You know where they cut through the belly and take the baby out," Iris reported, as she crossed her belly with two fingers from left to right.

"Oh, no...I have only just learned about that procedure in the book I am reading. It sounds like you shan't feel anything though, because they numb-up your belly good with an anaesthetic," Tina said, trying to sound positive and knowledgeable.

"Yes, I am not worried about the pain. Though, I won't be coming back here afterward. So, if I don't see you, I hope your delivery is easy and your baby is healthy," Iris said. She gave Tina a hug, as close as possible, with their two bellies in the way.

"Thank you, Iris. Will you give me your number before you go, so I can ring you up when I get out of here?" asked Tina.

"Okay. I will give it to you at breakfast," Iris assured Tina, and then drank the remainder of her water. "I need to take a nap!"

The pair walked back to the bedroom wing and closed their separate oak doors to the outside world until suppertime.

Luana set her book upside down like a butterfly to rest on the arm of her overstuffed chair. She needed to take a moment to digest the material she had read. The words seemed to float in her mind like a spiral staircase searching to reach its conscious destination. *I can't even imagine how it would feel to carry a baby for nine months, knowing it was never to be held in your arms*, she thought. Then, she remembered her internship in the late 1970s when she'd worked in a women's medical clinic. She counseled women who needed to make the heart-wrenching decision of whether to terminate their pregnancy. She would counsel their fears and wipe their tears as they talked of the personal circumstances, which at the time forbade the possibility of their becoming a mother. She informed them of all the alternatives, and then waited and supported their ultimate resolution.

Some women would continue their pregnancy and opt to give the gift of adoption to an enthusiastic couple. Others would choose to terminate their pregnancy and pray they were doing the right thing for everyone involved. Luana heard stories from older women who didn't think they could get pregnant at their late post- menopausal age. She also listened to the young teens who didn't think they could get pregnant "the first time," "underwater," or "if he pulled out." During that time period, on many nights Luana found herself deep in a dream helping a woman sort through her choices and her spiritual beliefs, to find a solution for her predicament. There were as many heartbreaking stories as there were numbers of women who appeared in her office for counseling. Then, halfway into her sixth year at the clinic, Luana could not listen a day longer. She continued her counseling career, but chose a different area in which to specialize.

Reflecting on both Tina's and Destiny's scenarios thus far, Luana felt pangs of sorrow in her heart. The stories stirred-up memories from her clinic days, and she began to search her own spiritual beliefs surrounding the enigmas of birth and death. She recalled the time in her life when she was confronted with the same type of deliberation the women in Charter Manor had experienced. She thought about Tina and how she had become pregnant. Then she reviewed Destiny's story to find a tidbit of truth to match her own sexual deflowering. She also reflected on her spiritual growth throughout her life, and accepted there was no need for blame. Her education and career in counseling had instructed that she reach the middle-of-the-ground thinking that most counselors employ to assure an unbiased viewpoint. As Luana closed her eyes to remember her younger self, she acknowledged that her life's story had similarities that matched both Tina and Destiny's tales within the intriguing book.

Luana was born on a cold rainy Christmas morning in 1945 to middle-class parents who worked hard to establish a home for their family of four. They lived in a rural location with fields of poppies and lightly wooded areas where she could run and play hide-n-seek with her older brother during the summers. Luana attended a local elementary school that was always ready to furnish her the next book to devour. She read several hundred books in addition to the required reading for all her classes taken through her high school years. Her mother could always find her sitting in her bedroom window-box with the streaming sunrays bouncing off a book page, highlighting her pale blue eyes and blonde hair. She was definitely a typical bookworm, reading vast amounts of literature to harbor in her brain's sanctuary, safe, until she recalled their powers to share with those who merited the savored revelations.

Luana thought of herself as a liberal-minded woman, open to whatever life had to offer. Her parents were an unconventional couple. One was a spiritualist and the other agnostic, which left Luana holding a blank ticket to use as she saw fit to discover her own viewpoints about life's eternal questions. She had that ticket punched many times. Sometimes she studied traditional religious thinking; and at others, she unraveled a stylistic combination of East/West metaphysical belief that resulted in her current eclectic spiritual outlook. While in the midst of searching for answers as to how the Universe works, Luana traveled to the Far East and found numerous rewards. She tucked them into her belief system, making sure to include the simple pleasures of giving and accepting the act of compassion and kindness. Throughout her counseling career, even when she felt she had nothing more to offer, Luana would pull out her compassion and kindness ticket and use it to open new doors with her patients.

Luana remembered one young girl who presented for counseling at the clinic, at barely fourteen years old. As she mixed the girl's urine pregnancy test, Luana prayed it would be negative. It showed itself as a clear positive. The nurse's examination revealed her to be approximately ten weeks pregnant. She was such a shy girl; Luana was surprised that she would even be experimenting sexually. As she explored the facts, it became clear the girl had not been voluntarily sexually active, she had been raped.

Luana could barely understand the young girl as she cried throughout the counseling session. In addition, she was Hispanic and knew little English. Luana had learned some Spanish in order to counsel the many Mexican American women who visited the clinic, but this client's accent seemed unfamiliar. After reading through the girl's paperwork, Luana learned her client had arrived directly from Mexico only a few months prior. Luana was able to discern that the girl had been raped by one of her cousins she was living with. At the time, her mother was saving all she could to eventually rent a place of their own.

With great care, Luana gave her young client all the informative pamphlets and explained all the alternatives to choose from. The young girl decided to terminate her pregnancy because of the nature of her impregnation. She assured Luana that if she had gotten pregnant by her current boyfriend, she would continue her pregnancy and they would marry. Luana asked her how long she and her boyfriend had been going together, and the girl admitted they had met just two weeks earlier. Luana took a lengthy amount of time to cover all the contraceptives available to her client to use after the procedure; but at the same time, she covertly intuited she would see this young girl at the clinic in the future.

This scenario seemed to be a theme in America during the 1970s after the well-known Roe vs. Wade Supreme Court decision passed in 1973. Although challenged many times, this United States federal law still stands and gives women the personal right to choose whether they want to continue or terminate a pregnancy. It also allows each state to regulate the restrictions on terminations. It was during these feverous and somewhat irrational years that Luana worked in the women's clinic. She was in her early thirties, and still struggling with her own sexuality, while at the same time explaining the subject matter to her clients.

On many days in that turbulent anti-choice decade, Luana would arrive at work to witness picketers circling the medical clinic. The crowd would shout obscenities to anyone entering the front entrance. She and the other employees would be forced to enter through a pair of sliding glass doors at the rear of the building. It was a fearful time for the doctors, nurses, counselors, and especially for the patients, who tried to cover their faces as they made their way through the barrage of naysayers.

On one evening, when the clinic was entertaining an open house for medical professionals in the area, Luana was asked to tour the doctors through the establishment and answer their questions. The night was going smoothly when she decided to take a break and sit in the kitchen to drink a cup of coffee. In an instant of thunderous noise and a flash of light, there were a million pieces of glass plummeting around her. Guessing a gun had been fired, Luana dropped to her knees and scrambled under the table. She looked up to witness a man's baggy clothes, a long gray beard, a green cap, and a bottle of booze all flying through the air in different directions! Several doctors dashed into the room like soldiers ready to do battle with whomever or whatever they found. One doctor rescued Luana from beneath the table and helped her to her feet while sheltering her with his body; others grappled the unknown man to the floor. The police were called and their discovery was that the intruder was not an anti-abortion fanatic. The man was just an old alcoholic who had stumbled into the sliding glass window, unaware of the cause for alarm he had set off that had swept through the entire building.

Yes, the 1970s in the United States seemed caught in a sexual revolution all their own. Luana's own first sexual experience occurred at the beginning of this decade, when she was twenty-six and on a date with a man she had been seeing for a few months. Luana felt she had made herself clear that she was looking for a long term relationship, not an intermittent meeting between two sexually starved people who couldn't wait to undress each other. Evidently, she was not clear enough. When they were enjoying a last cup of coffee at her apartment after a dinner-and-a-movie night, he forced her down on the floor and continued his demand until it was met.

The old memory jogged Luana back to her surroundings and she opened her eyes, not wanting to visualize the details of her so-called *first time*. She took this moment to reread the first page of her book describing Destiny's first sexual experience, and her eyes began to tear. She felt a deep connection with the likable heroine. *How brave Destiny is to be walking her journey alone*, she thought. Luana's eyes were still weeping as she removed the bookmark, opened the page wide, and followed the storyline late into the night.

Four

Destiny figured out the directions for the soothing vaginal cream, and then sat on her bed to write in her trusty journal.

> Journal—June 1976: I met a new friend, her name is Tina. She is a little wisp of a girl, barely fourteen. Her skin looks silken and her short brown hair is styled in a female version of the Beatles' bob. It seems such a shame that her fate is one of becoming a mum so early in life. Why would any God allow this to happen? Again with the God questions!
>
> I cannot wait until I leave this place and secure a job to be out on my own. I feel like a canary locked in a cage waiting for someone to open the door-latch to freedom. The staff is nice enough I suppose; but, I can't really relate to them. Tina seems to be my only comfort. For some reason, she draws me to her like one of Uri Geller's spoons, easily bending me to share what I am feeling. It's actually quite mystical.
>
> I think I will ask Tina if she wants to walk with me through the garden tomorrow. It is unbearably hot, but we could stay in the shade and get some outside air. Yes, I will ask her in the morning.
>
> I still believe my goals are clear and the doctor seems skilled. In less than two weeks, I will be released from this burden and able to get on with my life!

Destiny closed her journal and closed her mind to the muffled sounds within the manor. She fell asleep quickly and dreamed of the hot sun beating down on her while swimming in the ocean. The heat penetrated her body, as the cool saltwater softened her skin until it became baby smooth. Suddenly, a floating baby appeared beside her, reaching for her. Destiny awoke in a hot sweat that equaled any woman's denial of her impending ovarian cessation. Her soaked nightgown stuck to her body, sucking her swollen breasts. She had no idea what was happening, but went to shower hoping the cool water would remedy her uncharacteristic condition. She made a mental note to herself to tell Dr. Ellsworth about the unexpected experience, and then crawled back into bed and fell into a deep sleep.

The following morning, Destiny went looking for Tina to tell her about the strange dream and night sweats. She entered the dining room, sat in an empty chair and surveyed the table to locate her friend. The padded chairs were spaced evenly along the cherrywood table, a few sat alone, unoccupied. Destiny did not see Tina or Iris, the tall woman who had been sitting with her the day before. She ate her scone and eggs quickly, so she could go check on Tina. Destiny then walked back to the bedroom wing thinking perhaps Tina did not feel well and had purposefully skipped her morning meal. She knocked on Tina's door, waited a few seconds, and then knocked a second time to no avail.

Hoping to learn where Tina might be, Destiny went in search of the attendant Tina had spoken about. She walked the narrow hallway to its end, finding the nurses' station empty. Assuming everyone was still at breakfast, she decided to go back to the dining room to ask if someone might tell her where her friend had gone. By the time she returned, most of the women residents were walking to the lounge to watch the only Tele in the manor. Destiny spied Mary just leaving the table and walked up to her explaining, "Hi, my name is Destiny and I am a friend of Tina's…sorry, I don't know her last name. She is the pretty girl with the bangs and big belly that looks like a balloon ready to burst. She said you knew her well and was teaching her how to breathe or something."

"Hello, Destiny, I have been meaning to introduce myself to you. I will be your attendant and you can ask me any questions you might have," replied Mary as she gathered her files and rigidly propped them under her long arm.

"Hi, Mary. Do you know where Tina is? Maybe she is having another exam?" asked Destiny.

"No, Tina is not having an exam. She is having her baby! She started her labour last night and was taken to the hospital. I am not sure how she is doing, Destiny. I will be checking my messages soon and there should be an update coming in about her. If you want to follow me back to the nurses' station, perhaps we can find out some news," Mary explained, gesturing with her unfilled arm while trying to balance the patient files with the other.

"Oh, yes. I really want to talk to her. When will she come back to the manor?" Destiny asked, knowing Mary most likely could not answer the question until she had read through the messages.

"We'll see what the incoming messages say," Mary replied.

The pair walked back down the long hallway, turning into the area reserved for the nurses and attendants. Mary went to check her message box for news of Tina's progress. When she returned, Destiny noticed Mary's face was pale and drawn, and her lower lip was quivering. Destiny immediately asked, "What is it? What does the message say, Mary?"

"I am afraid Tina's baby did not survive the birth. This breaks my heart. Even though Tina was so very young to be having a baby, she wanted it so desperately. Destiny, Tina shan't be returning to the manor. Her parents have decided to allow her to return and she will be nursed by them." Mary began to cry a bit, and then stopped herself quickly. She didn't want the other nurses to see her crying.

"Oh, no! How terrible for Tina...and I will so miss talking with her. Thank you for sharing this with me, Mary. I imagine you are not supposed to tell us the details of someone's medical report." She wanted to go to her room to think about what she had heard about Tina, and said, "I am going to go lie down for awhile."

"I will talk with you later, Destiny. Let me know if you need anything," Mary offered, as she watched Destiny waddle back down the hall.

The afternoon heat seemed to penetrate the old manor, causing waves of nausea to flow through Destiny's stomach. She even felt a bit dizzy and decided to lie in bed for the afternoon. Her last exam with Dr. Ellsworth indicated she could start labour any day. She missed Tina. She became friends with Mary, although didn't disclose herself intimately as she had with Tina. Mary instructed Destiny in the breathing techniques to use with contractions, and helped her read through all the legal papers necessary to release the baby for adoption. Everything seemed to be going as expected, until an unfamiliar knock sounded at the front door of the Charter Manor.

"We're search'in for a young teen runaway. We need to talk to the person in charge here," the Bobby announced loud enough for everyone in the lounge to hear.

"I'll take you to Dr. Ellsworth. She is the head doctor of the manor," replied the pregnant woman who opened the door.

"Thank ye, little lady," said the Copper, as he followed the girl to the medical wing, disappearing down the hall.

Destiny could hear Mary's footsteps before she knocked on her door. She was a bit irritated to be interrupted when she had decided to take a nap. She opened the door to find Mary in tears, "What's wrong, Mary?"

"Destiny, a bloody Bobby just popped in! They are looking for a runaway teen! I know we haven't become real friends, but I wanted to warn you in case you were the girl they are looking for," Mary divulged, trying to catch her breath.

"You are sweet, Mary, but even if I *was* the girl they are looking for, it wouldn't matter. I just turned eighteen. I can muck about all I want and they could not touch me," Destiny said with a prideful smile.

"Oh, good…I mean, if you *were* that girl. They are talking to Dr. Ellsworth now, so the entire manor is a bit dotty," Mary said, waving her arms in the air.

"Well, do not worry about me, Mary. I am sure it will all work out with the lost girl," Destiny said, patting Mary's shoulder.

"Whew! I will let you rest now. Put a cold cloth over your forehead, sometimes that helps the body keep cool in this unbearable weather," Mary said.

"Okay," Destiny smiled and closed the door.

Destiny tried to get into a comfortable position on the bed. Finally closing her eyes, she thought, *At least the timing of my birthday worked out well for me to go through all this mess. Life sure throws a lot of shit at a person. I wonder why it has to be that way?* She drifted into a light sleep with dreams of ocean tidal waves turbulently overtaking small villages near the shoreline. Once again, she woke up soaked in sweat and needed to shower to remove the stickiness clinging to her skin. As she stepped from the shower bath, she came face-to-face with Dr. Ellsworth.

"Destiny, I need to speak to you when you have dressed. Please come to my office," the doctor stated clearly.

"All right, I will be there directly," replied Destiny, as she reached for the nearest towel to wrap what she could of her middle.

While dressing, Destiny played tapes in her mind that could defend any opposing question thrown at her. She felt confident entering the doctor's office. She sat in the familiar chair, positioned perfectly two feet in front of the old desk.

"Destiny," addressed Dr. Ellsworth, as she entered the room. "I was visited by a local Bobby this afternoon. He was searching for a young teen who had evidently run off from her home several months ago. The girl's parents are concerned and called for an official alarm." The doctor took a pensive breath to allow Destiny the opportunity to respond.

Destiny remained quiet.

The doctor continued her questioning as she stared straight into Destiny's eyes, "Are you that runaway, Destiny?"

"No, Dr. Ellsworth. I am eighteen. I come and go as I please. I am not a runaway," Destiny responded bluntly.

"I see..." the doctor lingered. "The name of the girl they are looking for is Destiny Collins. Have you heard of her?"

"No, I have not. Have you asked the other residents?" Destiny suggested.

"No, but I have informed the Bobby there is no one here by that name. I doubt that they will return. The young runaway may even return to her home before they complete their search," Dr. Ellsworth said, summoning a slight smile that eased the lines on her face. "You can go, Destiny. I am sure I will be delivering your baby in a few days. Go rest now."

"Well, that is too bad about the girl who thinks she can't live with her parents. I hope she finds somewhere to be happy." With that said, Destiny managed to get up more quickly than normal in her present condition and walked swiftly back to her room.

A blue and purple butterfly circled a waiting tulip trying to survive the morning heat. Destiny wiped her forehead for the umpteenth time while sitting in the garden filled with limp shrubs and reluctant flower blooms. She poured a bit of water from her glass onto a sad looking marigold, hoping the cool liquid would quench its thirst. The sun had scorched the leaves of the plants leaving a laser-beam trail of destruction. The landscape reminded Destiny of the film snippet that was being promoted on the Tele for an upcoming feature titled *Star Wars*. The film trailer displayed handheld laser tools that could destroy most anything in their path. Her broad imagination was enticed.

Destiny had always been a fan of science fiction stories depicting planets with unknown inhabitants possessing powers beyond human perception. When she was younger, she would go to the cinema to watch any new sci-fi film portraying foreign lands filled with tempting treasures and unheard of mysteries. At about ten years old, she was able to see *2001: A Space Odyssey* and thought it was the best film ever made. Around thirteen, she went to the cinema to view the raw film *Escape from the Planet of the Apes*, and then became fascinated with the possibility of evolution. She even found books in the library to learn more about Charles Darwin's theories.

Traditional religion had never set well with Destiny. She went to the proper services when needed, and listened to the priest speak of a world created by a god to be worshiped; but she always felt there was something lacking with the facts. She could not make sense of most of it. Sometimes, she would challenge the nuns' religious tales by asking questions, which many times, they had to admit were unanswerable. This made Destiny even more intent to believe only in what she could perceive with her five senses, or had experienced firsthand. She found no interest in learning about stories from two thousand years ago. She made up her mind that she was put on Earth only to go through the mundane experiences that accompanied being human.

"How could there be a god that would allow me to be raped and put in this horrific situation?" she inquired, while gazing upward as if to ask an invisible authority. She waited a full sixty seconds to make sure there was no reply. Suddenly, she felt a new sensation in her belly—not quite a pain, more like a hardening of her entire abdomen. She stood to stretch her arms and legs, which seemed to help ease the numbness. As she started to walk back through the garden, she again experienced the new sensation that caused her to stop and lean against the porch railing. She remembered what Mary had instructed about the signals of imminent labour, and assumed the discomfort was the beginning of Braxton Hicks contractions. Mary had explained that these contractions were named after a doctor in the mid-1800s, and would make her tummy feel like it was as hard as a brick. Destiny slowly made it back to her room to lie down.

After twenty minutes or so, Destiny's pre-labour contractions subsided and she lay on her back staring at the ceiling. She allowed her mind to slip into a nearly unconscious state where she felt at peace, somewhere between reality and a space-time she could not name. When she allowed herself this inner meditation, her questioning thoughts traveled in search of the reason for her existence. Destiny would allow herself to go far into the recesses of her subconscious to reach for answers and direction. Quietly, she whispered to the Universe, "I accept my life and my destiny to be challenged with trials to overcome, such as this pregnancy. But will I be able to accept my decision to set this child on a journey fettered by an unknown conception? If there is a better way, I ask it to be revealed to me now." She waited in silence. The room was silent. The world was silent. This was her answer.

Five

Luana had fallen asleep with her reading glasses stuck to the bridge of her nose. The book lay open, beckoning her to resume reading the moment she opened her eyes. Half-asleep, she rose to turn off the lights and snuggled down into the covers. Her thoughts drifted as conscious awareness floated to visions of infants crying and babies being born. As she dreamt, Luana's psyche searched for peace surrounding the issue of whether Destiny would continue with her plan, or change her mind.

Early the next morning, Luana savored the fact that she didn't need to go work in an office; she could take her time to savor the captivating novel. She didn't want to miss a single word that might shed a ray of light on the story's evolution. Envisioning the storyline's progression, Luana spoke out loud, "If Destiny is smart, she will realize what an important decision she soon has to make. If she continues with her plan, her life will be forever changed. If she picks her alternate choice, her life will also be forever changed."

Luana fixed her usual bowl of oatmeal with a touch of brown sugar and rice milk. She was tempted to prop the book up and read it while eating her breakfast; however, her thoughts soon chased the past. She remembered her own sexual encounter when she was twenty-six and all the inner turmoil she had felt. Her stomach lurched as she put her spoon down to truly feel the emotions that took over her body and mind. Luana recalled that after the forced intercourse on that horrific night, she had told her assailant to immediately leave and never return or call her again. Then she had quickly showered, crawled into bed, and never mentioned the incident to anyone. The experience stayed tucked in her subconscious mind for nearly three months, until it became apparent that she had missed two menstrual periods.

Luana knew better than to submerge herself in college studies to avoid the pending situation; however, she did encrust her brain with enough denial to restrain normal alarms that would alert her rational mind of the impending situation. Upon her third missed menses, Luana couldn't stop her obliviousness from reaching reality. Her brain screamed out what she knew must be the truth: "I am pregnant!" Panic sat unrelentingly in Luana's throat like a lump of hot coal that stopped the vomit in her stomach to spew. Limp and exhausted, she reached for her pink princess telephone to call her doctor. The appointment was made for the next day.

Throughout the rest of the day, Luana steadied her mind with gifts of denial. She offered it fabrications that mimicked: *Whatever happens, I am a strong independent woman and can handle anything.* However, her mind chose to ignore her deceit and displayed visions of scenarios filled with back alley butchers and the emotional anguish of having to give away her baby. Lastly, her creative mind handed her a vision of raising a child, which would surely end her educational pursuits and her career. In the middle of the night, she sat upright in bed to scold herself for allowing her mind to skid onto the denial path she had selected twelve hours earlier. She was unable to sleep until 3A.M.

The doctor's appointment was kept at 9A.M. sharp. She dutifully presented the nurse with a small plastic cup of yellow liquid to be mixed, stirred, and ultimately reveal its prediction. While the nurse was busy with the testing, Luana sat on the edge of the exam table ready to be poked and prodded. She tried not to jump ahead to the expected verdict, but found it difficult to concentrate on anything except her anticipated sound of the doctor's voice announcing, "Congratulations, you're going to have a baby!"

Luana wrapped her arms around her chest to ward off the involuntary shakes that were convincingly waiting to enter her body. The doctor entered the room, "Hello, Luana, is it time for your annual exam already?"

"Hello, Dr. Shelly. No, I am here because I believe I am pregnant," Luana said, trying to sound adult.

"Oh, then let me do a quick exam. I'll be able to tell if you are over three months, and the urine test—did you give the nurse a urine sample?" the doctor inquired.

"Yes, she has it. Will it show one way or the other? I have missed three periods," Luana explained.

"Yes. I should be able to easily discern if you are that far along. Lie down and let's take a look," Dr. Shelly said, as she placed each of Luana's cold feet in the colder metal stirrups. "Do you want to be pregnant, Luana?"

"No. It was really an unplanned event. I am not sure what I will do if I am pregnant," Luana replied, offering just enough information without getting into the whole rape issue.

"Oh, I see. You do know abortions are illegal except in cases of endangerment to the mother, don't you?" Dr. Shelly asked as she felt for Luana's uterus, withdrew her hand, and then removed the thin plastic gloves.

"Yes, I am aware," Luana said, retrieving her feet and regaining control of her legs from the atypical position.

"Let me go check on your urine test. You can get dressed. I will be right back," the doctor said, and turned to walk out the door.

Luana was using all her willpower to control her emotions that were exploding from her pores like invisible fireworks. She redressed and sat in a cold chrome chair feeling her flat stomach that indicated there was nothing growing inside. The nurse opened the door and asked Luana to follow her to the doctor's private office. Luana sat in the overstuffed 1970's avocado green chair and tightly crossed her legs as if to protect her private parts that had just been invaded. Dr. Shelly entered the room and sat behind her Maplewood desk. She set Luana's medical chart down, and explained, "Luana, your urine test came back negative, and my examination found your uterus to be of normal size. However, since you have missed three periods, I would like to do one last test to ensure you are not pregnant. The test is called a sonogram, have you heard of it?" the doctor asked.

"No. Why would I have missed three periods, if I am not pregnant?" Luana inquired.

"Well, there can be many reasons. You may be pregnant, but I need to rule out a few things before being completely sure.

Can you get to the community hospital by 3P.M. this afternoon?"

"Yes. I'll be there. Where do I go?" Luana inquired, not feeling any less anxious.

"Go to the outpatient area and they will take care of you. I'll see you again tomorrow afternoon at 2P.M., and then we should have a better idea of what's going on. The sonogram is a relatively new test that is not invasive, so it won't be painful," the doctor reassured.

Luana left the doctor's office bewildered and knew she would be unable to go to class. She drove directly home, turned on the television, and zoned-out until she needed to leave for the hospital. During the sonogram, she tried to get the technician to reveal the outcome of the test, but the tech adhered to the hospital's protocol of not discussing medical findings with the patients. Thinking she was still pregnant, Luana drove home feeling uneasy about her choices. She knew there were only three alternatives: Have an illegal abortion; give birth and allow someone to adopt her baby; or, give birth and raise the child herself. None of the options felt acceptable to her. She kept telling herself not to think about her choices, at least until she knew for sure she was pregnant.

Luana snapped back from her daydreaming and into reality. She finished her cold oatmeal, placed the unwashed bowl in the sink beside yesterday's tea cup, and settled into her reading chair. She needed to reread the last paragraph to refresh her memory of where she'd left off with Destiny's story. "I wonder why Destiny didn't choose to get an abortion?" Luana spoke aloud. "I know abortions were legal in England in 1976. I think they became legal in the late 1960s over there." She thought about Destiny's situation and compared it to what she'd gone through when she thought she was pregnant in 1971. Again speaking to herself, "I assisted so many women that were going through that harrowing circumstance. I can certainly understand the personal reasons a woman could not consider an abortion. I suppose that could be why there is no mention of that option for Destiny, at least so far." Until completing her thoughts about her own confusing situation when she was twenty-six, Luana found she couldn't continue her reading. Her memories streamed detailed visions of her past...

Following the sonogram, Luana's mind traveled to the age-old questions regarding life and death. She had yet to explore her own beliefs about abortions; she had no reason to, until her current predicament. Her college courses in Women Studies had touched on the issue, but only to cover the fact that women could not obtain abortions in the United States, at least not legally. Many students talked about the illegal procedures done in dirty buildings with hidden back-alley entrances performed by medical students to earn money to finish their studies. Then, of course, there were rumors of women actually dying from their own botched attempts from using metal coat-hangers and knitting needles, or drinking wild poisonous concoctions. Now, being confronted with her own emergent situation, Luana seriously contemplated her feelings surrounding pregnancy termination. *So much depends on when, or if, one believes a soul energy enters a body, and when. And that question cannot be answered until you have a firm grip of whether there is such a thing as a soul essence, which gives life to the physical body.*

That night, while waiting to receive the final results of her sonogram, Luana questioned her religious and spiritual beliefs. She thought about what had been preached in the community church she had attended when she was a young girl, and what several of the spiritual books that her mother had left lying around the house had suggested. Soon, her mind twisted in a maze of metaphysical laws and religious principles. Luana knew her spiritual beliefs were based on the concept that all living beings do, in fact, have a soul. She also acknowledged her belief that all souls survived death, and maybe continued on to other lifetimes as well. This awakening came to her in a flash of insight, as if waiting to be discovered at exactly this time in her life. With this ideology, Luana realized she believed a soul enters a physical body with its first breath, much like she had read in several religious texts. Armed with this spiritual perspective, she could now move toward accepting the possibility of having an abortion, if she chose that option.

The next morning, Luana lay in bed wondering what she could do until 2P.M. The appointment seemed like days away, instead of hours. She decided to make a list of her options by writing down their pros and cons, hoping a decision would be revealed to her somewhere between the lines. The words in each column spilled onto the next page, looking like a spattering of paint drippings racing to the edge of the paper. She recognized her heartbeat quickening when she read over the list under the heading "Give Up for Adoption." Because of this visceral reaction, Luana decided to eliminate that option altogether. The two options left were equally difficult to comprehend or consider because her inner voice kept shouting, "You don't even know if you are pregnant yet!"

Luana decided to go for a long lunch to occupy the few hours until her appointment. The café overlooked a small estuary where she sat outside. She soon spied a Blue Heron patiently searching the shallow waters for a fast meal and admired his elegant meditation. She closed her eyes to imitate his rumination and found herself thinking: *If I get through this, I promise to be more deliberate, more pensive with my time and decisions. I promise to be more aware of myself and those around me, so I can live the life I have planned.* Luana opened her eyes and wondered who she had been addressing with her bargaining promises. *Perhaps a part of my inner Self, or a Divine Power*, she thought calmly in answer to her own silent question. She knew logically that negotiations with a Divine Source were a futile attempt, but the process felt inherently natural at this stressful time.

She thought about her spiritual beliefs and sighed as she ate her spinach salad and drank her iced tea with lemon. She tried to make sense of why she would need to go through the experience of an unplanned, albeit, unwanted pregnancy. A group of colorful Mallards waddled up the shore below her table begging for handouts. She tore off a few edges of her sourdough bread and tossed them over the deck's railing. The ducks scrambled to the heap of crumbs sparring for the tasteful morsels. She glanced at her wristwatch to check the time, which had passed much faster than she expected. Signaling for her check, Luana applied a bit of lip gloss to her full lips, left the café and drove to the doctor's office.

Once again, rooted in the overstuffed chair that occupied her doctor's private office, Luana's heart began to race as she heard Dr. Shelly's voice in the hallway. She took two deep breaths, relaxed her shoulders, and turned her neck one way and then the other to release the tension residing there.

The doctor entered waving a medical chart in the air, "Well, Luana, you are not pregnant! I am glad we jumped ahead to the sonogram—it's the newest and best imaging tool we have currently."

"Whoa…I am so surprised! But, if I'm not pregnant, why have I missed my last three periods?" Luana asked with grave concern.

"Well, it seems you have developed quite a number of fibrous tumors in your uterus, Luana. We see this many times in older women, more rarely in women your age. Are your periods painful?" Dr. Shelly inquired.

"Yes, I have always had terrible cramping during my periods, even as a teenager," Luana admitted.

"That is a typical sign of fibroids. We can take a wait-and-watch approach, or we could remove your uterus. Of course, that would mean you could never have children," the doctor said matter-of-factly.

"Oh, my goodness! I can't handle a decision like that right now. I need to first assimilate the fact that I am not pregnant." She listened to the unequivocal words "Not Pregnant" echo in her brain.

"I understand. Why don't we make another appointment in three or four months to see how you are doing? I need to know when your periods resume," the doctor said, finalizing the visit without waiting to hear Luana's reply.

Luana left the doctor's office and headed to her parked car. Once secure inside, she released the tears that had been hibernating deep inside. Allowing her emotions their outlet, she quietly whispered, "Thank you…thank you. If my prayers were met by a Divine Being that oversees my life, I thank you. Someday, I would like to know why I needed to go through this ordeal. It feels like one of the biggest lessons I will ever learn in my life."

Several years later, Luana *did* understand why the incident of facing the possibility of an unplanned pregnancy had been necessary for her to experience. Without the inner turmoil she had experienced when she was twenty-six, she never would have become the empathetic counselor she had been when working with the hundreds of women at the medical clinic. She could identify with those younger women who often times found themselves in a sexual situation that had gotten out of hand. She could also identify with women who became pregnant, even while using a method of birth control, but could not face having a child at that time in their lives. In all the circumstances that were presented to her as a counselor at the clinic, she easily empathized with each heartfelt story. It was then that Luana recognized why her personal situation several years earlier had transpired, so she could compassionately help guide other women through their traumatic circumstances surrounding an unplanned pregnancy.

Luana fingered the pages of her book that was waiting patiently to present its next chapter. She concluded her mind rummage of her past and acknowledged that because she had gained such a valuable spiritual insight while a young woman, she could trust whatever Destiny chose to experience in her younger years would also be an essential lesson in her life. Selfishly, Luana hoped Destiny would change her mind and keep her baby.

Eager to discover the imminent decision, she placed her reading glasses over her nose, took a deep breath and began to read.

Six

In the haze of her drowsiness to get up to pee for the third time, Destiny realized she had experienced light contractions throughout the night. She could only imagine what was coming next, but felt ready; after all, she had made it this far. Settling back into bed, she stared once again at the stark white ceiling to resume her contemplation. The early evening's *silent answer* provided the sense of relief that her decision to give the baby up for adoption was the right choice. Destiny's brain housed only unanswerable questions, all spinning their tiny hooks to snag every crevasse of brain matter to leave her mind aching for silence. *How could I begin to explore my future while tending to a baby's needs? I certainly didn't ask to get pregnant! Why did that wanker have to rape me? Why should I be held responsible for raising a child conceived in such a horrible act? Why do I have to undergo this experience?* She was relieved and almost happy when the more intense contractions brought her awareness back to the present task at hand.

Destiny cherished a few hours early in the morning to drift in and out of a tormented sleep. Abruptly at 7A.M., she knew the time had come; she must call for Mary. She managed to get to the door, open it and shout down the hallway, "Mary, it's time!"

One girl on her way to the loo noticed Destiny clutching the doorway and signaled she would go find Mary. Mary came running down the hall just in time to catch Destiny as she sank to the floor with another contraction.

"Destiny, do the breathing I taught you, *now*. This one will pass and then we'll get you to the delivery room. Don't you worry none," Mary tried to sound professional and comforting at the same time.

Dr. Ellsworth was notified and Destiny was taken directly into the delivery room. "It looks like you have been going through labour on your own, Destiny, good job!" the doctor commended. "Now, let's get on with this delivery."

Destiny was silent throughout the entire process; she instructed her mind to retreat from reality. It was effortless to guide herself into fantasies far beyond conscious awareness. She visualized adventures in other countries, like America. She easily saw herself strolling along the Pacific Ocean's shoreline gathering shells and placing them in baskets purchased from vendors selling beach items to tourists. When she visited a favorite illusionary beach, she would journey on a pier held high above the waves by blackened pylons. Sounds echoed beneath the pier as each wave splashed against the wood causing a salty mist to linger in her hair. She felt the hot summer sand between her toes as she walked toward the warm water slapping the rocks and tumbling small shells to land at her feet. Standing silent, tall, and still, she allowed herself to melt into the wet granules and sink beneath the Earth.

Yes, it was easy for Destiny to envision exciting travels only she could create. Her mind was a rich mixture of creative exploration and realistic trivia filled with details devoured from hundreds of books read throughout her young life. If there was one book required for a class, she would read three. She had her parents' entire library at her disposal and learned to twist each book she read into an adventure of creative imagery. Some of Destiny's favorite books were the ones her mother had purchased that depicted the famous landmarks of the United States. Her mum had always wanted to travel abroad to see the famous Niagara Falls, but her father seemed too preoccupied with his work to venture beyond the countryside. Most of her life, Destiny had felt it necessary to retreat into her inner-mind travels to escape what she thought was a lonely mundane existence.

"Destiny? I said, do you want to hold your baby?" the nurse jarringly shouted in Destiny's ear, offering a bundle wrapped tight in thin blankets.

"What? No! Why would you ask such a thing?" Destiny yelled back at the shocked nurse.

"Nurse, take the baby to the nursery wing. Destiny is giving her baby up for adoption," Dr. Ellsworth announced to the uninformed nursemaid. Then while facing Destiny, the doctor said, "We will need one last signature from you before you leave to finalize your decision."

"Yes, yes, of course," Destiny complied. She closed her eyes to drift forward a few days to envision when she would leave the manor that had been her unwitting refuge.

Dr. Ellsworth finished sewing the delicate tissue between Destiny's legs and gave her instructions on how to care for the area. She mentioned a second time that she would need to see Destiny again before leaving the manor.

The following day, Destiny lay on the narrow bed in her room wishing her breasts would stop aching. She had been given the magic injection to halt lactation, but the laden glands were still swollen and tender. She closed her eyes to study her evolving intentions for the future. The primary issue was not to return to her parents' home. She was adamant that any plans she made would support that decision. Her next concern was to decide where she would live. She still had money saved, most of which came from graduation gifts. She had used much of it to harbor in the dingy motel for the past several months. Recounting in her mind what her bank passbook read, Destiny decided there was enough to rent a small flat for several months. She wanted to check out the suburb of Swindon Village near the outskirts of Cheltenham, just northwest of the borough. Tina had talked to her about growing up in Cheltenham, and the visits her family took to the countryside. It sounded peaceful and a perfect place to live. She envisioned herself living in a small cottage and walking or riding a cycle to work, probably in a pub or such. As long as the area had fresh gardens she could walk in and a library to visit, Destiny knew she would be happy.

Once, when Destiny was around twelve years old, she had a dream about living near a stream that flowed with the breeze past pastures filled with grazing horses. The vision crept into her consciousness and she felt the excitement of new possibilities. Slowly, Destiny turned on her side to reach for her journal to capture the plan:

Journal—July 13, 1976: I cannot wait to leave this place! The thought of having to work in a place like this gives me the creeps...not that everyone here hasn't been supportive. Oh well, in a few days, I will catch a ride to Cheltenham to scout about.

My breasts are killing me! The nurse keeps telling me to massage them and wait a few more days. So here I lie, too sore to move. I have no emotions about my decision; I know it is best this way. At least the kid will have a set of parents who can give it a home and raise it proper. Should I be more upset? Actually, I never felt like it was mine to keep, more like something that happened to me. I am glad it is over. I do wonder if it was a boy or girl; yet, I could not ask the doctor. I hope it grows up to be happy and very smart so it can live a proper life. I also hope it does not end up hating me...

Destiny stayed fairly secluded for the next few days; she didn't want to engage in conversations with other women. During her last visit to see Dr. Ellsworth, she asked about contraception and was told the nurse would go over the information. *At least I can make sure this will never happen to me again*, she thought. She was also given an e.p.t. kit for early pregnancy detection that was currently being tested by physicians. The doctor gave her the final adoption papers to sign, and stated there were a few months in which she could change her mind should she wish to do so. Destiny signed all the papers, albeit, with her fictitious last name.

On the morning of July 17th, Destiny left the Charter Manor. Her thoughts lingered for a moment on her short friendship with Tina. Tina had been the only person with whom she had dared to share herself, and maybe one day they would meet again. At the bus stop, Destiny asked the driver to take her to Cheltenham. Once there, she could find out how to get to Swindon Village. She settled on the furthest rear seat next to the window, and pulled out an old road map from the seatback in front of her. Following the crossing lines, Destiny judged the travel from Worcester to Cheltenham to be thirty miles. Heading south on the motorway, she watched the wild flowers desperately trying to survive the unfamiliar heat wave. The hilly landscape that would normally be dark emerald green was turning dusty brown, setting the theme for the looming drought. She lowered the window to feel the warm air sweep across her face. The breeze blew her golden brown hair aside to find the nape of her neck, and the hot air dried the damp beads of sweat clinging there.

Destiny had always thought of herself as a rather studious-looking girl, especially when she was wearing her spectacles with tortoiseshell frames. She was proud of her intellectual capabilities, and never apologized for her quick sense of comprehension when a new topic was introduced in a conversation. Her study grades were top of the class in all subjects; and she completed her studies by mid-term, in January. If she had decided to walk in her graduation ceremony, she would have received honors. As the bus motor continued its drumming noise, Destiny reviewed her privileged life, acknowledging it had transpired because of her parents' social status. She desired no part of that life for herself and her new chosen independence. She made a mental reminder: *When I am settled into my own place and have a job, I must call to assure Mum of my safety.*

Opening her journal, Destiny reread the last few lines she had written a few days earlier: "Will my feelings change? Will I later regret my decision?" An inner voice assured her: *You are doing the right thing for your life at this moment.* Destiny's inner voice had a clear connection to her higher consciousness, and she listened assiduously to each word it chose to reveal. Sometimes, she would ask questions to see if a miraculous answer would resound from deep within, but that usually did not happen. The voice was more a quiet whisper, offering tidbits of insight and assurance when she needed it most. Now comforted by the visitation from her inner voice, Destiny settled back into the leather-worn seat to envision the next step of her journey.

The bus came to a halt near a park filled with lush trees trying desperately to reach the airy clouds for a wisp of moisture. Destiny walked a few blocks around the centre, and then sat squarely on a waiting bench. She watched two young boys play with a leather soccer ball displaying its blue hexagon patches with bright red stars in the center. She had enjoyed playing soccer as a child, until some bully kicked the ball straight into her face leaving a deep purple bruise on her cheek for weeks.

Destiny's mind drifted to those years when life was fun and free, and her parents were not so worrisome. There were occasions in her childhood that were filled with excitement, like going on outings with her mum. They would shop for clothes, or sit in the library reading books, and then go for a pudding. Her mum, Helen, used to be happy and her face reflected the joy in her heart. Her physical appearance reminded Destiny of a beautiful painting she had once admired in a gallery. It was of a Victorian woman relaxing in a lounge chair reading a book. The woman's auburn hair loosely flowed over a bodice of cream silk lace, and her green eyes seemed hypnotized by the printed pages she held in her lap. *What happened to that mum I loved so dearly?* Destiny pondered. *I wonder what could have happened to make her so stiff and rigid?*

Soon, the two boys left the park. She spied a pub and walked to it, knowing she would be welcomed. Sitting at the bar, she asked for a Coke with a lemon wedge. Talking with the barman, she revealed, "I am looking for a hostel. Could you point me in the right direction?"

"Oh, sure, if you go down this street here and turn left, and then continue another mile, there's a fine establishment for travelers to stay. Will you be visiting awhile then?" he politely asked Destiny, as he served up the ordered drink.

"I am not sure yet. I am going to visit Swindon Village. Which direction is it?" Destiny squeezed the lemon in her Coke and took a long drink.

"Aye, Swindon? Well, it's hardly a village ye know, more like a little suburb. You'll find it going that way, northwest," the barman said, as he pointed to the direction with a towel-filled hand.

"Thanks…and for the Coke also," Destiny replied, and left payment on the dark oak bar top.

She made her way toward the hostel, stopping to look in shop windows to get a feel for the area and renew her sense of freedom. For a split second, Destiny thought of Tina and where she might live. Then she abandoned the thought, allowing it only to dwell in the back of her mind. The hostel was similar to most found in England—clean, cheap, and offering just enough comfort to spend a few weeks' lodging. She settled her things, which amounted to a small piece of luggage, tote bag, pocketbook and a light jacket. If she needed more clothes, there were several shops advertising the newest styles from decorated windows. Destiny sat in the cushioned oak chair near a small window in her room to deliberate her next move. Like a chessboard, she used her journal to jot notes in a logical order to ensure each move would result in both a job, and a place for her to live.

She figured that her first move to play was to meet people. Destiny had a flair for engaging strangers and knew this would benefit her search for employment. The choice to work in a pub in Cheltenham was not her most preferable choice, as much as a quick task to earn a living. Being a frequent visitor of the pubs where the college students hung about in Telford would now work in her favor. A positive note, she was now eighteen and had no reason to worry about getting thrown out for being underage. Destiny's mind ventured to stray her thoughts, so she decided to take a nap. It was early afternoon and she reasoned that waiting until evening to survey the village pubs would ensure more crowds, and then she could make her first tactical move.

Luana took a break from her reading to get a few errands done. It always happened that when she was heavy into a favorite book, her daily routine went off-kilter, leaving her house and her grooming quite unkempt. This time, Luana swore not to allow her preoccupation with devouring her newest book to keep her from living a more balanced lifestyle. She loved that her time was her own, however, it took a bit of systematic organization to keep her house clean and the car maintenance up to date. The idea of hiring a gardener and a housekeeper did not appeal to her. Luana was in good health and of sound mind, so felt it was silly to pay someone else to do ordinary everyday tasks. Maybe when she was into her eighties, she might recognize a reason to retain a helper now and then. In the meantime, she felt proud that she could carry out the trash, pull weeds, clean the house, fill her own gas tank, and do her grocery shopping. After all, she was only sixty-eight years old, not eighty-eight!

Luana reflected on how the years had a way of slipping into the ethers when one passes the age of fifty. When we are children, uncaring of life's daily procession of chores, the days linger among the cobwebs of our immaturity. We rise early, eager for the rush of new adventure, and fall asleep just as eager, to dream of flying like super-humans ready for whatever the following day may bring us. As Luana dutifully managed her day, she found her awareness roaming her inner child's mind. Some of her favorite memories were the days spent with her brother and their parents at the beachside. She would run down the shoreline to stream the wind through her long blonde hair just to smell and taste the salty mixture. Until the sun set, Luana and her brother would hunt for shells, placing them carefully in plastic buckets filled with ocean water to gently rinse them. They would inspect each one and decide those to be honored with the ride back home. The next day, she would fondle each shell as if it were a baby kitten and place it in a perfect position to display its beauty among her other garden treasures.

Luana's family trips to the beach were treasured memories that she had tucked neatly on the shelves of her subconscious mind. Often at bedtime, she would turn on her sleep machine with its continuous sounds to lull her into a deep dreamstate. Her favorite white-noise drone was the ocean waves turning their foamy surf over and over upon the shore, imitating the Earth's breath heaving in and out. This evening, after the day's business was complete, Luana reached for her hardback book. She removed the beaded bookmark and opened her cherished companion, knowing she would be up late once again.

Seven

When Destiny awoke, night had consumed the little room's window, declaring she had napped past midnight. The moon smiled across the bed cover as she unfurled it and crawled inside. *I guess I need more rest than I thought*, she surmised. She closed her eyes to the night and slept another eight hours. She did not dream of babies, or of her parents; she did not dream at all. Her body sought time to heal, and her weary mind finally gifted the unfettered sleep to begin the healing process.

With her body-mind working in tandem over the next few days, Destiny regained her physical strength and a renewed sense of calculated deliberation. She made a few trips to a nearby deli for food, local papers, maps, and to listen to hearsay about jobs for hire. Making notes in the margins of the newsy, she gathered enough information to feel confident there would be employment waiting for her when she desired it.

The original pub that Destiny wandered into the day she arrived in Cheltenham became a regular visit for her to appraise the local scuttlebutt. She ascertained from the gossip being bantered about that there were several pubs in the area. She also learned that the parish of Swindon Village had a creek named Wyman's Brook circling its outskirts. This tidbit of news triggered her dream of living in a quaint village with a stream running through it. Destiny decided to hitch a ride there as soon as possible. As she was inquiring about Swindon, a woman a bit older reported that she worked in a day spa in the village. She even offered Destiny a ride whenever she wanted to go visit. The woman explained that Cheltenham, and its suburbs, was considered a *ville d'eau*, a spa village. In the area, there were many public and private mineral pools, and most of the spas offered therapeutic massage treatments. Destiny listened intently to all this new information.

Feeling like her life was finally moving forward, Destiny noted in her journal how she was beginning to feel in control of her life again. Then she realized she had always been in control. She was the one who had decided to shut her parents out of her life. She was the one who put herself in an uncompromised situation by attending college frat parties. Not that she wanted to be raped, she felt totally out-of-control in that situation. However, she did have one hundred percent control over her decision to not have an abortion, but to give her baby up for adoption. Actually, she felt her decision against an abortion was not a choice; her small inner voice had guided her to complete the pregnancy. She also felt that it took self-control and lots of confidence to decide to give birth to a baby, especially on her own.

One day, when Destiny was walking around Cheltenham square to check out possible shops or pubs where she might find work, she discovered the public library. Anxious to surround herself with books again, she entered the great stone building that looked as if it was built a hundred years ago. She was familiar with how libraries were organized, where to find filing logs and such. On this first visit, Destiny decided to sit in a comfortable chair near a large window overlooking a garden, so she could survey the enormity of the old library. She always felt at home in any library, as if it could provide all the answers to her questioning mind and meet her needs on all levels.

While strolling through the aisles of books, Destiny knew she could not leave until taking out at least one. As she was perusing the Spiritual Books section, she turned abruptly and accidentally knocked a book to the floor. Picking it up to replace it to its home on the shelf, she glanced at its title, *The Nature of Personal Reality* by an author named Jane Roberts. She thumbed through the first few pages, reading the heading of Part One, "Where You and The World Meet." The first paragraph caught her attention, and she read: *The living picture of the world grows within the mind. The world as it appears to you is like a three-dimensional painting in which each individual takes a hand. Each color, each line that appears within it has first been painted within a mind, and only then does it materialize without.*

Destiny closed the paperback and started to tuck it back in the neverending line of books hugging the shelf, when her inner voice whispered, "Read it!"

"Whoa! Wait a minute," Luana said out loud, "I can't believe how Destiny's life is unfolding!" She set her book down spread-eagle on the arm of her chair to keep the current page saved for her return. She wandered outside feeling the cool breeze that gave her the energy rush she needed to drop back into her own reality. She sat on the lounge to reflect on what she knew of Destiny's life so far. The yellow-breasted finch were stressing over who should be the first to dine from the birdfeeder, and darted around her head as if to say, "Get out of the way! What are you doing outside on such a cold day?" Luana closed her eyes to meditate, allowing her mind to roam toward silence. Soon, she found a peaceful space where the birds were merely bubbles floating beyond her sense of time.

Luana meditated regularly and was an avid yoga enthusiast. She'd decided to look into meditation in the early 1970s, finding many techniques through the decades that captivated her sensibilities. After a few years, she realized all the methods she had experienced took her to the same place. She eventually chose a simple exercise in relaxing one part of her body at a time to arrive in a state of non-awareness, which always pacified her goal of inner silence. After enjoying a short twenty minute meditation, Luana opened her eyes and took a few deep breaths. She began to instruct her mind to digest her book's newest revelation. There were definite similarities between her life's path and that of Destiny's journey. It was a bit uncanny how some of their experiences seemed to overlap one another. And now, this latest discovery that Destiny was beginning to investigate the metaphysical world took Luana by surprise.

In her younger years, Luana was introduced to metaphysics and other spiritual practices when she began to study world religions in college. She developed an eagerness to learn about all types of spirituality, including meditation, yoga, self-hypnosis, color and aura healing, and the phenomena of psychics and mediums. By the time Luana was in her thirties, she was well versed in the metaphysical world, as well as the holistic healing arts. She even used some of these techniques in her counseling practice with positive results. The many Jane Roberts books were some of the first she'd studied in the metaphysical arena. They contained a portion of her current spiritual belief system in which she could truly believe and follow. Luana became fascinated with the author's accounts of channeling a nonphysical being. These books led her to read many others dealing in this area of psychic phenomena.

Another person Luana studied who had mediumship abilities was Edgar Cayce. Cayce was a renowned channel, or medium, who lived in the early Twentieth Century. After entering a deep sleep, or meditative state, he would verbally respond to the thousands of letters he received. The letters contained questions of all varieties, from health concerns to career choices. His secretary would take notes while he dictated his channeled answers, which helped guide the inquirers toward a decision to their question or a more healthy approach to living their lives. Luana had been amazed at the accuracy of Cayce's physiological and medical knowledge, even though he never studied medicine. Through the years, she had joined several groups that studied Cayce's life and his readings.

It will be interesting to see if Destiny is also drawn to read about Cayce, and other books that I have also read, Luana thought excitedly. *No wonder this book is one Susie thought I would enjoy!* She felt a cold chill dance along her spine and realized she had been sitting outside much too long. She stepped inside, closed the sliding door and fixed herself a light lunch. While eating her vegan chili beans, Luana's inner voice began to echo: *Your days of teaching are not over*. She let the voice sit alone without her attention, but made a mental note to recognize the guidance if revealed a second time. Luana was quite aware of the intuitive voice that directed her life. It was like a loving companion she could always count on, no matter what the circumstances. Her intuitional inner voice had become like a subconscious twin to her rational conscious mind. She felt the voice as an unconditional impression of Love, and likened it to how others described their Higher Power or Divine Self.

Luana had always believed there was something greater than herself, a force within her commanded that she have this belief. While studying the Hindu religion in India, she was told by a yogi that she would one day find her spiritual voice to share with others. At the time, she was not sure what the words meant, but perhaps there was a connection between his prediction and the current instruction she received from her inner voice. *Could I teach or guide others on their spiritual journey?* Luana thought, while listening to her question float in her head. Musing to herself, she arrived at a joint consensus between her twin minds that she, in fact, could instruct others in the area of spirituality. She was certainly equipped with enough education and knowledge to teach those seeking more metaphysical and spiritual insight. Luana decided to let the possibility germinate for the time being, so she could return to Destiny's journey.

Leaving the library with her new library card and an intriguing book to explore, Destiny stopped in a pub she had spotted earlier. She sat at the bar, ordered a Coke with lemon wedge, and started a conversation with the barman. He was a handsome fellow with curly ginger hair, freckles, and a slight limp to his gait.

"Have you heard of any pubs in need of a server?" Destiny asked.

"I did hear of an opening down at the Flat Iron, but I am not sure if it's been filled or not," the freckled chap replied.

"I am looking for a proper place to work. If you hear of something, I will be by again in a couple of days," Destiny said.

"I'll keep an ear out for you; surely, you need a proper pub," he said with a wink.

"Ta." Destiny waved as she finished her soda and left the pub.

Destiny was sure she would find employment. She was not worried; she had plenty of money for now. The hostel was cheap and she could stay there for a few months. She continued her walk, stopping at the deli for a bite to eat before heading back to her room.

"You've been coming here quite a bit lately. Have you settled in the area?" the girl behind the counter asked Destiny.

"Well, I am just staying down the street. The food here is smashing," Destiny replied, reaching over the cheese to pay the girl.

"I've been here for the past few summers. It's well enough I guess; but, I am looking to hang about with a proper job when I graduate," the girl explained.

"So, you are in college then?" Destiny inquired.

"Yes, my last year is coming up next. Then I can move wherever I want."

"Sounds like a plan. I will soon be looking for employment myself. I thought I might work in a pub for a bit. Do you know of any proper ones needing a server?"

"Well, I did hear that the Flat Iron was hiring...oh, wait! There's a new place, down about the centre...let me think what that name was...oh, yes, it's "Skittles." It's all set up with the game in the basement, they say. It brings in lots of older gents, I hear. Guess that would mean good tips!" she said a bit excited. "Perhaps I'll look into it too, and make a change this summer!"

"Thanks for the information. My name is Destiny...what's yours?"

"I am Gwen. Nice to know you, Destiny." The girl came around from behind the counter. "Do you think you will go investigate the new place? Maybe, if it's okay with you...I'll tag along."

"I will let you know tomorrow when I come in for coffee," Destiny promised, knowing she would not keep the pledge.

After leaving the deli, Destiny headed for the pub she had been frequenting to see if anyone there had more information about the new place in the centre. She ordered her Coke with lemon wedge, sat on a stool, and was quickly approached by a young bloke. "Hi there, my name is George. I've seen you sit'in here a few times. What's your name?"

"Hello, George, I am Destiny. Yes, this is a great pub," Destiny tried to sound friendly.

"Yep, I come most every day to unwind...I don't get tanked though. Do you live in Cheltenham?" he asked.

"No, not really. Do you know the area well?" Destiny inquired, without sharing too much.

"Aye, always lived here," George replied.

"Have you heard of the new pub "Skittles" down about the centre?"

"Aye, been by there to check it out. Looks like a bang on pub. It's set with games and such to draw in the crowds. I hear it's an off-shoot from Worcester's Skittles League try'in to get a start up here," George shared with Destiny.

"Thanks, George. I may check it out to be a server there," Destiny said, and then realized she was sharing too much and stood up to leave.

"Ye go'in already?" he asked with disappointment in his voice. "Yes, I need to get home." Destiny waved good-bye.

Once in her cosy room, Destiny blankly stared out the little window trying to envision herself working in a pub, carrying draught beers to old gents with smirky eyes. She watched a crisp orange sun dismount his side of the planet to allow night's moonbeams to fall once again upon her bedcover. Standing in the glow of night, Destiny felt a relaxing sensation seep through her body from head to toe. Night's darkness reminded her to sit in silence and regenerate her body-mind. Gently sinking into the cushioned chair, she crossed her legs one under the other, took a few long breaths and closed her eyes to the moon's smile.

Destiny listened to the quiet rhythms of her breathing, unquestioning their beginning or ending. When she stopped listening, her awareness left the room and traveled to inner-visions of warm seashores and white sand beneath her feet. The familiar pier was in the distance as she walked the wet beach that allowed the cool waters to splash her feet. There were only seabirds to guide her steps as her footprints disappeared along the sandy path. She walked until her body-mind was completely relaxed; and then, she found herself sitting once again in the small oak chair. The meditation was a needed retreat, and Destiny vowed she would make it a ritual each day.

Eight

When life throws us a curve, is it best to hide in a delusion of retreat until the frayed ends of an unknown world are magically mended? We have all attempted this ruse. Usually, the refuge does not unwind the dramas that so cleverly worked their way into our lives. No, retreat is not a decision for brave women who meet each day armed with an inner mantra to squeeze every drop of existence and *joie de vivre!* from their being. Destiny is one of those young women who accepts Fate's responsibility, properly carrying it upon her shoulders to climb over each obstruction placed on her path. She has learned to stare Fear in the eye, defying its stubborn stance to reach from deep within for enough self-love to snide its confrontation. Yes, Destiny is a rare young woman indeed.

The words seemed to flow from Luana's pen without effort. Had she become possessed by the book she was reading? Was she drawing on some inner knowledge not yet recognized by her conscious mind that was teasing the creative force of literary writing? Or, was she channeling a mysterious entity whose only purpose was to inspire humans to unlock their psychic talents hidden like old shoes in an attic? What was happening to Luana's mind to guide her to sit by the fireplace and write about this novel she had not even finished reading?

Puzzlement washed through her as she glanced into the intense dehumanizing flame. Luana felt as if she had experienced an out-of-body event, causing her to pose inertly between reality and the unknown dimensions of existence. She sat fixed, frozen and silent, questioning the inner recesses of her mind. Unable to stop herself, she compared her life to what she had read about Destiny's journey thus far. *How have I lived my life?* Luana's inner voice asked. *How did I survive my life's traumas? Was I strong when standing in the face of Fear, or did I retreat hoping to reap Luck's rewards?*

Luana felt there was a message lurking within her that wanted to be discovered. She felt the message would be important to others, as well as for her to ascertain. Redirecting her eyes from the yellow blaze jolted her cognition to resume reality. She reread the written paragraph that had automatically revealed itself. Realizing a sense of perception not gained until the words became visible, Luana whispered into the burning fire, "There is a reason I am supposed to be reading this book, an important reason. This book is a link to my future..."

Luana had always been a believer in listening to the whispers that raced through her mind, darting from one thought to the next in search of an action. She did acknowledge that she had devoted less time to her meditative practices when she was in her thirties. It had been difficult enough to keep her marriage intact, and at the same time, try to expand her counseling career. She admitted that the rigors of life had robbed her of the treasured retreats at a time when they would have been most valuable. She would try to sit quietly in the morning hours before the day's routine found her, but the stressful years had raided her inner-awareness and her moments of Zen. It took a finalizing event to awaken Luana to the realization that she could not survive without consistently visiting her innermost core.

The year of 1984 was like no other Luana had experienced. Her practice was thriving, even growing weekly with referrals from past patients and local doctors. However, her marriage was lacking in its original promises of fiery passion and travels to unknown places. The couple's unexecuted pleasures of joint adventure had wrapped a drab film of trepidation around the relationship's search for libido. There was a gapping juxtaposition exposing their love and their regrets. In that year, when Luana was thirty-eight, a mutual compromise surfaced between her and her husband of ten years, and they separated. Perhaps, the fact that the marriage did not produce the child her husband had anticipated took a toll on the relationship. He argued that was not the case, but Luana could not allow the presence of the issue to exit her mind. Luana's other guilt, which sat lodged between her logical and illogical brain-mind, was the lack of time she had spent nurturing the relationship because of her burgeoning career.

Luana and her husband both had a passion for traveling before they were married. They visited the foreign lands of India and Turkey, which brought wild adventures with the Kama Sutra and eating exotic foods to ignite their hidden passions. One of their journeys concluded their retreat with being harbored in a second story flat in Paris surrounded with depictions of coitus and vast amounts of aphrodisiacs. Now, nearly thirty years after their divorce, Luana still labored over what she could have done to strengthen her marriage bonds with her first husband. Sometimes, it is not as easy as it sounds to let go of the remorse spurred by past relationships. When she executed couples counseling, and before acknowledging a marriage could not be resolved, Luana would insist upon one last session to ensure all avenues possible be dissected. Through the years, as she watched the national statistic imbalance hedge toward divorce, she always felt a pang of disappointment when a couple admitted they were giving up on their marriage vows.

As Luana reminisced by the warm fire, her thoughts turned to her own inner mantra that kept her head above the waters of Fate's spineless tsunamis. She had learned to be self-sufficient throughout her younger years, which brought solace to her soul's desire for solitude. Within this solid state of independence, she began to realize why her life's path had traveled in the directions it had. She spoke aloud, asking herself, "So how did I survive my life's traumas? Was it because my upbringing was filled with love and exposure to the positive feedback I received from my parents? Was it due to my relentless search for recognition and praise during my educational years? Or, have I survived many of life's obstacles because I have an inner strength not acknowledged? Certainly, it has taken me many mornings of meditation, and many nights of self-deliberation, to arrive at this stage in my life. Have I truly lived my life as admirably as I could have?"

Once again, Luana began to write in the ruled notebook she recently found stuffed in a desk drawer. The notebook had waited until this moment when she felt a strong instinctual pull to uncover the talent perhaps experienced in a past lifetime, but never explored in this one. After reading hundreds of educational texts, and writing the same number of papers to satisfy her professors' demands, she never imagined weaving her words together to complete a manuscript. After writing for an hour, Luana smiled as she listened to her first written paragraph dance over her tongue as she reread the words. She was delighted to discover this passageway into a new form of creativity. Paired with her passion for reading, Luana knew this new adventure would bring her hours of joy. But for now, she reached for her companion book and began to read once again.

Destiny awoke the next morning feeling more rested and balanced than she had in ten months. She sat crossed-legged on the bed, studying her journal. There had always been a secret writer lodged within her psyche, and the journal gave the muse its outlet. All of her journals were stacked in the back of her clothes wardrobe in her parents' home, hidden from the wandering eyes of maids. Since she was ten years old, Destiny had been preoccupied with writing in diaries and journals. There was a powerful and mysterious quality to the act of writing that enticed her creativity, which no doubt came from forming a sentence to stimulate a vision in her mind. For several years, she even studied poetry to detect the rhythm of words written by the masters like Whitman and Longfellow. To Destiny, words were as powerful as any drug she could have scored. They could make or break an ego; direct good or evil forces; and harbor or release the array of emotions from compassion to rage.

There was one short poem Destiny had cherished since her childhood. She wrote it on the inside cover of all her journals. While she had been searching for an old piece of poetry written by Reinhart Nordness in her parents' library, another book caught her attention. The volume sat beside the one she had intended to peruse and silently called to her. She decided to randomly open the book, telling herself the words would be the ones she would carry with her always. The poem contained no metered rhythm or rhyme, and the author was unknown, but the words touched an internal cord when she read:

As a tree stands, I am strong
As the river flows, my Being grows
Life delivers life
Death is but a song

Destiny's devotion to the written word helped guide her through the years to graduate secondary school. Many times, a teacher would remark to her that she should consider writing as a career. Although she took the praise with merit, she did not seriously reflect on the suggestion until school year thirteen. The headmistress took her aside to say, "You are at the top of your class, Destiny, and I want to commend you. Each professor you have studied with here at the Charlton School for Girls tells me they believe you are a bit of a writer. I encourage your pursuit in this area. If I can help with recommendations to university, let me know."

"Ta, I will think about it," Destiny replied.

The conversation took place in the fall, just before Destiny discovered she was pregnant. Now, sitting in her hostel room, her dreams hung in midair waiting for inspiration. She wrote a brief journal entry just to appease her writing muse, and then dressed for the day's adventure. The goal for the day was to visit the new pub in the centre for a possible serving position. Realizing the establishment catered to older gents, she put on a plain dark blue dress with simple lines that she kept from school. She wound her hair up behind her head and put her tortoiseshell specs over her nose.

Arriving at "Skittles," Destiny asked for the landlord. She stood tall and sturdy like the tree in her poem. Soon a stout older man with a grey beard walked over to her with an outstretched hand. "Good day, young lady. I am Jon. What can I do for you then?"

"My name is Destiny. I am looking for a position...are you in need of a server?" she asked.

"Indeed I am! Do you live here in Cheltenham then, Destiny?" Jon inquired, while smoothing the ends of his beard.

"Currently, I am at the hostel. I intend to find a more permanent flat soon," Destiny replied, standing straight and tall.

"All the better then…I'm lookin' for someone who wants to stay for a spell and not run off, ya know…" Jon reported.

"Yes, I plan on staying in the area permanently."

"Aye then, have you ever done serving before?"

"Well, I have been about pubs for many years…never actually worked in one, though I am a quick study!" Destiny replied, with a smile displaying her white teeth.

"Well, then, I think we should try you on a bit! You'll have to mind the gents then." Jon put out his hand for a contractual shake.

"Brilliant! I can start whenever you like," Destiny said, feeling secure that her second game move had been played successfully.

For the next few days, Destiny arrived early at the pub to learn her duties and scope it out. She was, in fact, a quick learner and serving lagers to old gents came easily. Jon provided some black Capri pants and a few shirts with "Skittles" embossed on them for her to wear. She was glad not to have to buy clothes for the new job. She met the regulars who went directly downstairs to play the games, and a few of the locals who would stop by to have a pint and chat a bit. Jon had put her on the daytime shift that ended at nine o'clock. That worked for Destiny, because then she could sleep in and stop at the library on her way when she desired.

The hot summer months passed and soon the leaves in the park centre turned yellow and red. Destiny still wanted to visit Swindon Village to see if there might be a flat she could rent. It was definitely time to move out of the hostel that was beginning to host new vacationers. She remembered the woman from the pub who said she would drive her to Swindon, and decided to ask about the offer the next time she saw her. There was also a bus she could take, or she could rent a cycle since the village was only a few miles from Cheltenham.

The new serving job was easy, and Destiny wrapped the older chaps around her little finger. She had plenty of time on her breaks to sit and enjoy reading the books she took out from the library. Sometimes before work, she would go to the park and sit for hours beneath the trees to immerse herself in the world of words. Her mind was expanding daily with the guidance honed from books like the one that fell off the shelf on her first visit to the library. She found other books by Jane Roberts, and felt a connection between herself and the channeled entity, Seth. Destiny learned a significant truth from these books. It was written simply and clearly within one of them: *You make your own reality. There is no other rule. Knowing this is the secret of creativity.*

Armed with this new insight, Destiny began to consciously realize how she was creating her reality. She reread many of her journal entries, and reflected on her teen years that had led to the recklessness she enlisted. Destiny's search for her Higher Self and her spiritual beliefs coincided with her search for the meaning of life. Each new book she devoured, even if revealing only one sentence to fit the puzzle, spurred her mind toward a greater understanding of how the Universe works. A sense of comprehension collided with Destiny's awareness like a Tequila shot landing in the pit of her stomach when she came to understand that she had control over her life *through her actions and reactions.*

Nine

Two weeks flew by with the autumn breeze; however, Destiny had not run into the woman who had offered the ride to Swindon Village. She decided that on her next day off, she would rent a cycle and ride to the suburb. After asking around, she located a bike shop that rented to tourists. The night before her trip, she packed a small lunch of grapes, water biscuits, and a can of Coke. The directions on her map were clear: Head northwest for about three miles. Once on the road, Destiny felt a sense of freedom. Her body appreciated the exercise as the crisp air streamed through her hair. At one point, she spied a little creek and decided to stop. She knelt down to touch the rushing water and splashed a bit on her face. Cupping her hands, she took a sip of the cold liquid and let it slowly slide down her throat.

A little further down the roadway, she came to a sign that named the creek, Wyman's Brook. She remembered her fantasy of living in a village with a stream running through it, and she began to pedal faster. She came to a full stop when she looked up to view a blossoming village with rows of bungalows lining the near end. The billboard read: Wyman's Brook Cottages. *Am I in heaven?* Destiny thought. *This place could not be any more like my vision!* She dismounted and walked her cycle to the centre square, eyeing each unique building. Off to the right, she saw a large church and over to the left a few shops. There were some small mansions and various manors scattered throughout the village with long walkways furrowed with flowers of every colour. There was a park in the square and Destiny decided to leave her cycle in a rack to tour the neighborhood more closely.

The village was surrounded with greenery. There were several wandering lanes with abundant trees shadowing streaks of sunlit fog. Destiny turned into one of the lanes and followed the trees that eventually ended at an impressive brick building that reminded her of a lodge that should reside in the high country. The building could barely be seen as it was drowning in ivy and flowers that covered the entire grounds. She did not want to venture too close, but there was a small sign she wanted to read hanging in one corner of the entry door. She tiptoed up the cobblestone footpath close enough to read: "Leisure Centre Health Spa." Destiny walked back to the centre square and sat on a bench to eat a bit of her snack. She pondered to herself, *I bet that place is where the woman works that I met in the pub! It looks like a lovely place to hang about.*

Destiny found herself gazing intently at the old church at the far end of the roundabout. It was a curious building with a bell tower constructed with six unequally sized walls. She had never seen a church with this architecture and wondered when it had been built. She packed up her lunch and hopped on the cycle to go take a closer look. At the walkway entrance an engraved plate named the church, "St. Lawrence." Even though Destiny could not envelop Catholicism as her parents did, she had a fascination with the belief system, but found it difficult to believe in a god that possessed such vengeance as the nuns' declared. On the plaque, placed under the name of the church, it was noted that the structure had been built in the Twelfth Century.

Riding back through the village, Destiny decided to stop at the bungalows she had passed to inquire if there were any to rent. She spoke to a woman who was leaving one of the cottages, "Hello, do you know if there are any cottages available?"

"Hello there, I am not sure, but you can ask the manager. He lives over there," the woman said, as she pointed to one of the units.

"Ta." She walked her cycle down the path and knocked on the door.

"Enter," a voice sounded from within.

"Hello, my name is Destiny and I am looking for a place to rent. Are there any cottages available?" The fellow was sitting on the couch in front of the Tele.

"I do have a unit coming up soon. Where are you staying now?" the chap asked, while looking sideways at Destiny so not to miss the show he was wachting.

"I am at the hostel in Cheltenham. I work at "Skittles" and would like a more permanent place to settle." Destiny offered the information knowing she would need to tell him eventually, if she was to be considered for tenancy.

"Oh, then you like the job, do ya? I haven't been to that pub, but had intended to soon. I tell you, come back next week, and I'll give ya a look at the cottage. Does that suit you?"

"Oh, yes, that would be fine. I will return next week," Destiny said with conviction.

Destiny was so excited while riding back to the bike shop, she didn't even remember passing the little brook she was going to sit by to refresh herself a second time. She turned in the rented cycle and headed to her favorite pub. She ordered a Coke with lemon wedge and sat at a table to think. *Could this truly be my reality? If it is, I am creating exactly what I had envisioned!*

Destiny's enthusiasm lasted for the entire week. On her next free day, she again rented a cycle and rode to Swindon. In his cottage, the same fellow was glued to his Tele when Destiny knocked. "Hello, remember me, I am Destiny? I am here to look at that unit you said would be available."

"Oh, yes, Destiny. Follow me, I'll show it to you, young lady," the man said, while turning off the Tele. "It's small with only one bedroom, but I bet it'll suit you fine. My name is Ben, by the way."

"Nice to meet you, Ben." She followed him on a narrow path to the rear of the bungalow property.

"Now then, what ya think?" Ben asked, as he opened the door to show Destiny the cottage.

Destiny walked through the small bungalow that basically had three rooms; the living area, a kitchen with a table and two chairs, and a bedroom with a small loo off to one side. Destiny spun around quickly to ask Ben what the rent would be, and then nodded in agreement when he told her. Just before leaving, she looked out the little window over the kitchen sink and a smile adorned her face. There was a sparkling stream just yards away, and on the opposite side was an open area with low forested hills. Destiny felt blessed in those few minutes, but kept her delight on an emotional leash as she followed Ben back to his cottage to sign their agreement.

The pair agreed she could move into the cottage whenever she liked. Ben explained a few policies, and then they shook hands. Destiny rode back to Cheltenham once again as if floating on a cloud. When she arrived at the bike shop, she asked the owner if he had any used cycles for sale. She bought an older model and rode it back to the hostel. Sitting in the chair by the window, she felt like she was inside a dream that she had created long ago. She wrote in her journal:

> Journal—October 1976: I feel so happy! Finally, the Universe is working with me, and my life is moving in a positive direction. The cottage is bang on! It's just far enough from work to give me a workout cycling. I cannot wait to explore the wooded area with the little stream out back, and the rest of Swindon Village.
>
> Tomorrow, I must remember to return my books to the library and take out new ones. I want to find more books about how to create my reality. I have certainly created a dream come true these past few months. Coming to Cheltenham was a spot-on choice, and my job will be fine for now. I have found a perfect place to live, and I feel strong again. If there is a God or Higher Divine Source of some kind which has directed me, I give thanks and gratitude.

To the end of that year and well into 1977, life for Destiny was a steady mixture of work, reading, and exploring. She decorated the little cottage with flowers from the yard, and added a few colourful touches like pillows and curtains. One day, deep into winter with the fog dripping over Swindon, Destiny ran into one of her neighbors. She literally ran him down! While riding home from work, soaked from head to toe with thick fog and barely able to see her cycle's front tire, Destiny ran into Jess. She hopped off her cycle to make sure the chap was all right. "Oh, no! Are you okay? I am so terribly sorry! This dotty fog totally blurred my vision," she apologized.

"Hello there! Yes, I am fine, really. My name is Jess. I see you riding almost every day. You must live in one of the bungalows," Jess said, while offering Destiny his umbrella for shelter.

"Hi, I am Destiny. I live just over there, in the back unit," Destiny said and moved closer under his umbrella.

"Maybe it's time for you to spring for a motorcar, Destiny! The winter weather will only be getting worse, you know?" Jess suggested with a smile.

"Yes, probably so." She looked up into Jess's face, and then back down at her feet.

"Well, I hope to see you again, Destiny, but not like this!" Jess remarked with a wide smile. He leaned forward to walk down the pathway, but not wanting to leave Destiny in the dreadful weather, he added, "Can you make it home okay?"

"Oh, yes, of course. Have a good evening," Destiny said, and moved from under Jess's umbrella so he could leave.

"You, too, Destiny," Jess said, as he left and vanished into the abysmal fog.

This was the first encounter Destiny had with anyone living in the bungalows. She figured Jess to be in his late twenties, a nice-looking fellow with blondish hair and deep blue eyes. After removing her wet clothes, she sat at the kitchen table to nibble on water biscuits and cheese. She thought about how her body had reacted when standing so close to Jess; she had not felt those feelings in a long time. She began to realize how she had become a virtual hermit for the past six months or so, and it was so unlike her. "I guess with all that I have experienced in the past year, my life has dramatically changed," she announced to her little cottage. "It has been good for me to take the time to recoup and plan what I want to do with my life." Then, again, Destiny thought about her parents. She had not followed through with the promise to herself to ring up her mum. She made a mental note to do so the next day while at work, just to let her mum know she was well and doing fine.

That night, after putting on her warm cotton pajamas, Destiny picked up her latest library book, which proved to be intriguing. It was a new release and was featured on the "New Books" shelf in the library. Even though she was only about a third of the way into it, she found herself totally involved with the author's use of words and inner vision. It was a small book, not even two hundred pages in length. It read like a fiction book, but it captured her sense of relevance so thoroughly that she swore it was a true story. The book was titled, *Illusions: The Adventures of a Reluctant Messiah*. That night, Destiny could keep awake only long enough to read a few more pages. It had been a long day at work, and the cold fog drained her energy. She drifted to sleep remembering what Jess had said a few hours earlier about getting a motorcar.

Luana again found herself amazed at what she was reading. She set the book down to roost on the arm of a chair, thinking she would enjoy a few sips of hot tea. She thought back to the late 1970s when she was introduced to the little book, *Illusions*, and the others written by one of her favorite authors, Richard Bach. One of Bach's first books, which had made it to the top of the best sellers list, *Jonathan Livingston Seagull*, had introduced her to a more creative way to look at life. Just reading Bach's books and knowing there were others who had a metaphysical bent toward reality was reassuring to her sense of how the Universe works. *I definitely see how Destiny's greater sense of reality is unfolding,* Luana thought. *Now, to see how she handles allowing a man to enter her life!* "That will be a big test for her!" she muttered under her breath. "I wonder if she is truly ready?"

Luana reminisced how her own turbulent twenties had unfolded. After the incident with her so-called boyfriend, she didn't allow herself to date for a full two years. Then she met James, whom she married in a short few months. In hindsight, Luana knew she had jumped-the-gun in marrying James, but he'd seemed so right for her. He was an advertising executive in a noted firm, and as handsome as they come. They met at a mutual friend's cocktail party and began dating soon afterward. Luana told him fairly soon in the relationship that there might be a problem with her having children, but he seemed confident his manhood could overcome any obstacle she might possess. As it turned out, that was not the case.

When Dr. Shelly informed Luana a second time that she had the choice to remove her uterus, she couldn't bring herself to do it. Luana felt that if there was even the slightest chance she could become pregnant one day, she wanted to leave the possibility open. After five years of trying and no pregnancy, Luana accepted her fate to be childless; however, James never gave up his desire to become a father. At the time, the process of in-vitro fertilization techniques was only being concept-ualized, but not widely known by the medical community. Luana's physiological makeup of uterine tumors also countered the use of this scantily tested method of impregnation.

It was in their tenth year of marriage when James brought up the issue of separation. Of course, her heart was broken, but on an inner level of consciousness, she knew it was best. They had been living separately for a few months when James had his lawyer serve her divorce papers. It was during this time that Luana retreated into her spiritual-self to cope with her loss and the stressful situation.

During this time, it was uncanny how her life issues seemed to attract patients with the same type of concerns. Luana found herself time and time again working with people whose lives and emotions actually ran parallel to her own. She began to believe that she was creating, or drawing to her, those patients that could teach her as many lessons as she could offer to them. It became an intriguing game for her to listen intently to patients relate many of the same issues that she, herself, was trying to work through. Her text books might have called this phenomenon "counter-transference," but Luana never thought of it that way. It was a metaphysical synchronicity that many of her patients presented with some of the same issues that she was also working through in her own life. She read many books like Bach's that spoke of creating one's reality and the Universal laws of attraction. Luana liked to think these metaphysical laws were guiding her patients to her, and the symbiotic relationships ensued.

Luana was grateful for each patient who allowed her into their private life, and felt honored to be of service. When counseling, she listened to her words flow through her lips, as if being channeled by another's wisdom. Many times, she learned new insights about herself while counseling her patients. Her life had been filled with loving and grateful people who enlisted her direction to guide their lives on a new path. As her patients became strong, Luana also found new ways to explore and create her own desires.

Luana snapped out of daydreaming. Eager to continue her reading, she put down her cup of tea and began the next chapter in Destiny's life.

Ten

When Destiny had read about halfway through *Illusions*, a quote perched itself starkly upon a single page:

> "You are never given a wish
> without also being given the
> power to make it true.
> You may have to
> work for it,
> however."

She reread the few lines over and over to cement the words within her consciousness. She was beginning to understand that she really was in control of her life. She realized that she alone had the power to mold it by being aware of her actions and reactions. She thought again about her name and why her mother had chosen it for her. *Perhaps,* she thought, *it had something to do with teaching me that I have the power to create my own destiny.*

While on a break one spring afternoon, Destiny took a few minutes to enjoy reading her newest book. The winter's fog had lifted and once again the sunlit shadows danced upon the flowers in the centre square. Her mind drifted to her parents and she decided this was a good time to ring them up. She put her book into her pocketbook and went to use the telephone in Jon's office, but then she hesitated. *What will I tell them?* she silently asked herself. *Do I tell them about the rape? the pregnancy? where I am living?* This slight hesitation turned her good intentions into trepidation. She left the office, honoring the apprehension she felt in her gut. *One day will be the right day for me to contact them,* she thought, *but not this one.*

The pub was working out to be a rather familiar routine of chatting with the older gents and serving up their lagers. Destiny began to sense a bit of restlessness within her. She had hoped that a friendship would have started with Jess, the chap she nearly ran down with her cycle. She found herself purposefully leaving her cottage at the same time she saw him stroll by, but the prearranged meetings only earned her a casual, "Good day." She began to think he might be batty; but then, she noticed a woman leaving his bungalow late one evening and nixed the thought. She made a mental note to herself to begin a more engaging conversation the next time she saw him. Luckily, when she went to her favorite pub, Jess was sitting on a stool at the bar. She walked up, and said, "Hi, Jess! I haven't seen you here before. How are you?"

"Oh, hello, Destiny. I am fine, and yourself?" Jess asked, focusing his dark blue eyes on her brown ones.

"I am just getting off work and thought I would muck about with my friends here. I come here all the time. How was your day?" Destiny asked, trying to sound sincere.

"The day was an exceptionally good one actually. I was recently promoted, and will be transferring to the States! I guess, in a way, I am celebrating tonight," he announced with a big smile that revealed straight white teeth.

"Oh, congratulations, Jess! That's bang on...but now I won't be able to get to know you better. When do you shove off?"

"In about two months. I will be living near San Francisco to work in a quite large architectural firm. I have been so busy lately that I haven't had the time to talk to anyone, except my sister who comes to visit. Maybe we could chat one evening before I leave. Do you want to plan a time to hang about?"

"Well, okay, that would be nice. How about this coming Saturday, after I return from work?" She was a bit unsure if she really wanted to learn more about this man who made her heart race.

"Great, then. I will stop by your place about nine-thirty," Jess said, revealing that he knew when Destiny arrived home from her work at the pub.

"We shall make a toast to your new position, then!" She rose her glass to tip it with the one Jess had in his hand. "May it be all that you *wish* it to be!"

That next Saturday, Destiny's stomach was performing flip-flops all day at work. She knew there was an attraction between them, and was more than a little nervous about getting to know Jess better when he would soon be leaving for America. She tried to tell herself there was nothing wrong in starting up a friendship with him, even though she wished it could be more. Bach's words about making wishes come true kept ringing in her ears. Finally, she was able to calm herself with the realization that it takes two to form a relationship. And at this point, she had no idea if Jess had an interest in her other than a causal friendship.

After riding home that night, Destiny changed from her work clothes into a pair of black velvet tights and a white loose-fitting rayon blouse that draped over her slim hips. She decided to put her hair up in a ponytail, thinking she looked older that way. Just as she finished dressing, she heard Jess' soft knock on the door. "Hi, Jess, come in," she said, as she opened the door wide.

"Hi, Destiny. How was your day at work today?" he asked, and sat on the pillowed couch.

"Oh, fine. It's getting to be quite dreary and routine. I could do it blindfolded!" Destiny remarked, throwing her hands in the air.

"I guess that could be a positive thing. I mean, at least your day is stress-free."

"I guess, but I think I need a bit more of a challenge. I was even thinking of looking into becoming a massage therapist to perhaps work at the Leisure Health Spa here in Swindon. Have you been there?"

"As a matter of fact, I have. It's a great place to unwind. Sometimes, I even go to their yoga classes. Have you ever tried yoga, Destiny?"

"No, but it does seem like a good way to loosen up the muscles!"

"Oh, it is indeed. You know, there is a massage school right in Cheltenham. I think you would enjoy that line of work. Go visit the spa and let them know you are interested. They are a fine group of people. Where are you from, Destiny?" Jess asked, starting a more personal line of conversation.

"Well, my parents live in Wellington. I moved here last July and really like it. I feel as if many of my dreams have come true since being here. Do you believe we have the ability to make our wishes become a reality, Jess?" she asked, with a slight hesitation.

"Oh, yes indeed. I truly believe we co-create our reality. My beliefs may be a bit too New Age for you, but I strongly believe in the metaphysical principles and laws of the Universe. Have you studied metaphysics?"

"I am always reading a book or two, and many of them have to do with spiritual and metaphysical insights. Right now, I am really into the new book *Illusions* by Richard Bach. Have you heard of it?" Destiny reached over Jess, pointing to the book she had earlier placed on the end table.

"Oh, yes indeed! I have been meaning to buy that one. It sounds fascinating. Is it a good read then?" He picked it up to peruse its cover.

"Well, I am sure learning some good things from reading it. When you said you believe we *co-create* our reality, what did you mean?" Destiny asked, tilting her head.

"I feel people have a spark of the Divine within them. And, with that spark, we co-create what we wish to happen in our lives. This is what some term *freewill*. For example, I have been dreaming of living in the States for some time now. I have directed all my energy toward that dream, and now I am moving there! I certainly feel as if I have had a part in creating my life. Do you understand?" Jess studied Destiny's big brown eyes.

"Yes, I know exactly what you mean, Jess. It difintely is nice to talk with someone about all this stuff. I haven't had anyone to share my thoughts with about it all. Now, I really *wish* you were not moving away!" Destiny stared right back into Jess's blue eyes.

"Well, maybe one day you can come to visit me…I mean if you wanted to, some day. I have to tell you, Destiny…I am holding myself back from kissing you right this second. Do you feel the same?" Jess asked, as he touched Destiny's cheek.

"Yes, I certainly do…it is okay to kiss me, Jess," she agreed and put her arms around his neck in encouragement.

"But, we really shouldn't start this up. I will be so far away in just a few months!" He could not stop his desire and leaned in for a kiss as Destiny leaned forward. Their lips touched in a soft short embrace, and then resumed for a longer second meeting. Jess reluctantly pulled away and whispered, "Well, now I need to ask you, Destiny...are you willing to stay in touch with me after I move?"

"Oh, definitely, Jess...but I don't even know your last name!" Destiny said laughing.

"Drew... Jess Drew. And what is your full name, Destiny?"

"Collins. Now that we know each other's names, does that mean it's all right to kiss again?" Destiny smiled.

"Most definitely...Miss Destiny Collins!" He answered her question by pulling her closer to envelop his lips around hers once again.

After Jess left that evening, Destiny ran the piece of paper that he had given her through her fingers. Written on the paper was the address he would be moving to in America. She read it several times, as if she needed to memorize it: 8 Shady Lane Drive, Mill Valley, California. She pictured the residence in her mind. She envisioned a narrow windy lane with light fog dancing on the top of tall Pine and Redwood trees. A white two story manor sloping down the hillside with gables displaying windows squared with panes. Destiny placed the paper neatly inside her journal to keep it safe.

Jess promised he would meet her several times before his move, and on the following Sunday, he knocked softly on Destiny's door. "Hey, do you have time today to go scouting about with me?" Jess picked her up to spin her around.

"I guess...now put me down," Destiny ordered.

"Right...I am excited to show you around our little village, are you game?"

"Oh, yes. I have wanted to see more of it. I just haven't taken the time. What a perfect idea!" Destiny said with an air of excitement in her voice.

"Great, there are several things you should know about in this village. Have you seen the St. Lawrence church yet?"

"Yes, but not inside. Can we go inside?"

"Well, today would not be a good day with the services and all. It is best to go on a weekday. How about the spa, then? I can show you around and see if you feel comfortable there," Jess suggested.

"Oh, brilliant idea!" Destiny jumped up and down a few times, and then felt like a child and stopped. Instead, she gave Jess a quick hug.

"We can walk, if it's all right with you?"

"Okay. Let me go change my boots," she replied, and went into the bedroom. While she was putting on her walking boots, Destiny shouted to Jess, "Do you know yet what day you will be pushing off for the States?"

"The first week in May…" his voice trailed off as he felt a pang of sadness that painfully acknowledged how much he would miss Destiny.

Destiny felt her stomach lurch as she stood up to reenter the living room. She walked directly to Jess, put her arms around his neck and gave him a big kiss. "I think I am going to miss you terribly, Jess."

"I know…me too. But we have today…let's go scouting!" he said, and took her hand as they left the cottage.

"Do you know anything about these bungalows?" Destiny asked, trying to change her mood.

"I know they were first developed in the 1960s. Before that, Swindon Village did not have much housing. Aren't they lovely? I love my little cottage. I will miss it for sure. I hope my new place will be as quaint. I was once told that the name Swindon came from a hill around here where the swine were kept back in the Eleventh Century!" Jess laughed out loud.

"Oh, how funny!" Destiny began laughing with him.

The couple held hands as they strolled through the lanes to the health spa. "I think this area was a large settlement in the Roman era. Of course, in those days everyone had massages and pools to soak in!" Jess remarked, as he showed Destiny around the large swimming bath. "They hold classes like the yoga that I go to over in that building, and all body therapy practices are performed in that one. There is also a steam room, a gym, and halls to play games like basketball, hockey, and racquet sports. Can you tell that I love this place?"

"It sure is a lot bigger than it looks on the outside! Everyone seems to be having a relaxing time, too," Destiny remarked.

"If you do decide to learn massage therapy, I bet this place would be happy to hire you." Jess turned around with a big smile. "I could even come to get treatments from you when I am visiting from the States."

"So, you will be traveling back and forth?"

"Well, I could take my vacation time to fly back, even if the company doesn't send me," he hinted to get Destiny's reaction.

"I like that idea," Destiny said, squeezing his hand.

"Have you seen the stadium yet?"

"No. I had no idea there was one here."

"I hear there is also another stadium in the works that will be completed in a few years. It's supposed to be named the Prince of Wales Stadium," Jess announced.

Destiny was so happy learning about all the places she had not taken the time to visit in Swindon. After thoroughly scouting about, the couple held hands and strolled through the lanes, and then went back to her cottage.

"How about I take you out for dinner tonight? We can drive into Cheltenham where I know of a little café that serves up the best pizza pies! Want to go?" Jess bent down to kiss her cheek.

"That would be lovely, Jess. Give me a bit to clean up and come around again about six o'clock," she suggested.

"Brilliant! I will pick you up at six." Jess held Destiny in his arms as gently as a child. He rocked with her for a moment to feel her body next to his, and then walked back to his cottage.

Destiny buzzed around her cottage to get ready to meet Jess for dinner. She needed to bathe, do her hair, and change her clothes. She acknowledged the excitement she felt, not pushing it aside this time. "Jess is so perfect!" she announced to her cottage. "He is everything a girl could want. Why does he have to go off to another country when we are getting on so splendidly?" Destiny looked into the lavatory mirror to see a glow to her face she had not seen before. She asked the reflection, "Are you falling in love?"

Jess arrived and drove them to a small Bistro that was decorated with glowing candles made from empty wine bottles sitting on white tablecloths. The waiters were dressed in black and white. Destiny was very impressed and smiled as she surveyed the menu. The pair ate pizza and drank a pitcher of ale while sharing aspirations for their future. After eating, Jess reached over the table to play with Destiny's fingers. He leaned across their devoured platter of food and whispered, "Let's leave and go back to your cottage."

Driving through the foggy narrow roadway to Swindon, Destiny slipped her right arm around his left. Jess smiled and felt content to drive with one hand. Once they were settled on the couch, they resumed their discussions of life and how the Universe works, all the while, both silently desiring a bit of intimacy for the evening. Jess made his move by tenderly cupping Destiny's face in his hands and parted her lips with his own. The rush of passion came fast for Destiny, and she felt her limbs go limp as she melted into his arms. Coming up for breath, she whispered, "This is all so new to me, Jess. I am not sure I am ready to get this involved."

As Jess held her face firm in his hands again, he whispered, "Oh, Destiny, I have such deep feelings for you. I have never felt like this before. I want to honor our relationship and keep it wrapped in my heart forever. Perhaps, it would be best if we stopped now so we can treasure this experience, especially since I will be leaving so soon."

"It hurts to think that you will be so far away," Destiny winced.

"I know," Jess said, "but I can ring you up and write even more often. I will make sure I'll be able to come back for visits. I think I am falling in love with you, Destiny." He stood up drawing Destiny close. Again, he swayed their bodies together in a rhythm-dance while holding her tight against him.

Destiny whispered, "Me too…"

Eleven

The next few weeks found Jess and Destiny mystified in a passionate romance neither one wanted to discontinue. They met most every day after work to trace their younger years with descriptive words so each could visualize the other's childhood memories. They talked of their families, describing each member with light humor to hide the loss of an emotional upbringing. While Destiny skipped past many of the outrageous experiences she instigated as a younger teen, she was truthful when telling Jess about her parents. Jess mostly shared about his sister and their strong sibling connection. He also talked of his love for design and how he became driven to secure a career in architecture. Destiny shared her love of books and described her parents' library, and how she would lose herself in the poetic rhythm of the words she read. The couple talked constantly when they were together, trying to relate each detail within their lives before Jess needed to leave. The fact that there was a deadline to their time together led them both to bare their deepest beliefs to capture the other's approval.

Destiny concluded that Jess was an enigma. His Capricorn nature directed a journey toward achieving the height of his profession. At the same time, he possessed a clear metaphysical bent toward his spiritual beliefs. She could listen for hours as he explained his opinions on the universal knowledge of consciousness, and how each of us contain the power to create our reality as we desire. She felt Jess verbalized much of her own philosophy, but had acquired far more comprehension beyond her limited knowledge. She became fascinated with listening to him describe his theories on the Big Bang and evolution, and found herself asking questions like a school girl. Of course, this encouraged Jess to delve even deeper into his own beliefs. Soon, he brought literature he had studied through the years to share with her. She was delighted to thumb through the material as they each questioned what they were reading. Jess had been studying the popular works of Carl Sagan and his opinions on the Earth's origin and research on planetary astronomy. When he told Destiny of his intuitive connection with Sagan, she could totally relate and they both savored much of Sagan's writings.

March quickened the time of spring and renewal, which spurred the couple's passions. Jess was willing to control his lust; it was Destiny who made the bold advances that awarded her a sense of belonging. She had never felt the turbulent pulsing of her body as much as when Jess wrapped his arms around her to sway in a slow motion rhythm masquerading as a dance. With only a few weeks left before Jess would leave for the States, Destiny placed his hands on her young breasts, encouraging a night that would not end. Jess gazed deeply into her pleading eyes and relinquished to her powers. They stood in the middle of the little cottage as clothes slowly dropped to the floor. Standing bare to each other, Jess and Destiny acknowledged the bond between them. With exploring hands, silently they kissed as if nothing mattered but their souls finding one another again.

Arms entwined, the pair found the softness of Destiny's bed and gently lay as close as two lovers could without sexual intercourse. Quietly, Destiny whispered in his ear, "It is okay...I have protection." She rolled over to open the drawer of the night table and fumbled for a condom. Jess received the gift with a sigh of relief and resumed his foreplay. Words were not needed between them; they made love over and over as if their life depended on each receiving a perfect orgasm. Then a sense of guilt triggered Destiny's hidden shame and she sat upright, weeping. She covered her face with a pillow to muffle her sobs, but Jess lowered it and brought her close to his chest.

"This isn't your first time, is it?" Jess whispered.

Taking a full minute to calm herself, Destiny whispered in return, "No, but..." She could not bring herself to voice the words that must be shared.

"But what...?" asked Jess, as he cupped her face gently.

Do I dare tell you? What will you think of me if I tell you? Destiny silently thought. Not wanting to hear her words as they entered the space between them, she slowly and silently mouthed, "I was raped." The room stood still. The air went stale and she could not breathe. She managed to whisper, "Please do not hate me, Jess, or judge me."

Jess released his hands surrounding the cheeks he had grown to cherish. His slow reaction to respond stunned Destiny and her body jerked uncontrollably, alerting Jess to verbalize what he was feeling. "Oh, my god, Destiny! I am so sorry...do you need to share what happened? I understand if you do not, but I will listen if you do."

Destiny folded the sheet around her naked body and began to share the incident that kept her imprisoned within her shame. She was not intending to disclose the entire event, however, as her emotional words hung like a holographic vision in front of them, the details revealed themselves. Surprisingly, Destiny found a sense of relief in sharing her episode of pain and shame. It was the type of relief that comes with successfully removing the binding placed by one who enjoyed stripping away another's sense of dignity. As she approached the issue of her becoming pregnant as a result of the attack, she hesitated. She felt Jess had heard enough of her past plight for one night. Sinking back into his arms, she surrounded herself with his unconditional love and acceptance for what she had gone through. She silently entertained the fact that she may never share her entire past with Jess.

Time skipped its normal pace to bring the lovers to the edge of their togetherness. They agreed to take the last week off from work to spend the days walking in the woods and to spread a blanket to sit and talk of all the issues concerning love, life, death, and rebirth. The blanket was spread atop a patch of dry leaves left to mulch the new seedlings pushing the ground to announce their arrival. Destiny brought a picnic basket filled with enough food and drink to last the hours engrossed in topics ranging from supernovas to reincarnation. On one such afternoon, Jess read from *The Prophet*, poetic prose that was unmatched by any other in his eyes. One line held Destiny's awareness, as if the author had appeared before her and whispered the verse to capture and hold it tight to her breast. As Jess continued reading, she felt possessed by the previous words that lingered as an echo within her: *And let today embrace the past with remembrance and the future with longing*. It was at this exact moment when Destiny knew one day her trials from the past year would need to be released, so she could begin a new journey with the man which she had fallen so deeply in love.

As Jess continued reading the poetry that softly ebbed from his lips, Destiny visualized a future filled with laughter and love between them. Her creative mind took her to a white sandy beach with a crisp sea breeze ruffling her hair as Jess raced her to the foamy waves. They held hands and together jumped the surge of seawater that rolled over their feet. Soon he ventured beyond the breaking waves and sank beneath the darkened water. Frantically, she tried to spy his head bobbing up and down or an arm signaling he was safe...

"Destiny? Destiny, are you okay?" Jess asked, as he paused his reading and touched Destiny's shoulder. "Your face has gone so pale."

"Oh, my goodness! I guess I was lost in the words for a minute. Jess? You will never leave me, right? I feel we should be together forever!" Destiny leaned over, pushing Jess down on his back so she could lie on top of him. "I do love you!"

"I love you, too, Destiny. I will never leave you. After I get settled with my job, I will return...I promise," Jess assured her. He kissed both of her eyes, and then her lips. "I have one last passage to read you from this book." Jess sat upright and opened to the final page and read:

> The noontide is upon us and our half waking
> has turned to fuller days, and we must part.
> If in the twilight of memory we should meet
> once more, we shall speak again together
> and you shall sing to me a deeper song.
> And if our hands should meet in another
> dream we shall build another tower in the sky.

Jess left for America on a foggy day just before Destiny's nineteenth birthday. Two weeks slipped by, and then four, but still no posts were received. Destiny had written a few letters adorned with hopes that his new home met his desires and, of course, a few touches of *missing you* notes. She had no phone number to ring him up, but expected a post soon after his arrival informing her of the number so they could talk directly. She waited a full six weeks after not receiving a post before getting terribly worried. The earlier vision returned of Jess drowning in the ocean waves, most likely to aggravate her fears that he had forgotten her. But, it wasn't possible for her to believe that Jess Drew was not the sincere man he presented himself to be. She continued to believe she would hear from him.

As the months passed, Destiny began to wonder why the Universe would bring Jess into her life only to take him from her. She could never admit that perhaps their relationship was created to help guide each of them toward a new path. One day, she recalled what Jess had shared with her about the massage school in Cheltenham, and decided to investigate where the school was located. She made an appointment for a tour. When she followed the instructor through the building where the classes were taught, she felt a strong sense of liberation. Taking all the literature home to read thoroughly, Destiny again noticed a surge of freedom that she had recognized only a few times in her young life. The sensation reminded her of when she'd decided to ignore her parents' demands and moved forward with her own desires. This intuitive reaction affirmed that she should enroll in the massage therapy school and move forward with her life.

Once into her new adventure of learning professional massage, Destiny knew she had chosen a meaningful path. Her hands seemed to know where to go and how to release the tension in each muscle of her clients. She was eager to learn about the human body, as well as the holistic issues relating to stress and relaxation. She read each text with great care and obtained supplemental reading at the library. Her cottage held stacks of books and journals in each corner, dictating that if one stack was removed the bungalow would surely collapse. She attended school in the morning hours before work, learning everything from the newest methods of massage treatments to helping a client de-stress their life. After she returned home each night from the pub, she would study and write her papers to ensure her grades would earn the sought-after certificate.

Destiny was a bit shocked that she had no problem touching and massaging the other students to practice her techniques. As a child, she had not been hugged or touched that she could remember. However, while learning how to use different therapy techniques on others, she felt completely comfortable. When it was her turn to receive bodywork from other students, she had to adjust her demeanor to release a bit of her uptight defenses. The instructors were well informed on the psychological blocks people use to prevent from relaxing their body, and they counseled the students on how to let go of their fear and inhibitions. Because of this, Destiny found herself looking forward to the classes in general psychology that were taught in the final semester of instruction.

Her first priority was to keep her mind busy. She didn't want to allow herself to feel the unlabeled pain held next to her heart, knowing better than to express the hurt that might unleash the waves of anguish held there. She actually made a pact with herself after Jess didn't reconnect with her, to never again allow anyone to enter her private sanctuary. During the week of her twentieth birthday in May of 1978, Destiny received her Massage Therapist Certification. Two weeks prior to graduating, she visited the Leisure Health Spa to leave her Resume for any available positions. She was greeted by the head bodyworker, Stephen. He was a big Swedish fellow with a body to make any bodybuilder envious. In his broken English, Stephen told Destiny that her name would be placed on the short waiting list of therapists who desired a position at the spa. He liked that she was living in Swindon, and hinted it would be a plus during his consideration. In the meantime, she practiced her techniques on the other students at school and was told she had the magic touch.

Destiny's extended reading and research habits finally paid off; she gained the highest approval of all the instructors. The administration department notified her of several job openings available in Cheltenham. They also suggested to her to consider being a candidate to continue her studies to become an instructor. She felt honored and was intrigued by the offer; but for now, she knew she needed expierence and where she wanted to be employed, the spa near her cottage in Swindon Village.

The wait was not long. Just when the summer fog began to float atop the St. Lawrence bell tower, she received a post from the Leisure Health Spa stating a massage therapist position was going to be available in two weeks. On her way to work the following day, she rode by the spa to confirm she was interested in the opening. She talked with Stephen, who reported that she could start working at the spa in ten days! Destiny continued her ride to work with a big smile etched across her face. She gave notice to Jon, telling him how grateful she was to have had the job at the pub. He understood her need to move forward with her life, and gave his blessing, "Now, you come in once in a while to give ole' Jon a hug then. I want to know ya got on properly."

"I promise," Destiny said, giving him a big hug.

One needs to be at peace with their past to be able to accept the present, so they can create their future...the words echoed in Luana's mind as she penned them. This truism had been an important lesson she needed to learn many years ago. After her divorce, Luana had immersed herself in her patients' traumas, thus shielding her own pain and remorse. Through the years, there were times when she second-guessed her decision to not fight for her marriage. The passionate and adventurous travels intermittingly encroached upon her memory. Late one night in the summer of 1987, Luana shouted to the ceiling, "I let you go, James. I must move forward with my life. I must not allow my mind to travel backward to be consumed in dead memories of our lust. I affirm now, this night, to be the beginning of the rest of my life without you haunting my thoughts and dreams."

That following morning a red-tailed hawk flew straight into Luana's closed front window and dropped to the ground. Running to reluctantly view a dead heap of feathers, she instead witnessed a miracle. The stunned hawk stood perched on the porch railing as if waiting for Luana's arrival to impart his message of wisdom. She distinctly heard in her mind: *Do not allow the walls of life to hinder your vision.* Luana watched the spiritual messenger gently take flight and soar into the morning sun rays. Her heart felt grateful as she savored the hawk's message. She knew from that moment forward, she was to accept Hawk Energy as her personal totem. She had studied with a few Native American shamans and easily adopted many of their spiritual insights. Luana especially enjoyed being a participant in the healing medicine wheel rituals. She likened the experience to becoming one with nature and spreading healing energy to the Earth, and all those upon it.

Currently, after thirty years, Luana could reflect on her first marriage with compassion. Once she had totally allowed herself to fully realize that the love she shared with James was real, it became evident that the marriage was just not meant to continue. It was then that Luana could forgive both herself and James. She accepted that she could not provide James with the family he so desired, and acknowledged that dissolving the marriage was essential so he could pursue his dream. It had taken years for Luana to stop harboring the guilt of not being able to conceive a child, but eventually did forgive herself and accepted her infertile condition. In early December of 1987, Luana had the hysterectomy that her doctor had suggested so many years prior. After her recovery, she was finally free of her guilt and shame, as well as her menstrual pain.

During the summer after her surgery, when Luana was forty-two, she accepted an invitation from her girlfriend, Jill, to vacation in Hawaii. Jill's family owned a condominium complex where they could stay, making it an easy answer for Luana to say, "Yes!" She had traveled to many countries, but she had never been to one of the most sought-after destinations in her own. She acknowledged a sense of excitement in her body as she packed for the trip. It had been a long time since she had explored a new environment. She even ventured to think that she might meet an interesting man or two. Luana's mind kept jumping from being protective of her demeanor to allowing herself to be completely open, or even lose control! She had a full three weeks to play on the party island of Maui, and she was not shy about sharing her intentions with Jill.

After the first few hours on the island, it took Luana and Jill only a few minutes to set up a mutual system to signal each other about when they desired privacy. The system was easy. When either of the women knew she would not be home for an evening, or through the night, she would leave a message on the motel phone: *Not home tonight.* They did want to keep tabs on one another for safety reasons, but also allow each their own way to enjoy the island. The plan worked perfectly.

One evening five days into their vacation, the women dined together at one of the many gourmet restaurants found on Maui. Toward the end of their meal, Luana's eyes locked with those of a handsome gentleman sitting alone at a table nearby. She was able to openly return his smile, and then alert Jill of the connection. Soon after they finished their meal, the man walked over to their table and introduced himself. "Hello, ladies. My name is Victor. I would love if you would like to dance with me," Victor spoke in a broken foreign dialect.

Victor's jet black eyes were fixed on Luana. "Yes, yes of course. I'd be delighted." Luana rose quickly from her chair, taking Victor's outstretched hand followed him to the dance floor.

The dance steps she had once known many years ago came rushing back to her, and the two floated in unison over the tile floor. Luana could feel her heartbeat quicken when Victor took her arms and placed them around his neck, pulling her tight against his chest. He was wearing a causal tropical shirt revealing bountiful chest hair that enticed her touch. Luana laid her head on his chest and heard a heartbeat worthy of a young man; however, Victor was not a young man, but well over fifty. His dark eyes penetrated Luana's as he commanded the lead, spinning her like a limp flower in his grip.

Other than telling Victor her name, they danced for nearly an hour without speaking. Then he whispered in Luana's ear, "Would you like to walk on the beach? There is a full moon tonight."

"That'd be wonderful," Luana managed to answer. She walked beside Victor like a robot, willing to follow his every command.

Once on the sandy beach, Luana removed her gold-studded sandals and they walked hand-in-hand gazing at the full moon. When they were away from the noise of the restaurant, Victor turned and asked Luana if she would allow him to kiss her. She nodded affirmatively. Victor cupped her face between his hands, tenderly touched her lips with his two thumbs, and then placed his lips on the fullness of hers. They stood locked in a kiss that seemed to last until the moon cried for them to stop.

"Who *are* you, Victor?" Luana was able to ask, as they sank to the sand to sit side-by-side.

"I have come to visit this gorgeous island…never expecting to meet such a woman as you, Luana. Tell me more about who you are," he said, putting his arm protectively around her shoulder.

"I am here to vacation and enjoy the island as well," she offered, and then asked, "Are you visiting alone?"

"Yes. I am alone here," he said.

"Does that mean you are not alone somewhere else?"

"Yes, I am afraid it does. You see, my dear Luana, I am married. My wife has decided we are not to be together much longer. She is on holiday with another man. I decided to retreat and come here." Then, taking Luana's face in his hands once again, he added, "I have no intention of staying married to my wife, Luana. Do you believe me?"

Luana looked toward the waves glistening beneath the moonbeams. She sighed, and said, "Victor, I have no reason to not believe you. However, I do not wish to develop a lasting relationship while on the island. Do you understand?"

"Yes, my dear Luana. Will you allow me to enjoy your company for the reminder of your stay?" Victor whispered.

"Let me say that we can take one day at a time during my vacation. I have no entanglements here, or at home," she said, hoping Victor would understand her proposition.

"I am happy we can share our time together while we explore our adventure here." Victor pulled Luana's body close to his. Later that night, Luana's phone message to Jill divulged the tryst: *Not home tonight!*

The days and nights overlapped, and then fused as one for the couple whose desires ruled their actions. Victor's lavish suite became their rendezvous. Most of Luana's belongings were spread throughout the rooms, affirmaing her presence. Victor applauded her nonchalant demeanor, which proved to spur her lack of inhibition even further. Luana found herself thoroughly reveling in her passions once again as her tall, dark, foreign stranger took her in his arms exploring every mound and valley of her willing body. There was newness to their lovemaking that delighted Luana, and she gave herself freely to each passionate exploration. Victor was a thorough and ardent lover whose sensual touch made her explode in ecstasy.

"My love," said Victor, "you are a jewel found once in a lifetime. Will you not consider flying with me to my country to be my consort?"

"Oh, Victor! Are you from a royal family in some faraway land?" Luana jokingly laughed.

"Yes, I am. You must have assumed my status by my companions who are always near, did you not?" Victor said.

"Well, to be truthful, Victor, I had not even noticed anyone around us! I've been so filled with your passion that my mind has become oblivious to anyone else. Oh, Victor, I cannot travel with you, or become anything to you. I'll be but a memory tucked in your consciousness prompting a vision of a few short weeks of romance under the Hawaiian skies. I'm sorry if you assumed there would be anything more." Luana took a bit of his black curly hair to twirl between her fingers. As she spoke her words, even she was surprised there was no remorse for her actions. She felt strongly that Victor could only be a reminder of the passion she possessed that might one day be offered to a man who would capture her heart.

On the day before Luana was to leave her paradise, and her bold lover, Victor gave her a small silver ring with a large deep blue gem stone. He told her, "I want you to take this home with you dear, Luana. Wear it when you want to remember our days here together. Wear it when you desire to feel the passion we have experienced so freely. Wear it to envision me next to you in your bed, touching you gently. Wear it to remind you how truly beautiful you are."

Twelve

The fog cast its ghostly shadows along the lanes of Swindon Village, keeping the promise that the winter of 1979-80 was going to be exceptionally cold. Destiny had become a highly popular massage therapist at the spa, her days and evenings filled with appointments made by both locals and tourists. Visiting her favorite pub to catch up with random friends whose names were usually drown in a draught beer, became the only social time she allowed herself. She kept her promise to herself not to get involved with another man, even when she was approached by a chap now and then from the spa or pub. One older gent she regularly provided bodywork for invited her to be his personal massage therapist and travel with him on his yacht! After that invitation, she knew she could survive without the attentions of anyone who might not treat her appropriately.

Jess Drew had become a vague memory Destiny had shoved to a far corner of her mind. She allowed herself to visit the corner only during full moons to dream of the passionate kisses he'd placed upon her lips. He had been the first to explore her willing mouth with open kisses to ignite her lust. She would never forget the sensual feelings that pulsated between her thighs when Jess took her into his arms. Now to curb her physical needs, she made only intermittent solitary visits to satiate this seat of pleasure.

Nearly a year and a half escaped Destiny's life while she dutifully worked at the spa. During one cold February evening, when sitting in the pub, she was approached by a young man whom she could not ignore. He seemed like a standup kind of fellow, dressed in a dark blue suit and matching tie. He slid onto a stool next to her at the bar, and reported, "Hello, I am Ian. I am new to the area, and actually I will not be here long, but I wanted to say hello to you. I've seen you here before."

"Hello, Ian. I like coming here, it is a spot-on pub. My name is Destiny," she said, sticking out her right hand for a shake.

Ian quickly took Destiny's hand in his and held it gently turning it over to one side, and then the other in a strange fashion. Finally, he released his grip, and said, "Do you believe in destiny, Destiny?"

"You must know I have heard that one before! To answer your question, I do believe we all experience adventures and lessons that our souls have chosen before we incarnate in a lifetime. Is that too deep for you, Ian?" Destiny said with a wink.

"Ummm…no, not too deep at all, Destiny. In fact, I can't believe you would share such a personal insight to a virtual stranger," he said with a big smile. "I feel honored."

"Well, I do have certain beliefs that I have no problem sharing to those who want to listen. Besides, you are the one who started the topic of conversation with your question about destiny." She smiled back at him.

"Yes, you are right there. Do you want to sit at a table with me to discuss more of your insights? I may even share a few of my own."

"Splendid! It is early and I haven't had much to drink…not that I get tanked often. I actually would not mind talking about metaphysics with you. Let's sit over at that table in the corner where it is a bit more quiet." Destiny pointed to the far end corner of the pub. Ian approved with a titled nod of his head. She noticed that he seemed a bit younger than her, and a very chipper fellow.

The pair sat at the table, not too close, just close enough to hear each other above the patrons of the pub. "Are you a spiritual person, Ian?" Destiny asked, starting the conversation.

"Yes, I guess you could call me spiritual. Although, I am not one of those *New Agers* you hear about today. I do believe each person co-creates their own reality."

"Are you a book reader?"

"Yes, I love to read."

"I recommend you get a little book called *Illusions*. The name of the author is Bach. If you read that book, you just might see the New Age philosophy a bit differently. Do you believe we each have a soul?"

"Yes, I surely do believe that, Destiny. Deep inside me, I even know our soul lives on Earth many times," he whispered across the table.

"Oh, yes! I believe that too…reincarnation. Not many people I know believe in it, but I know it to be true. I'll tell you something I have never told anyone, and I am not sure why I am telling you. I have had visions of myself in other lifetimes!" Destiny whispered back.

"Brilliant! I have been to India where everyone seems to remember a past life or two. I have no doubt in my mind that you've had visions of yours…that is so exciting! Would you like to share one of your visions with me?"

"No. It is just too private. You understand, right?"

"Right, of course. May I ask what you do for work, Destiny?"

"I am a massage therapist at the Leisure Health Spa in Swindon. It has been a good job for the past few years now. I am a bit bored with it though. I may look into getting on with more classes so I can teach it at the massage school. The position might introduce me to a whole new adventure." Destiny wondered why she was divulging so much information to her handsome blond stranger.

"Now that sounds spot-on! Once you become a teacher, you could live most anywhere," Ian explained, as if he knew firsthand how Destiny's future would unfold. "Well, I better shove-off then. It has been a delight chatting with you, Destiny. Maybe we will run into each other again before I leave."

"It was nice to meet and chat with you, too." Destiny stood to shake Ian's hand. Once again, Ian held Destiny's hand for several seconds before letting go, and then he said, "Destiny, you will find your niche when you begin to trust yourself and others." He gave her a quick wink, turned and left.

After a few weeks had passed with no sign of Ian, Destiny wondered if she would ever see him again. She kept visualizing him sitting across from her again at the pub, so she could ask him questions about his premonitory statement about trust. He dashed off so quickly, she had no time to respond. *Did he see something in me that gave him the impression that I did not*

trust people? she silently asked herself. She reached for her journal to make a note of the experience:

> Journal—March 1980: I met this fellow named Ian, a few months ago, and I am still thinking about him. He was a friendly sort of chap who asked me questions about my spiritual beliefs, which I find odd and rather intriguing at the same time. I haven't met anyone else, except Jess, who wanted to know such personal things about me. This Ian chap also had a way of making me think about what I really do believe spiritually. It is just like in all the books I've been reading.
>
> The weirdest thing about Ian is that I think he may be psychic! Just before he left, he acted as if he were telling me something about my future. He stated: You will find your niche when you begin to trust yourself and others. A bit weird to be sure.
>
> Note: Check to see if there are any psychics in Cheltenham to help shed some light on my future.

Destiny closed her journal, shut out the lamp beside her bed, and climbed under the bedcovers. The early spring moon was full as it rested behind a blanket of fog that surrounded the little cottage. Dreams entered and then left Destiny's sleep throughout the night. When she awoke the following morning, her mind was swimming with memories of two of her dreams that needed to be written down. Sitting up, she opened her journal to a new page and wrote "Dreams" as the top heading:

> Dream #1: I was searching for someone, but I could not remember who it was. I was determined to find them and kept running down a long hallway. Soon, I came to the end and there was a single door closed tight. I tried to turn the doorknob but it would not open. Then I woke up…
>
> Dream #2: I was in a classroom with about twenty students. But instead of being one of the students, I was standing in front of them at the head of the room. I was telling the students to open their books to page #78. Then I woke up…

For a few minutes longer, Destiny thought about the dreams she had remembered, and then got out of bed to dress for the day. It was a Sunday, and she had decided two weeks ago to visit the St. Lawrence church to experience the services. Due to her working at the spa, she had met several residents in Swindon who spoke of attending the church. Many of these local people also requested Destiny to perform their bodywork at the spa. She took this loyalty as a compliment of her massage methods, not thinking they might also be fond of her. It was still difficult for her to receive friendly gestures, or develop friendships.

Destiny chose her dark blue skirt and jacket to go with a light grey rayon blouse to wear to church. She put on her black Mary Janes and fixed her long hair in a bun at the back of her neck. She walked the short distance to the church, and met others walking as well. She found herself waving in return to several people who made the friendly gesture. Once seated inside the church, she took in the beauty of the damp old building with its unique hexagon bell tower. She was told that services in the church were brief, not traditional. The building was considered a historical monument, and the Sunday services were mostly directed toward entertaining the tourists visiting the village and its spa.

After the service, she followed a group to the outside garden. The misty fog surrounded her as she enjoyed her commune with nature. After returning to her cottage, she changed into jeans and a sweater. She reached for a piece of fruit on the table she had bought the day before, and sat on the couch fingering her journal's pages. She thought about how easy it had been to sit quietly and listen to the Latin words resound through the church, and was a bit taken aback that she had actually enjoyed the entire experience.

Opening her journal to write down this new insight, her eyes fell upon her last entry. Rereading her previous words about the morning's dreams, Destiny felt a strong urge to open a book to page number seventy-eight. Would there be something valuable for her to discover? She remembered her mum had introduced this spontaneous trick-of-inspiration to her as a child. She reached for the first book on top of the closest stack beside her;

it was one of the Jane Roberts' books. Opening to page #78, she read from the top:

> "In this case, also your reality colors your beliefs, and your experience is a direct result of your conscious attitudes. By such attitudes as these just mentioned you put clamps upon your inner self, purposely hamper your experience, and reinforce beliefs in the negative aspects of your being.
>
> Only by examining these ideas of your own can you learn where you stand with yourself. Now I do not mean to stress the negative by any means, so I suggest that you look to those areas of your life in which you are pleased and have done well. See how emotionally and imaginatively you personally reinforced those beliefs and brought them to physical fruition—realize how naturally and automatically the results appeared. Catch hold of those feelings of accomplishment and understand that you can use the same methods in other areas."

Destiny sat back, lowered the book to her lap, and took a deep breath. *These two paragraphs were meant for me to read right now*, she thought. Then addressing her cottage, she affirmed, "I promise to work on...no...I promise to change my way of seeing the world. I will open myself to others around me. I will accept their friendships and gestures of kindness without thinking they have ulterior motives in mind. I will create my life only in positive ways. I will focus on my future instead of my past." She felt good about her new affirmations and quickly wrote them in her journal.

There was definitely a change happening within Destiny; she felt it, and others sensed it. Her demeanor took on a more positive frame and she found herself smiling when a client entered her massage room. Even her hands seemed to emanate a radiant glow of healing energy that amazed those who received her touch. During the early summer, Destiny enrolled in the first of several classes necessary for her to become a massage instructor at the school. Again, the task of learning new material became an easy challenge. In the spring of the following year, 1981, she became an instructor at the massage school in Cheltenham.

Finally, Destiny took the driver testing and received a driving license. She purchased an older motorcar, and even ventured on small outings on her off days. Her twenty-third birthday was approaching and her parents once again entered her thoughts. It had been over five years since she ran away, and she still had not contacted them. She knew it was time to reconnect and divulge the truth about why she had left without as much as a note of explanation. She decided to plan a road trip to Wellington in her new motorcar. A straight through jaunt would be less than seventy miles; or, she could take two days and stay midway. The road map showed an easy route straight off north from Cheltenham, and then heading west a bit to arrive at Wellington. "Should I call before showing up or just arrive with a surprise entrance?" she asked her cottage walls.

Destiny's birthday was weeks away, so she felt there was no rush in deciding whether to alert her parents of her plans. She continued her routine of working a few days at the spa and teaching a few days at the school. Her favorite pub was always there for downtime on weekend evenings and to mess about with the locals. One night while she was at the pub, a fellow crossed the darkened room and tapped Destiny on the shoulder. "Hey there, Destiny. Remember me?"

Destiny spun around quickly and poured half her drink onto the tall blond who stood beside her. "Ian! Oh, I am so sorry! Here, let me help clean you up," she exclaimed, and grabbed a pile of napkins from the bar to begin rubbing Ian's shirt.

"No, no…that's okay, Destiny. It will dry quickly, don't worry. Do you want to sit down at a table with me to catch up a bit?" Ian asked.

"Yes, that would be lovely. Are you here for just a short time again?"

"Yes, I had business to tend to this week. This is my last night and I thought I would pop in to see if you were here," Ian revealed his intentions outright.

"Oh, I feel honored!" Destiny said with a wink, and took a seat at the table. "I actually took your advice from the last time we chatted."

"And what advice would that be?" Ian inquired, winking back at her.

"Well, you had mentioned that I might become a massage instructor, and...well, I did! Also, just before you left the pub last year, I remember that you mentioned something about my perception toward trusting others. I have been working on that one, too. I feel certain I am making progress." She beamed, as she gave Ian a big smile.

"I am happy to hear that, Destiny. You are a brave young woman with many talents, and it's good to share them. The fact that you are letting go of past wounds is a big plus for moving forward with your life. What's next in your plan book?"

"Well, in fact, I do have a trip planned in a few weeks around my birthday. I am going to visit my parents. I have not seen them in several years. I am not sure how they will receive me just arriving at their door...?" Destiny heard the tone of her voice shift with a slight inflection that made the statement seem more of a question.

"I believe they will be joyously delighted with your visit, Destiny. It's always good to reconnect with our relatives, no matter how much time has passed. There is a new glow about you! It is a most pleasant effect that I know will draw only positive experiences and positive people to you," he predicted, being careful not to overly detail the strange statement.

"I have to ask, Ian, are you psychic?" she whispered as she leaned toward him.

"Now, why would you ask such a question?"

"I guess it is just the way you say things. It's like you know me and what's going to happen...I don't know, it was just a question." Destiny almost retreated, but then asked, "We talked last time about people being able to create their reality, or co-create it, as you put it. Tell me more."

"I did purchase the book you suggested and the storyline certainly offers a fair insight to believing that possibility. I would say in part, that I believe...we have a part in creating our reality by the choices we make, and by how we respond to the outcome of those choices."

"Well, with my new approach to life and how I feel, I am consciously helping to create it. I feel like I am just beginning to also appreciate it. What a late bloomer I am." Destiny laughed.

"Better late...well, you know. I wish you well on your journey to visit your parents, Destiny. Use your new insight of trusting others. I have a feeling you will learn much more than you share," Ian said in his premonitory way, and then he also laughed. He told Destiny he needed to leave the pub to get an early start for the airport in the morning, and then stood from the table. "It is always a pleasure to chat with you. I'll be back in the area again and will be sure to stop by the pub when I can."

"Good to chat with you too, Ian...have a safe journey." Destiny gave him a light kiss on the cheek. She gazed in his blue eyes intent to tell him something profound, but her lips did not move. The two shared only their good-byes.

Thirteen

Spring arrived in an aroma of colours that Destiny could taste the moment she opened the back door of her cottage. The flowerbeds were in full bloom, and the blue birds sang their highest notes to command their song be heard. She had eagerly laid out her plans for the trip to visit her parents. If she wanted to arrive on her birthday, she'd need to leave in less than two weeks. This Sunday, however, she had decided to explore the open fields and orchards behind her cottage. She packed a small backpack with water and snacks, and started on a hike she would never forget. The birds voiced their alarm at Destiny's intrusion as she forged a path through the ivy. The fog retreated, allowing a vast landscape to appear before her. Adjusting the straps of her pack, she closed her eyes and took a deep breath of crisp air, releasing it through her mouth to form the universal sound, OM. The vibration of the deep tones saturated her very being. She repeated the chant three times to penetrate every cell of her body as she instructed her mind to relax.

Over the past few years, Destiny had used many new techniques to help guide her clients toward complete relaxation. She also automatically employed many of these de-stressing methods herself. As she stood among the flowers, she recognized the soft sounds of the stream splashing its way downhill. She opened her eyes and stepped forward to the cool water's edge. She began to hum an unknown tune, as if it needed to be released to bless the stream's existence. She continued humming as she crossed the stream by hopping on the flat stones that unknowingly revealed a passageway. The wooded area located on the far side of the brook was spotted with birch and fruit trees within an array of unfamiliar larger ones. The trees were just beginning to don their leafy coats. Destiny hiked through the fields and into the woods. She kept the sounds of the stream within range, so she could retrace her steps back to her cottage.

After hiking for nearly an hour, she decided to sit on an old log that had been created when a large tree fell to make room for new growth. The log was damp from the fog's early morning rest. She opened her pack and nibbled a bit of cheese, and then took a few sips of water from her canteen. The woods felt holy to her as she reveled in the scenic views and surveyed the painted hues of browns and greens of every shade. She stood on the log and twirled around with her arms outstretched to the sky. Shouting out loud, she yelled, "I am alive! I am free! I am grateful, and I am happy to be me!"

Destiny felt as though she had scaled a mountain as she balanced herself upon the willing log. Silently, she thanked the fallen tree for being a new harbor where she could open herself to the wind and talk to the sky. She thanked the woods for their part in the life cycle of nature, and thanked herself for creating such a perfect environment in which to live. Destiny's gratitude came easily as she began thanking everyone she had ever known. She even thanked her parents for their part in shaping her into who she had become. She thanked the nurses, attendants, and Dr. Ellsworth from the manor that was her temporary home. She thanked her special friend, Tina, who offered such genuine friendship. Then, as abruptly as she began her verbal *Thank You Parade*, Destiny stopped in mid-sentence. Her eyes filled with warm tears as she softly mouthed the words, "Thank you dear one whom I did not meet...for bringing me to this point in my life. Without you, I would not be exactly where I am supposed to be."

At dusk, Destiny retraced her steps along the path that only her feet had touched, and returned to her waiting cottage. As soon as she entered, she reached for her journal to submit her newest reflection:

> Journal—April 1981: I had a revelation today! I realized how important it is, as we walk our life's path, to take note of how we arrived where we are. It is so obvious to me now that each year, each class, each experience, and each person with whom we interact has an impact upon our lives in some manner. As we step

onto a new adventure, our life changes in ways we might not recognize but for the choices we made. What a revealing insight it is to actually see how I have created my life! To be so close to understanding how we create our individual reality is mind-bending.

I marvel that the books, which seem to fall into my lap at the library, are the exact ones I have needed to read. They have guided me toward understanding how I really do co-create my reality. The little book, *Consciously Creating Circumstances* and Bach's *Illusions*, have taught me to focus on what I want to bring into my life, and how to draw it to me. I am so grateful for every choice I have made and each step I have taken. I can easily retrace my journey to understand why it was necessary for me to go through the experiences that I have so far.

Affirmation: I vow to continue to be conscious of my choices and focus on creating my reality the way I wish it to be!

The days passed quickly, and soon Destiny was packing for her road trip to visit her parents for her birthday. There was still a bit of trepidation lingering in her mind when she locked up her cottage. Her heart raced as she turned the key to start her motorcar's engine. She glanced at the road map that lay on the passenger seat announcing its bold black line, dictating a direct route from Swindon Village to Wellington. Tuning into a radio station that blared a popular rock sound, she put her foot on the pedal to begin her next adventure.

Luana's organized inner-adult instructed her to relinquish reading her book to tend to her late fall garden. Even though the book's storyline was foremost on her agenda, there were daily duties that her conscious mind commanded. As she removed the weeds creeping toward the rows of winter vegetables, her mind recaptured the intuitive words given to her earlier: *Your teaching days are not over.* Luana pondered the possibility of teaching a Women Studies class at the local college, and then directly nixed the idea when the political nuances of being a college professor crowded her vision.

"What about a nice small group of women gathering in my home?" Luana asked the yellow squash peeking from beneath its vine. She continued her one-sided conversation by noting, "I could post a flyer at church and on my Facebook page with all the details. I could also put the word out to the local women's clinic, the library, and the community college. But, how would I decide which topics to discuss? I guess I could leave the issues open to be explored by the group and whatever is current in their lives. Or, I could present a list of topics to choose from at each meeting." Luana quickly pulled the remainder of the weeds trying to steal her harvest, so she could go inside to jot down an outline for her evolving thoughts.

Even though Luana had worked as a counselor for well over half of her life, she thought of herself first and foremost, as a teacher. She'd even taught a few college courses when she was younger, but found the paperwork and administrative duties to be tedious and filled with politics. She turned down subsequent offers to teach, and resolved that counseling others was clearly related to teaching. Her file cabinets were overflowing with articles and papers that held her life's work of guiding patients toward their goals. She realized that all this information could also be valuable teaching material to use in a group setting.

Going to her home office, Luana randomly pulled out one file folder that was neatly tucked in a cabinet that was labeled "Grief." She read through the papers to appraise whether this topic might be one that could be addressed within a group. She thumbed though several other files, all visibly labeled in thick black letters, until she had chosen an even dozen. With a flare of excitement and confidence, Luana began to write an outline for facilitating a women's group. "Perhaps my teaching days really are *not* over yet!" she mused loud enough to broaden a smile.

Satisfied with her outline, Luana tackled making a flyer that would list the advantages of joining her group. She was actually surprised when she realized all the various topics that she could teach. The flyer came together nicely and she placed it into a folder to take to the nearest printer to run-off copies. Content that she could begin a new adventure at this time in her life,

Luana was now ready to sit cross-legged in her reading chair like a youngster to pursue her book. She was eager to learn what newest adventure Destiny would bring to *her* life's journey.

Destiny followed the line on her map and drove north on the M5 motorway. She was in no rush and casually absorbed spring's colourful scenery. Soon, she recognized a bit of landscape, which exposed the fact that she had traveled the route before. She thought, *How many years has it been since I sat on the leather seat in the bus from Worcester to Cheltenham? I wonder if the manor is still housing desperate women with no other place to go?* She quickly shook her head to stop more thoughts from entering her awareness. She had not considered that her subconscious mind would offer memories from her past, and was quite shaken by the flashbacks attacking her. Finding an outlet where she could exit, she pulled onto a small roadway and drove a few miles west. At this point, she needed to halt the intruding thoughts and slow the pace of her racing heart. Coming to a stop near an enormous tree that whispered her name in the breeze, Destiny turned the ignition off and stared at the thick old branches bending down to sweep the ground.

Had it been almost six years? Destiny's mind automatically retraced the events of 1975 and '76. She lingered for nearly an hour as she sat frozen in her bucket seat as if in a daze. Finally, a gust of wind blew a tree limb onto the bonnet of the motor-car. She jumped and turned around to make sure no one was near. The avenue was quiet, promising not to divulge her secret musing of her past. Not wanting to belabor her emotions from five years ago any longer, she said a silent affirmation to attest that she had moved forward with her life as she had envisioned during her walk in the woods. Yet...a small voice crept along her consciousness until she had to acknowledge its presence. "What? Visit *that* manor? There is no one there that I want to see again," she argued out loud with her inner voice. Taking a deep breath, she started the engine, placed her hands firmly on the steering wheel, and returned to the main motorway.

Tomorrow was Destiny's birthday, and she was actually excited to be able to spend it with her mum and dad. She wanted her visit to be a positive one. She envisioned her parents' excited faces as they opened the door to witness their daughter standing in front of them. She felt calm as she drove the rest of the way through Worcester, and could feel herself blocking the awareness of the manor that had harbored within her for several weeks. She subdued her inner voice by focusing her thoughts on what she was going to tell her parents. Would sharing the fact that she'd fled so quickly that winter night to hide until she gave birth to an illegitimate child even be relevant today? Maybe she should start her conversation by sharing all her accomplishments and where she had settled. She could tell them about Swindon Village and how much she enjoyed living there, and also about teaching massage classes in Cheltenham.

As Destiny approached the half-way point of her trip, just south of Birmingham, she convinced herself there were many things to share with her parents, other than her brutal rape and its culmination. She wanted to tell them how she felt like a whole new person—an independent woman not afraid to take on new adventures and explore new ideas. Destiny also had many questions she wanted to discuss with her mum, if she was brave enough to ask them. The motorcar was running splendidly, but Destiny was not used to driving and her back was beginning to ache. She decided to look for a motor inn where she might spend the night. Her stomach was also signaling she needed to eat supper.

Veering off the roadway, she turned onto a lane lined with quaint older manors with long driveways, some continuing in a half-circle. Many of them reminded her of her parents' home with rows of greenery and roses etching out garden paths. She noticed a signpost announcing food and lodging ahead, and focused on spying the inn before passing it. After a few miles, she spotted the signage and pulled into a space for guests to register. Once in her room, Destiny sat on the end of the firm bed and felt rather proud for getting along so well with her unaccustomed travel.

After a light supper at the café next to the inn, she opened her journal to write a list of the questions she wanted to ask her mum:

> Journal—May 6, 1981: I seem to have gone foggy about my life since living on my own. My upbringing has faded away and seems so insignificant now. I do love my parents, albeit, the emotional element I once had for them as a young child is gone. Do we outgrow our parents?
>
> I would like to question Mum about my name again, and why she always hedges around the topic when I ask her. I know I was a bit dotty in my younger years and caused both of them trials of tribulations... but don't all teens? I guess I was quite a handful. Too bad all families cannot be like the chummy ones on the Tele.
>
> I wonder what kind of mum I would have been if...Oh, god...I can't go there! I have been able to keep those thoughts from my mind for five years. I guess I am more afraid to talk about it with Mum than I thought. How in heaven do I bring it up? I will see how the visit goes before starting to worry about sharing what happened to me.

Destiny stretched and rubbed her tired eyes. She wanted to arrive in Wellington early, so she decided to shut out the lamp to invite sleep to enter her exhausted body. Somewhere between 2:00 and 3:00A.M., she awoke in a panic and felt as if she could not breathe. A vision of a potent dream encompassed her thoughts, and she switched the lamp on to write in her journal:

> Dream: The ocean waves consumed me; I was drowning. Suddenly a white Light appeared above me and I was able to see the surface. I reached my arms toward the Light and found the air my lungs required. Gasping for breath, I silently thanked the mysterious Light surrounding me...and then I woke up.

Unable to close her eyes for fear of dreaming the same vision, Destiny lay rigid on her back, staring at the grey ceiling. Her mind raced with various meanings for the disruptive dream. She had recently found several books in the library that listed interpretations for these subconscious plays that come to share their illusive guidance with us. She remembered that water, especially large bodies of water, meant emotions within a dream. The books agreed that if the body of water appeared calm, it represented peaceful emotions. On the other hand, if the water was turbulent with tidal waves, the dream signified there were unsettled emotions residing within the dreamer. Destiny acknowledged that she, indeed, had unsettled feelings about meeting her parents. She instructed herself to enlist her meditation practices upon rising in the morning to calm her emotions before continuing her road trip.

Fourteen

Mastering Our Dreams

Where does our consciousness stray as we enter a dream deep into the night? Why do I dream of running or falling far from sight? Does my brain lie idle while visions escape my control, or does it realize my dreams are but fancy flight?

We all dream. Some may not remember the visions that visit their unconscious awareness; however, we all experience the illusive images that sweep through our subconscious mind as we enter the realm of deep sleep. Dreams can border on being an insanely rich creative aspect that roams throughout the dream state known as REM (Rapid Eye Movement). Emotional scenarios exploit our brain as we toss and turn in our sleep; and many times, we awaken just enough to edge the play to ensure the final production ends happily. At other times, our semi-conscious efforts are not received and the dream-play ends in a tragic conclusion.

Humans have speculated about dreams since the beginning of time, and little has been conclusively accepted by all genres of education. The physiological components of a person while in the dream state have been well studied, but the metaphysical, or mystical aspects have only been touched upon by the great dreamers themselves. Carl Jung (1875-1961) was one of those dreamers that ushered in the concept of dreams having common themes and coined the term "dream archetypes." He believed there was a symbolic factor associated with the images one envisions within a dream and related their mythology or origin, from a "collective unconscious." Thus, with this new theory, dream journals began to be written by those determined to unleash the meanings attributed to their dreams.

Luana set her pen down to reread the beginning paragraphs of her newest writing adventure. Each time she took the time to sit and write, the words continued to flow from her mind without the slightest interruption or question. Her wide body of knowledge afforded her a great pool of information to choose from for her articles. Once she began to write down her thoughts on that chilly evening in front of the fireplace, she was unable to stop the words held within her. Luana submitted her articles to many of the current e-Magazines and was delighted when each were posted on a web site or Blog for the public to read. She realized her articles coincided with the storyline of the book she was reading, which suited her just fine. That way, she didn't need to search her brain for new topics to explore. For Luana, Destiny's life was the muse guiding her pen.

During the next few weeks, however, Luana was so consumed with her new project of starting a women's group that she had little time to sit and read, or write. Still, Destiny seemed to be on her mind constantly. She concocted several scenarios in her mind of what could happen when Destiny arrived at her parents' manor. But, she also realized it was important to begin her group before the holidays. This time of the year was when so many people experience loneliness and self-doubt, and usually became aware of their destructive family dynamics. The phone rang just when she was walking out the door; she turned to listen to the message machine as a young man was stating that the printed flyers were ready to be picked up. She decided to drop by and get them on her way to the health food store. When she returned home, Luana stacked the flyers on the dining room table in several piles.

Looking down the list of the locations she had chosen to post the flyers, she decided to start with the women's clinic. She changed her slacks for a rose print dress with matching jacket. Then she ran a comb through her gray hair and cinched it with a hair-band to form a perfect ponytail like she wore when she was younger. Luana studied her reflection a bit longer than usual to assess whether her face had aged since her last birthday. In little over a month, she would be close to seventy;

she shook her head in disbelief. *At least my life has been a happy one*, she thought. But, *it has passed by so quickly!*

She sat on the edge of the white down bedspread neatly arranged over her memory-foam mattress. Grabbing one of the silky blue pillows that formed a pyramid at the headboard, Luana placed it snug at her lower back for support. She scrolled through her memory of important life events as if a reel of movie film to assure her life had been a happy one. Her smile broadened as she envisioned one experience in 1990 that brought the imaginary film reel to a halt. The event was the summer she met her second husband, Edward.

Forming a clear vision of the event, Luana remembered the holiday party she had attended. It had been hosted by one of her therapist friends who lived near Laguna in the town of Corona del Mar. She had tried to talk herself out of going, but reasoned she needed to meet new colleagues who might refer potential patients. She pictured herself in the short black dress she wore that evening. It was a formfitting design with an open scoop back. Her jewelry was a pair of simple gold hoop earrings and a gold beaded bracelet. She decided to wear black three inch high-heels that made her appear much taller than her five foot four inches. She turned to recheck her reflection in the full-length mirror, and thought, *not too bad for a gal my age!* It had been two years since Luana's Hawaii vacation, and her heart ached for another romantic adventure.

Darcy, a longtime friend, was the hostess and welcomed Luana with a hug. There was a crowd of people gathered on the outside deck waiting for the expected fireworks display to begin. The yard was decorated with red, white, and blue lights that danced upon the faces of the men and women politely attempting conversation as they stood sipping their drinks. Luana wandered through the unknown couples to a garden fountain at the far end of the yard. A server appeared out of nowhere to ask if she desired a drink. "Yes, thank you. I'll have a glass of white wine, please," she replied.

She sat on a wooden bench to inspect the water bubbling its soft rhythm. Tiny water plants bobbed up-'n-down as if dancing to the water's tune. A few silvery crystals lay beneath the sparkling water, and a gold Buddha statue sat happily accepting a baptism from the stray droplets.

"Here's your wine, miss," the server offered, and gestured Luana to accept the delicate wine glass.

"Oh, thank you," Luana said a bit startled. She took the stemmed glass with her left hand accidentally touching the handsome man's fingers.

"May I ask your name?" the server questioned, as he stood erect with his piercing eyes directed to Luana's blushing face.

"Well, yes, I guess that's okay…it's Luana," she replied, thinking it strange he would ask for her name, however intrigued at the boldness.

"My name is Edward. I noticed you when you arrived and knew we had to meet," Edward announced, slightly bending at the waist in a typical server's gesture of greeting.

"You *are* a server, aren't you?" asked Luana.

"Oh…I could see why you would think so. But no, I am not a waiter," replied the dark-haired mysterious gentleman.

"I am so sorry…I thought you were, well, I must have sounded very…well, you know, cold. What did you say your name was again?" She felt her cheeks flush.

"Oh, that's quite all right, Luana. I did sort of presume you would want to talk with me. My name is Edward, Edward Hollingsworth. I have a practice in Torrance. Are you a therapist also?"

"Yes, I have an office in Laguna Beach. Torrance…now is that up by Santa Monica?"

"It's just south of there, but still near the ocean. What is your specialty?" Edward took a seat on the bench next to Luana.

"Well, through the years it has changed; but currently, I am working mostly with women. And you?" she asked, taking a sip of her wine.

"I work with couples. May I ask if you are single, Luana?" Edward boldly inquired, looking into her blue eyes.

"Yes, you can ask…I am, indeed, single. Well, I am many years divorced…and you, Edward? I assume you are single, have you been married?"

"Yes…but I am also divorced. I guess that's why I work with couples. The divorce rate just keeps going up each year. You would think we counselor-types could at least keep our own relationships together!" He laughed.

"Yes, one would think…" she laughed openly.

Just then the fireworks erupted and interrupted Luana and Edward's conversation. They stood together for the entire display. Edward smelled of musk oil and peppermint. He was about five foot eleven with black hair and dark secretive eyes that Luana found enticing. She guessed him to be about fifty-five years old. After the fireworks ended, they agreed to leave the party together to find a restaurant where they could get a bite to eat and continue their question bantering. It was obvious they were attracted to each other, and during their conversation they uncovered many common interests. It took only a few subsequent outings together for each of them to realize they were falling in love.

As Luana's memories flooded back to her, she told herself to revisit them later to savor the twenty years she lived and loved her dear Edward. She needed to get back to the task at hand, she rose from her bed and replaced the pillow to the top of its pyramid. She quickly checked the mirror a last time to adjust her dress collar. On her way out the door, she picked up one of the stacks of flyers from the table and headed for the clinic. It was a crisp October day, and she was glad she remembered to throw her heavy sweater in the car. As she walked into the main lobby of the clinic, Luana felt confident that the manager would allow her to post the flyer on the public bulletin board and leave the rest on a nearby table. The agreement was made. She tacked up her flyer to the board with a sense of anticipation and excitement.

It took only a few days for Luana to distribute all her flyers. The first group meeting was set to begin in three weeks, just before the Thanksgiving holiday. Now, she would wait for at least six women to respond and agree to the initial pre-group interview. Luana always felt it was necessary to interview a potential group member to make sure each person was aligned with the dynamics within a group setting. In the meantime, she would go through her materials and suggested reading list to make sure there was enough information to introduce to the group for at least eight weeks. Luana decided to make this group a *closed group*, meaning no new women could join it after the first meeting. That way, the members would be able to share their personal history and concerns, knowing they would only need to do so once. She also felt a closed group initiated an accelerated sense of trust between its participants. Once Luana felt everything had been executed to ensure a positive group outcome, she relaxed and waited for interested women to contact her.

She was finally able to resume her reading and was trying to remember where Destiny's tale last ended, when her mind forced her to again reminisce about her years with Edward. Being a couple's therapist, Edward had no problem keeping his counseling practice busy. It was a few weeks before he found the time to invite Luana to visit his office, which was nestled between two commercial buildings off the main streets of west Torrance. There were only four tenants within the distinctive office building, his being on the top floor. The door opened to an inner waiting room decorated nicely in soft colors of tan and subdued greens. Several live plants adorned the room, continuing a sense of oneness with an atrium that could be viewed from a large glass window. The atrium was filled with various plants, flowers, and water fountains. The flowing water sounds were transported through audio speakers to resound their vibrato. The seating consisted of two dark tan sofas, sitting back-to-back in the center of the room. Each sofa possessed its own coffee table proudly displaying an array of current reading materials.

Luana was quite impressed as Edward opened the inner door to the main office that exposed an even larger view of the atrium's assortment of plants and water features. A dark cherry wood desk and matching chair sat on the opposite side of the room. She sensed the atrium's mesmerizing effect and the invitation to relax beckoning her from one of the overstuffed chairs.

"Oh, Edward, what an absolutely marvelous office you have!" Luana announced, as she allowed herself to melt into the chair as her feet made their way to the top of the ottoman.

"Thank you, Luana. I guess it has its good qualities, for sure." Edward took a seat in the opposing chair and leaned toward Luana as he asked, "What is your office like?"

Sitting up a bit, Luana answered, "Well, it is also very relaxing, but nothing as elegant as this one!"

"You'll have to show me one day. I'd like to know where you work. Perhaps next week you might let me visit?"

"That's a date," Luana smiled back at him. "The ocean must be near...I can smell it in the air. I adore living near the sea, don't you?"

"I do. In fact, we'll overlook the ocean during our dinner tonight. It's only a few blocks from here. My home also overlooks Torrance Beach. Would you like to go there after dinner?" Edward reached for Luana's hand and pulled her to her feet.

"Yes, I would like that..." she said, trailing her words as they hugged tightly.

The pair stood together for as long as it took them to pull away, and then they stared into each other's eyes—his, the color of dark coal, hers, the ocean waves on a sunny day. Their eyes talked of a love affair filled with passion and a romance to last a lifetime. Luana's pale blue eyes broke away first, and she placed a single finger to his lips as he caressed it with his tongue. The ensuing kisses aroused the passions within each of them. Silently, they agreed to pause their peaking temptations to keep their dinner reservations.

Edward drove Luana to a casual restaurant a few blocks from his office that touted a menu of fresh fish and a lengthy wine list. The view from within the café witnessed a pounding sea upon blackened rocks, hushed by a moonless night. Ordering a bottle of Chardonnay, Edward insisted Luana try one of the fish specialties of the day and she easily allowed him to order for her. Throughout the evening, their conversation included comparing notes on counseling methods. The two therapists had much in common when it came to counseling techniques, and raised their glasses often to cement their joint approval.

Declining a dessert, Edward offered, "How does a good cup of coffee sound? We could drive to my house, and I'll whip up a blend of the most aromatic beans you've ever tasted!"

"That sounds fabulous," she replied with a wink.

Luana was eager to know where Edward lived. She imagined a darkened bachelor's house filled with old self-help books, racks of music albums, and sports equipment flung on the floor. The narrow road twisted up a hillside lined with beach cottages that squeezed themselves onto every square foot of existing acreage. As they reached the top of the hill, Edward pushed a remote button and a garage door opened to welcome the vehicle home. It was a dark night and Luana couldn't readily see the outside of the house, but did notice some Calla lilies snuggled together waving their white cones in the sea breeze.

"Oh, I love Calla lilies, they are my favorite flowers!" Luana broke the silence, as she exited the car door being held open by Edward.

"Me too...I had them planted all around the house. They seem to do so well here in the ocean air. Let's get inside, I am anxious to show you around and make that cup of coffee for you." Edward led the way through the backdoor into the kitchen.

Luana was amazed at how neat the kitchen looked as she noticed the color-coordinated dish towels. Edward took her hand and walked her through his beach cottage one room at a time. As he pointed to cherished pieces of artwork and various mementos, he explained where he had found them. As he ushered Luana into the master bedroom, he turned and whispered, "Are we ready?"

Luana nodded, and dropped her summer jacket on the floor. She shook off her black heels to stand barefoot as Edward towered over her removing his jacket and shirt. The moment played out rhythmically. They surged toward their urgency, each allowing the other to explore and explode their desires. Luana lay beside Edward throughout the night with a calm heart and peaceful mind.

Fifteen

The remainder of Destiny's drive was uneventful, except for the recurring anxiety spinning in her stomach. She easily followed the road signs through Wellington that directed her to a roundabout and onto a more familiar roadway. When she knew she was within a few miles of her parents' home, she pulled over on a side road. She looked up into the rearview mirror and removed a strand of hair that had fallen over her tortoiseshell frames. Silently repeating her arrival speech, she turned toward the manor where she had been raised.

Quickly scanning the property, she noted that nothing had changed since she'd left five years ago. She drove up the hedge-lined driveway that introduced the front of the estate. Parking her motorcar, she sat with her eyes closed to calm her stomach, and then took a few deep breaths. She reminded herself it was her choice to visit her parents, and that she had control over how long she would stay. *If the reunion does not go smoothly,* she told herself, *I will leave.* She felt a formal attitude lurking in the air that dictated adherence, even by runaway daughters. She approached the front entrance and decided to knock to be received by the maid.

The door opened, but Destiny did not recognize the woman, so politely said, "Hello, I am Destiny Collins...the daughter of Helen and Henry. Are they home?"

"Why, yes, Destiny, come in. I'll go let them know you are here," the woman said with a hint of excitement in her voice.

Destiny entered the large receiving room and sat on the familiar couch. Thinking she might not stay long enough to unpack, she left her baggage outside. She glanced around and noticed that everything was exactly as it had been for decades.

"Who's here? Oh, my! Is it really you, Destiny?" Destiny's mother squealed, as she rounded a corner to enter the room.

"Yes, Mum, it is really me. I have come to visit you and Dad on my birthday today. I hope it's all right?" Destiny stood up to receive her mother's attempted hug.

"Well, let me sit down a moment and gather my thoughts. I have prayed you would come to your senses and come home to us, but never thought I would see this day," Helen said, and sank into a chair.

"Is Father home?"

"No, dear. He is out for the morning. He will be home this afternoon. We both think of you, Destiny, especially on your birthday and at holidays. Are you all right, dear?"

"Yes, Mum. I am fine. In fact, I am great! I want to tell you all about my life, but would like to wait until Dad is home so he can hear about it too. In the meantime, I need to know...are you terribly upset with me? Should I have even come for a visit? Will Dad be upset that I have come?" Destiny quickly asked her mum questions to appraise if she should stay or leave right then.

"Destiny, I am glad you have decided to return. I am not mad at you; however, I do not understand why you left. We were terribly hurt," Destiny's mother confessed, beginning to show a bit of emotion.

"Mum, I have not returned to stay. I have a wonderful life on my own, and have no intention of returning to live here. I knew I should have rung you up years ago, and I tried; but, I just couldn't get myself to follow through with it. So much has happened..." Destiny's voice trailed off as she noticed the tears welling-up in her mother's eyes. "Don't cry, Mum, I am really okay..."

Wiping her eyes with a tissue, Helen told her daughter, "I am just so happy to see you again, Destiny. I know we were never the doting type of parents. For so long, I have thought your father and I caused you to be so...rebellious. I am sorry, Destiny, for not showing you the love I have for you. It is just that...well, I have not had an easy life either." Helen did not relate details.

"Oh, Mum, it is so good to hear you say that...I remember a time when I was little and you were happy and smiling all the time. What happened to make that happiness go away?"

Destiny asked the question she had wanted to ask her mother for years.

"Dear Destiny…your memory of me makes me smile. Now that you are a grown woman, I will share something with you…and hopefully, you will understand my situation."

Helen rose to sit beside her daughter and took Destiny's hands in her own. Looking behind her to check that no one was near, she whispered, "Destiny, five years after you were born, during the summer of 1963, I became pregnant again. After you were born, your father was clear that he did not want another child. So when I discovered I was pregnant a second time, I told the doctor I could not have the baby. He told me that he could help my situation… and, well, I agreed to have an abortion. I never told your father about the pregnancy, or what I did. You are the first person to whom I have revealed my horrible sin."

"Oh, Mum! I am so sorry… for all you went through and that you felt you had to keep it a secret from Dad," Destiny cried, and wrapped her arms around her mother in comfort. "No wonder I remember you so differently when I was little. You still have not shared this with Dad?"

"No, dear, and you must never mention it to him, or anyone, ever. It is a burden I must carry to my grave." Helen put a finger to her lips with a hush. "Now that I have acknowledged the truth of my sin to another, perhaps God will forgive me."

"Oh, Mum…it is *you* that needs to forgive yourself…" Destiny whispered, and held her mother even tighter. Destiny made up her mind that she would stay on a few days soon after hearing her mum's unpredicted confession. The two shared a light lunch and waited for Henry to return.

The reunion with her father was far less revealing, or emotional. He raised one eyebrow upon entering the room, acknowledging his daughter's presence. Then he announced he had made plans to be with the fellows at the club that night. The brief conversation between Destiny and her father was dry and uninformative. She told him she would stay on a few days for a visit, and then would be returning to her new life. He did not ask her any questions, and Destiny did not bother to remind him it was her birthday.

Helen Collins rose early the following morning. She felt a sense of relief and confidence after revealing the details of her choice to have an abortion so many years ago. She acknowledged it was time to release her past, and embrace her natural inner joy for life. There was a spirit of excitement surrounding her as she dressed to spend the day with her daughter. She turned to gaze at her reflection in the antique mirror resting in the corner of the master bedroom. She pulled on a pair of pleated slacks that had not seen the outside of her clothes wardrobe in twenty years. Her green eyes studied the older woman's reflection, and then imagined the younger-self she wanted to embrace once again. Putting on a loose-fitting cream blouse and pale yellow sweater, Helen was determined to reflect the mum that Destiny remembered as a child. She brushed her auburn hair and twisted it at her nape, adjusting the bun with two Asian hairpins given to her by her father when she was a child.

"Destiny? Are you up, dear?" Helen's voice echoed down the long hallway as she knocked on Destiny's bedroom door. The room had not been touched in hopes its resident would return one day.

"Yes, Mum. I am awake, come in," Destiny replied through the closed door.

Bursting through the door, Helen exclaimed, "Oh, Destiny, I feel so alive this morning! I want to take you shopping like we used to do, and maybe even get a pudding together! How does that sound to you?" Helen asked her daughter who was sitting cross-legged on the bed focusing on a book. Not waiting for an answer to her first question, she asked another, "What are you reading, dear?"

"Mum, I didn't know you knew about Cayce. I did not sleep well last night. So, I went to the library to find a book to read and found this one, *Many Mansions*, about the life of Edgar Cayce. I have been reading about his work in books borrowed from the library in Cheltenham. Isn't it fascinating to learn that our souls may return one day? Sometimes, my mind just gets so boggled with all the new things I read about! I truly wish you would have shared more of your spiritual beliefs with me when I was growing up."

"Ummm…well, first of all, I was just barely beginning to explore other types of spiritual thinking when you were a child. Then, when…well, you know what happened…I guess I just retreated into a religious cave and did not come out. I would not allow myself to look beyond the reality of my guilt. I am happy that you are unraveling new ways to view your spiritual beliefs. Perhaps one day, I will get back into my studies as well. In the meantime, let's go out and play!" Helen jumped up from the corner of the bed and twirled around.

"Okay, Mum. I will get dressed and meet you downstairs for a quick scone." Destiny rose from the bed and gave her mother a big hug. She then held her mother's shoulders at arm's length and gazed into her green eyes, "I love you, Mum."

Helen's eyes began to tear as she said, "I love you too, Destiny."

The day was planned to include clothes shopping, a luncheon, and then a pudding. Destiny was transported back to her five-year-old-self as they laughed and giggled the entire day. Only once did she allow the thought to enter her mind of telling her mum the real reason she had left so suddenly five years ago. She wanted the time with her mum to be filled with positive memories, and feared her secret would spoil it all.

As the dinner hour approached, Destiny felt the pangs of disapproval she knew her presence would evoke from her father. She sat on her bed to meditate to release the tension in her stomach. Just as she was feeling more relaxed her mum knocked softly, and whispered through the door, "Destiny, may I come in?"

"Yes, Mum, the door is unlocked," Destiny replied, and stretched her hands over her head to release the immobility of sitting in meditation.

"I want to share something with you about your father. I know he seems rather harsh, but inside he is a good man, Destiny. He shared with me how his heart was crushed when you left; he really was devastated. I think your arrival yesterday has been quite a shock to him. He shared with me last evening before retiring that he was glad you were safe. Please do not be too hard on him, dear. He is trying to understand you, but it is more difficult for him to admit any wrongdoing. Can you understand?" Helen asked, tilting her head to one side.

"Okay, Mum. I will be gentle with him tonight," Destiny smiled. "Can we talk later, after dinner? Just you and me?"

"Why yes, of course, dear. Is something bothering you?"

"I just have something I want to tell you. Since you shared so much of your past with me, I want to share some of my life with you." Destiny hugged her mother and they walked down the hallway hand in hand.

Henry always sat at the head of the table for his meals, whether or not anyone was dining with him. He positioned himself firmly in the European chair that displayed a festive floral print. The meal was already arranged on the table for the reunited family of three. Henry politely asked his wife about the day's events and listened as Helen related her and Destiny's outing. He could sense a difference in his wife's tone and manner, but did not voice his awareness. Directly after their dinner ended, Henry rose to excuse himself and disappeared into the library.

Destiny and her mother quickly adjourned to the privacy of the bedroom to reconnect their budding friendship. "Mum, come sit over here, next to me." Destiny motioned for her mother to sit beside her on the bed. She placed her hand down in front of her, and Helen reached to hold it tight.

"Mum, it is very difficult for me to tell you why I needed to leave so suddenly that day five years ago. Please be patient with me as I try to gather my thoughts about how to begin."

Helen sat fixed with horror as the details of her daughter's rape were revealed. She was astonished and bewildered that Destiny could not share the horrific event with her directly after it happened. She was also speechless to learn of the subsequent pregnancy, and that she had a grandchild she would never meet.

Silence hung in the air between them, then finally, Destiny said, "I know you must be hurt that I did not come to you when all this was happening, Mum, but you must see now that I am fine. Please do not dwell on my past; I want to share with you what my life is about now. I want to share with you how I was able to move forward, away from those events in my past. Will you please say something?"

"Where do I begin? My heart aches for you and what you have endured alone. I wish you would have confided in me. I am also in shock that you can talk so candidly about giving birth to a child, and giving it away. After all, it is my grandchild...did you not think that I might want to raise him or her? Do you even know if it was a boy or girl? I am not sure what you want me to say, Destiny. I am so shaken by all this..." Helen's voice trailed off into silence as she stared out the window to view the perfectly kept lawn weaving between the flower beds.

"Mum, I was a different person five years ago. I thought I was in total control of my life. I recognize now that I was on a self-destructive path, one which could not have ended positively. I am not like that anymore. I have come to realize that I have choices in creating my life, and now I choose to make positive ones. My life is totally different than it was back then, Mum. I have completed a college certificate in bodywork. I work in a spa and also teach massage therapy in a college. I am good at what I do, and I enjoy it. Please do not be upset with me, Mum. I did what I thought I had to do at the time. I cannot change my past choices, just as you cannot change your decision, or that you have kept it a secret all these years. Do you understand? Can you forgive me?" Destiny pleaded.

"Destiny, I do love you...more than I can say. I will talk with you more tomorrow when I am rested and have a clear mind. I shan't tell your father about this. I will keep your secret until you, yourself, are ready to talk with him," Helen promised, and left Destiny's room to be alone.

Destiny's sleep was again filled with tidal waves flooding through her dreams, culminating with a headache that awoke her in the middle of the night. She retraced her decision to share her past with her mum. Needing direction, she sat alone in the library. Once again, she sought guidance from random words on a page in a book chosen with her eyes closed. Stepping onto the library ladder to the third rung, Destiny closed her eyes and let her right hand inspect each book's spine within her reach. When her fingers touched raised letters centered on a leather-bound book, she pulled it to her breast without looking at the title.

She sat in one of the cushioned chairs, clutching the sacred volume. Revealing itself, the book fell open when Destiny lowered it to her lap. She put a finger tight between the pages, and then closed the book to inspect its title. A single word on the ragged cover was revealed: Longfellow. The wine-coloured leather was worn, and the edges were frayed exposing an inner-padded cover. Beneath and to the left of the titled letters were etched depictions of white birds in flight. With one glance, Destiny knew when she read the words on the page that had initially opened that they would guide her toward the inner peace she was seeking. Studying the page, she read:

> And thou, too, whosever thou art,
> That readest this brief psalm,
> As one by one thy hopes depart,
> Be resolute and calm.
> O fear not in a world like this,
> And thou shalt know ere long,
> Know how sublime a thing it is
> To suffer and be strong.

Destiny reread the brief passage several times to infuse the lines into her memory. She felt calmness wash over her. A subtle glow, originating from nowhere, seemed to surround the book as she placed it on the polished wood table in front of her. She retreated up the staircase silently repeating a few lines of the poetry, and enjoyed a peaceful sleep the rest of the night.

Sixteen

Upon waking, Destiny immediately sat up in bed to read the lines of poetry she had entered in her journal from the night before. *There is a sense of strength in these words*, she thought. *I must read them to Mum. Perhaps they will encourage her strength to shine as well.* She heard a soft knock at her bedroom door, and inquired, "Mum, is that you?"

"No, Destiny. It is your father," Henry spoke softly. "May I enter?"

"Just a moment, Father." Destiny jumped out of bed to find the pink robe she left hanging in the clothes wardrobe. "All right, you may come in now."

"I did not want to awaken you, Destiny. But, I would like us to have a chat before you leave," he said, and took a seat in the corner window-box.

Henry was well over six feet tall with brown eyes that morphed to green in the sunshine. As he sat in the early morning sun, Destiny felt a renewed affection toward him, and joined him in the sunny nook. The alcove had warmly hosted her many times as she sat in the sunshine to read books from the family library. "Is there something else you wanted to discuss, Father?" she asked respectfully.

"Well, first of all, I am glad you are well and safe, Destiny. Your mum and I were quite worried when you up and ran off. We even put out an official bulletin with the authorities. But, that's not why I am here this morning. I want to know if you need our help. Where did you say you were living?" Henry asked in a mellow tone that Destiny had not heard since childhood.

"That is so nice of you to ask, Father. I currently live in Swindon Village. I rent a perfect cottage that is near both of my jobs," Destiny answered with just enough information to satisfy his question.

"I am glad to hear you are happy. Frankly, I was not sure if you would ever straighten yourself out, Destiny. Will you continue to stay in touch with your mum and me?" He smoothed his greying mustache.

"Yes, if you wish me to, Father. I will ring you up directly to appraise you of my whereabouts and such. You do know that I did not mean to hurt you when I left, don't you?" she asked, and reached forward with her hand to touch her father's knee.

"It is hard to imagine why you would leave us so abruptly without a note or word of your intentions. However, the past is the past, and it keeps its own secrets. Let's not dwell on it at this moment. I am here to make sure you are happy in your life, and if we can offer you help in some way. Are your funds holding out? Would you like to take some of your belongings with you?" Henry asked, and then reached in return for his daughter's hand. He held both of Destiny's hands as if pieces of fine china. Without letting go of her hands, he rose from his sitting position to tower over her, and then offering his outstretched arms, he said, "Destiny, I want you to know that I love you…I will always love you."

Destiny stood up to hug her father, but waited for his arms to move toward her before wrapping hers around him. The pair stood silent, enjoying their long-awaited reunion. Destiny pulled away first, saying, "Dad, I love you too. I did not mean to hurt you during my turbulent teen years. I was searching for myself, my individuality and the like. And now, I believe I have found who Destiny really is—I am an independent woman with high ideals who likes new adventures and making people smile. I know I am an intelligent person and have much to offer. I have discovered I am interested in metaphysics and learning how the Universe works. You would be proud of me, Father, if you could see me as an adult and not that bratty child that must be haunting your memory."

"I see you, Destiny. Maybe for the first time since you were a little girl, I truly see you. When you are ready for your mum and me to visit, we would like to see your cottage."

"That would be lovely. I will ring you up soon with an invite. I am leaving today. I am so happy you have come to chat with me this morning. Is Mum up?"

"Yes, she is awake. We had a long talk last night and…well, things will be different around here." Henry smiled with a wink. Before leaving his daughter's room, he acknowledged he would be home later to see her off. Destiny could not ever remember seeing her father wink! She quickly dressed to go find her mother.

"Mum, may I come in?" Destiny asked, as she knocked softly on the master bedroom door. She was excited to share with her mother about the chat she had with her father just minutes earlier. Knocking a second time with no response, she walked to the wooden staircase and down to the dining room. Passing an empty dining room table, she made her way to the kitchen. "Has my mum come through yet this morning?" she asked one of the staff.

"No, miss. Your mum has not yet requested early tea."

"Ta," Destiny acknowledged, and then turned to swipe a warm muffin from a blue and white platter.

She wandered through the study to the library. She found her mother sitting in a large ray of sunlight that streamed through her hair, highlighting its deep red hues. "I thought I might find you here, Mum. I have something I want to share with you." Destiny nestled in one of the overstuffed chairs.

"I was up early this morning, dear. I like to come here to read a bit when my mind needs clearing," Helen said softly.

"I like to do that myself. In fact, I used to come here often to read from books that would seem to jump from their shelf into my lap. Last evening, when I could not sleep, I came here and found a very old book of poems by Longfellow. I read one of the poems that I actually thought you might like to hear. I have memorized the most important part of the poem, would you like to hear it?" Destiny asked, hoping her mother would agree.

"Oh, yes…please recite it for me, dear."

Destiny spoke the words of Longfellow in a slow rhythmic rote, and then asked her mother, "Don't the words just make you feel strong, Mum?"

"Why, yes…they do indeed. Much of my night, I was also awake thinking of my life, my decisions, and my past. Then all at once, I felt I needed to tell your father about my pregnancy from so long ago, and what happened. I awakened him and related the entire event. He astonished me by his tender comforting manner. He said he had no idea that I had gone through the experience. He did say, however, that he had noticed a distinct change in me during that time period. I do believe that the emotional walls between us have started to crumble, Destiny. It makes my heart feel so much lighter." Tearfully, Helen stood to offer her daughter a hug.

Destiny quickly stood up to accept her mother's hug, and whispered, "Oh, Mum, I am so happy for you both! One day, I may even find that I can share my past with Father...but not today. I cannot deal with it now."

"Are you really leaving today? Can you stay just one more day?"

"Yes, Mum, I need to get back to my work. I am so happy that I came for this holiday...we have connected in a way I never thought possible. And Father came to my room earlier, he seems happier also. I do love you," Destiny said, giving her mother a second hug.

Destiny went back upstairs grinning to herself, and thought, *I would have never thought this visit would have gone so smoothly. I feel like my sharing with Mum what happened to me, may have been just what I needed to begin letting go of my guilt. Wait, do I have feelings of guilt?* She grabbed her journal to write down her thoughts:

> Journal—May 1981: Why should I feel guilty? I didn't ask to be raped or to get pregnant! What do I have to feel guilty about?
>
> Yes, I did suffer...even though I didn't ask for the experience, and I do admit I feel a bit guilty for not telling Mum at the time. Now that I know how she would have reacted, I guess I should have shared my situation with her at the time. Suffering makes us stronger...that's what Longfellow wrote. My suffering certainly has made me stronger. But why is guilt still haunting me? It's not because I chose to give birth instead of abort the baby like Mum did—oh, she must feel such guilt! Poor Mum, I wonder what I could say to help comfort her more?

Do I have a bit of guilt for not keeping the baby? But that certainly was not the correct move for me back then. I might choose differently today. Aha! That's where this tiny word with a capital "G" seems to tug at me! I must forgive myself for the choice I made to give the baby up for adoption. I only did what I thought was the best thing for both of us at the time. What more could I have done? That is exactly what I told Mum. I guess I better take my own advice.

Note: I officially release the guilt that has haunted me.

The goodbyes to her parents went smoothly. As Destiny pulled from the circle drive, she spied in her rearview mirror her father standing with his arm around his wife. She felt pleased that her visit may have rekindled her parents' affection. Her motorcar was packed with several pieces of new clothing and some she decided to take with her from her old clothes wardrobe. She also took a few books from the library that looked interesting. She could actually feel a sense of happiness swell within her as her motorcar hummed in approval.

She hadn't planned her return road trip, leaving the day's schedule open to either driving straight through to Swindon, or stopping again halfway to spend the night. After a few hours of driving, she pulled over for a snack of chips and a Coke. A motorbike roared near where she was sitting outside a deli. A young chap jumped off the sleek machine and walked past her to buy some food. After receiving his order, he sat on his bike and yelled over, "Ever been on one before?"

"No. No reason to take my life up in risks like that," Destiny shouted back, "though, it does look like fun!"

"Yep, it's risky all right. But it's good to be spontaneous and take a few risks, or you never learn what you can really do in life! That's my philosophy anyway," the fellow shouted in return with a mouth full of chips.

"Right, then!" Destiny rose to return to her motorcar.

As she drove down the roadway, her thoughts searched for an answer to her self-imposed questions that had been encouraged by the young chap on the motorbike. *What is my philosophy? What are my ideals?* Silently, she methodically sifted through her conscious awareness for valuable qualities that she could claim. She settled on two, *being honest* and maintaining a *personal truth*. Talking to herself, she said out loud, "Yes, honesty and truth, those are my ideals. I think I have been honest in my life, except for revealing my past to Father. My personal truth is that my life is an open book—no pretenses, nothing fake, just me being who I am." Destiny gripped the wheel with both hands and felt secure with her newly invented self-philosophy.

The return drive was going faster than her previous trip a few days earlier, most likely because the route was now familiar and she felt more secure in her driving, and her spirits had been lifted by the visit. As she entered Worcester, more than halfway home, she was confident she could drive the remainder of the way in one day. At a rather confusing roundabout, however, she took a turn that deposited her in an unfamiliar area. She decided to pull to the side and study her map. As she looked around for a landmark to pinpoint her location, her eyes froze as she saw the old manor. *Oh, my god…why would the Universe direct me here? I don't need to be reminded of it all. Wasn't going through the experience enough?*

Taking a few deep breaths, Destiny sat rigid while staring at the massive Charter Manor. "Hold to my truth," she whispered, while glancing back and forth to make sure no one was watching her. *But, why would I need to see this place again? Is there a reason for me to be at this location at this exact time? Do I need to release something more?* Destiny recalled the Longfellow poem and quietly said, "Yes, I suffered. But I am strong, probably stronger than most. I choose to release the pain. I release the emotion. I release my guilt. So be it!"

She folded her map, pointed her motorcar in the direction that felt right to resume her travels, and allowed her intuition to guide her to the correct roadway. She knew she wanted to get out of Worcester as quickly as possible. She drove straight through to her waiting cottage. Without unpacking, she flopped on her bed and slept soundly.

Late the next morning, the birds outside the bedroom window sang Destiny awake. She decided to lie in bed a bit longer to unravel her thoughts. She felt the trip was certainly a positive one, including her being able to share her secret past with her mum. What she had not expected, however, was her mum sharing her own secret. "What was it that Ian told me might happen when I visited my parents?" she asked her cottage. "Oh, yes! Ian said I would learn *much more than I would share.* He was so spot-on with that prediction!" Musing to herself, Destiny thought, *I am truly grateful that Mum and Dad shared their past with each other and are getting on again. I do so want a relationship with that kind of understanding and love. But, I am in no rush! I have a perfect life right now. Why risk it for the unknown?*

Destiny knew she needed to get her thoughts written down in her journal while they were fresh. She got up from her bed to dig through her baggage for the cherished binder, but it was nowhere to be found. "Where could I have left it?" she spoke out loud. "Oh, no! I must have left it in my old bedroom bureau." She told herself not to be concerned; no one ever went into her room at her parents' home. She made a mental note to herself to buy a new journal in Cheltenham that day.

Destiny's days were filled with massage appointments and teaching classes. Her schedule left little time for socializing. The weather was warming slightly and the hillsides were dotted with greenery and flower blooms. On her days off, such as this one, she sat in her backyard listening to the stream and reading books. The library was about all the socialization she afforded herself for the time being. After visiting her parents a few months earlier, there was a new surge of independence about her. She felt as though her life was finally her own, created just the way she directed it be. As she explored more topics surrounding the metaphysics of life, she sensed a feeling of self-control over her destiny. At one point, she even believed her life to be perfect.

What was it that the bloke on the motorbike said? Destiny looked upward as if the answer was written in the sky. Remembering the fellow's words, she repeated them out loud,

"...it's good to be spontaneous and take risks, or you never learn what you can really do in life." Her voice echoed the challenge, and she countered with, "But what of the risks? That fellow was taking a tremendous risk in riding that bike. I could never take that kind of a risk. Should I stay true to myself and not take risks, or take risks spontaneously and enjoy the ride?"

Destiny studied her thoughts and decided to jot them down in her new journal:

> Journal—July 1981: Do I miss out on life by not hanging about with people who take risks? I see people all day long; I wonder what risks they have taken? I mostly just want to be alone when I have the chance. So, what's wrong with enjoying a good book, or a hike through the woods to sit and meditate?
>
> I feel I might go a bit dotty if I never chatted with anyone. On the other hand, most of those I meet are rather fogged...what could they possibly chat about that would interest me?
>
> I guess I could pop in at the pub more often. It has also been awhile since I looked in on Jon. Not much of a risk there, but I should pop in on him and let him know how I am getting on. I sure wouldn't mind running into Ian again either.

She closed her journal and made up her mind to change her clothes to drive into Cheltenham. She planned to stop off at "Skittles" to say hello to Jon, and then see who might be at her favorite pub. Destiny pulled on a pair of black boots and a black pair of tight jeans. Her hair was mussed a bit, but she left it long at her shoulders. Deciding on a sapphire blue satin blouse, she applied extra lip colour, telling herself she could take risks like anyone else.

Arriving at the pub, she chatted briefly with Jon to let him know she was getting on, and listened to his banter. Then, she headed to her local hang-out. As she walked through the door, the smell of alcohol took her by surprise. She was not a big drinker, and hadn't been drinking for quite awhile. The pub smelled especially off-putting this night. She found a stool at the bar and signaled for a Guinness, stronger ale than her usual. Almost immediately a bloke walked up and began telling her about his day. Destiny found him a bit nippy, but displayed an appropriate gesture of interest. His name was Chester and was employed as a tradesman. He asked her all sorts of questions, at which she either nodded or politely gave a short reply. As the night progressed, Chester seemed like a friendly chap, and they agreed to meet again at the pub in a few days.

Seventeen

Luana was pleased that five women had signed up for her women's group, only one spot remained. She was ready to begin the first meeting in one week. The moon had just eclipsed the sun and Mercury resumed its direct flow; she took this as a positive sign that the last place in the group would be filled. She always followed the guidance of the stars, and studied numerology as well. When she'd attended graduate school, many students were interested in such metaphysical and holistic traditions. During this time, Luana learned to conduct group meditations and medicine wheel ceremonies, as well as some of the mysteries of astrology. She was prepared to figure and construct each group member's natal astrology chart. After giving the women their personal astrological information, she knew each would be better equipped to understand the other members' various life paths. She had always done a natal chart on her patients at the onset of their counseling. The nuances of an astrological chart helped guide her to a better appreciation of her patients' psychological, emotional, and spiritual makeup.

Now, nearly three-quarters of the way through reading her novel, Luana was anxious to get back to learning more about Destiny's life. On the other hand, she knew her time would soon be consumed with her women's group. She reluctantly set the book aside on her night table, thinking she would savor a few pages each evening before bed. She was still confident that the young woman's trials in life were somehow connected to her own journey. Glancing again at the artwork on the cover of the novel, her mind roamed to thoughts of her cherished ocean. She realized it had been way too long since her bare toes had dug into the moist sand. In a spontaneous decision, Luana readied herself for a trip to her favorite beach.

Living in touristy Laguna Beach had its moments of frustration; however, Luana knew the locals' pathways to hidden coves. Placing a heavy knit sweater over her sweatshirt, and pulling on a pair of warm walking boots, she was ready to hike the few blocks to Shaws Cove. She could be observing the ever-changing waves in less than thirty minutes. The passageway to the cove weaved between narrow trails lined with beach cottages, and then a long stairway led down to her secluded retreat. Even now in the fall and winter months, the sun would part the clouds for her to sit and meditate on the ocean's sandy blanket. This day, she spread out her bamboo beach mat and sat cross-legged facing the magnificent sea. She closed her eyes, relaxed her body, and slowly breathed in the salty mist. Her loud deep-toned chanting awakened a flock of seagulls and they dispersed beyond the rocks of the little cove. Luana's consciousness also flew past her awareness as her repetitive Vedic intonation surged from her being.

She sat still, eyes closed, silently listening to the foaming water swirl near her. A vision came to her of a tall young woman with long blonde-streaked hair. The woman's face was highlighted by the sun and she had a rather pensive expression on her face. Then Luana envisioned the unknown woman sitting in a circle of women. She opened her eyes and the mysterious woman's face became even clearer in her mind. Trusting her intuitive insight, she was sure the woman would be the last member of her group. The clouds began to darken, signaling her to begin the hike home.

The following morning the clouds had not retreated, so Luana decided to drive to a favorite coffee spot where locals gathered to chat about the weather and the upcoming tourist season. As she passed by a public message board on Forest Avenue where she had pinned one of her flyers, she noticed a tall woman glancing at the announcement. Deciding to introduce herself, she tapped the woman's left shoulder, and said, "Hello, I am Luana. I posted that flyer. I just happened to be walking by and noticed you studying it. Do you think you might be interested in the group? Can I answer any questions for you?"

"Oh, hello. Well, I am new to the area and thought perhaps a group like this might be a good way for me to meet other women. When will the meetings begin?"

"Next week, if you decide to join. You'd be the final member needed to begin the group. If you're interested, I would like to have you over to my home office to go through a pre-group interview. It would take only a few minutes of your time. I have all potential group members do this, just to make sure we are on the same page. My phone number is on this card. Give me a call in the next few days and I'll be happy to give you more information and answer your questions. Oh, what is your name?" Luana asked as she handed the tall woman her business card. She instinctually recognized the woman as the one she had envisioned in her meditation.

"All right, Luana. That would be great…my name is Emma Wells. I'll give you a call soon." Emma offered her hand for a shake to confirm her statement.

Driving home, Luana repeated a gratitude mantra she had learned while visiting India. She learned the mantra from the same yogi who had taught her the Universal laws of attraction and the principles of karma. He was also the one who said her life would be filled in spiritual service. During her stay in India, she learned the ways of several different yoga paths and their meditations. Learning the art of manifestation and creating one's reality, were Luana's favorite lessons. When she and Edward were together, they would consciously practice this spiritual law of attracting one's desires. They could combine their manifesting energies to create their relationship as they both desired. It took diligence and patience; but most times, they created their life together with happiness and material success.

A case in point, after they were engaged, Luana and Edward were sharing what they individually envisioned for their wedding ceremony—a casual affair attended by a few friends. The scene included a view overlooking a turquoise ocean while standing from jutting cliffs. They both intuitively knew their wedding was to take place on one of the Hawaiian Islands. Edward and Luana meditated together on this for several months, each describing to the other exactly what the entire day's celebration would entail. When they shared their plan with the friends they had invited to attend, all the pieces quickly fit together. The friend whom Edward chose to be his best man had relatives with a vacation home on the big island of Hawaii, and it was available to accommodate the entire wedding party. It was situated on majestic cliffs overlooking Hawaii's turquoise ocean, just as they had imagined. The arrangements were made, and Luana and Edward were married exactly one year after they had met at the 4th of July party in 1990.

Luana's cottage was perfect to host small groups. Gentle water sounds emanating from the fountain on the patio could be heard in every room. While sitting in the living room, a person could close their eyes and imagine they were hearing ocean waves softly dashing upon the shore. Luana was such a generous host; each group member had several different sitting options, all placed in a circular pattern. The women could choose from large pillows on the carpeted floor, overstuffed chairs, a beige sofa, or a traditional wooden chair. The women were invited to sit wherever they felt most comfortable. They introduced themselves, and then Luana offered a few simple group rules like keeping confidentiality, and the logistics to the available restrooms.

After the first group ended and everyone had left, Luana sat on her sofa and draped her legs over the cushions to contemplate the six women who would share their lives with each other for the next eight weeks. The women were a mixture of two young mothers, two older women, one younger woman, and one woman about forty years old. Luana was satisfied with the exchanges that transpired between the members during this first session. She smiled approvingly to herself for having the courage to begin what she knew would be a healing, spiritual group.

She had advertised the group to be "Spiritually Enlightening." She posed her feet up on a yellow print pillow, closed her eyes, and pictured how the women would share their secret desires, joys, and fears with one another. She envisioned all the women in the group as being supportive, offering their guidance and caring to each other. She also imagined them hugging each other upon arrival and at the end of each session. With her intuitive-eye, Luana's vision included all the women sitting cross-legged in a circle on the floor to meditate and send healing energy out to others. She was pleased with her group selection, and actually felt a visceral excitement as she thought about what would transpire within the next meetings.

The day before the second group meeting, Luana checked her outline and notes to be sure of the material she wanted to introduce. The list read almost like a college course. There were several book titles listed, and she still wanted to complete each woman's astrology chart. She looked down the lengthy book list and thought she might introduce Shirley MacLaine's newest book, *I'm Over All That*. Luana had read MacLaine's *Out on a Limb* the moment it was released in 1986; she also thoroughly enjoyed the movie by the same title. She had followed the famous movie star's journeys through the decades and identified with her robust energy for life. When MacLaine spoke about reincarnation, her words matched Luana's own ideology. She was quite happy that she and MacLaine shared so many spiritual concepts. She took a few moments to savor a sentence or two from this new book:

> When one understands karma, reincarnation (the physical re-embodiment of the soul) is paramount. "What the soul sows, so shall it reap." This means that every human soul is in control of his or her destiny. Depending on what each human needs to work on the next time around, the soul lives on and the learning of self continues.

If Luana shared just this one paragraph from *I'm Over All That*, she knew it would spark an in-depth conversation between the women in the group that might last the entire eight weeks. However, at this stage in the newly formed group, she felt it was not the right time to introduce the topic of rein-carnation. Instead, she chose to ask each woman to write out what they would like to discuss and share within the group. At the end of the meeting, the women were to turn in their papers to her. With this information, Luana would have the benefit of knowing each woman's individual issues and be able to guide them to topics that were relevant. Setting MacLaine's book to the side, she found six tablets for each woman's personal journal to write in as the weeks passed.

Luana explained to her group members that one way to use their journal was to write out dreams they remembered. Dreams had always been an essential method for Luana to receive messages from what she considered her Divine or Higher Self. Since her childhood, she had had many prophetic dreams and learned to analyze them with great success. When she handed out the journals to her group, she instructed them to record the dreams that seemed important for them to understand. She told them they would be sharing a few dreams with the group to help gain insight from each other. She also had several dream dictionaries, and other sources, to guide the women through interpreting their dreams.

The first woman to share a dream was the youngest member of the group, Marcie. The dream she shared surrounded her current boyfriend with whom she was getting mixed signals. Luana was pleased with how the other women offered their perspective of Marcie's dream. She reassured Marcie that she herself needed to be the final person to interpret her dream. "The dreamer is always subconsciously aware of a dream's meaning. Explore it further on your own, Marcie. Jot down a few notes. I am sure you will receive your dream's message."

Through the holidays, the women's group became more intimate. The women bonded and shared more of their lives with each other during each meeting. In January, with only one group meeting left, Luana suggested the women decide if they would like to continue with the group for another eight week period. She explained that every member would need to agree in order to keep the same group momentum, and that no others would be invited to join the established group. During the final meeting, all the women agreed to continue with the group. Luana was ecstatic she had facilitated such a close group of women.

The first few months of 2015 were colder than most, and Luana found herself bundling up with several layers of clothing. The sea breeze was intense and the sun rarely peeked from behind dark clouds to encourage her to visit the cove. She wondered if her astrology magazine was correct in predicting a new Age was emerging. She also felt there might be some new energy rising within her that needed recognition. In between holding her weekly women's group, Luana was constantly writing. The articles were easy for her to write and submit for publication or to post online. It was the more profound writing that streamed from her consciousness that she questioned. She was unsure what would become of the mystifying, yet methodical words posed on the sheets of paper arranged so neatly on her desk. The lines seemed to flow intuitively from her mind to her fingertips that lightly touched the lettered keys on her computer's keyboard. Sometimes, she felt like a spirit was dictating the sentences that transformed into pages. *Perhaps it will be a novel like the one I've been reading*, Luana thought to herself. Then she exclaimed out loud, "Oh, I must find that book and catch up with what has happened to Destiny. I haven't picked it up in weeks!"

Luana's group was well into its second set of eight week meetings when Emma Wells began to share her life with the group. Emma had lovely fair skin and light brown eyes. With her overly frosted blonde hair, she had that beach resident appearance. However, Emma told the group she had only moved to the area a few months earlier. She currently lived in Balboa, just north of Laguna. She also shared that she was twice divorced and was not interested in meeting any other men. Before moving to California, she'd lived with her parents who were now in a retirement community in Maine. Emma shared that she was ready to begin a new life, "I feel like my life has been bound with secrets. I so appreciate being able to share with you all. I have never shared much of my life with anyone, not even my mother."

"I'm so happy you found our little group, Emma. Please feel free to share your concerns with us. You can be assured, we'll all support you in any way we can," Luana stated directly to Emma, and searched her brown eyes for confirmation.

"I feel so comfortable here with you all, especially you, Luana. I feel as if we are connected in some way. Do you feel this too?"

"I feel connected to each one of you," Luana said, as she scanned her living room filled with caring women. "Perhaps we all have had other lifetimes together!"

Luana was not going to address the topic of reincarnation for another few meetings, but could not pass up this opportunity. She began telling the women about her spiritual beliefs surrounding reincarnation, and the possibility that those we have had a relationship with in one lifetime, we may have had in another. The topic was one the group immediately delved into with great interest and curiosity. Three of the six women in the group totally agreed with Luana, and even suggested that each of them had been destined to meet.

Remembering something she had read in MacLaine's book, *I'm Over All That*, Luana decided to introduce the women to Shirley's writings. "In this book," Luana said, while holding it up for everyone to see, "Shirley writes that we all have freewill and destiny. She states that sometimes we can move out of sync with our destiny when we use our freewill, and that is why it is so important for us to be in touch with our true Self. If we recognize who we really are, and what our purpose is in life, we can complete our soul's destiny for this life."

"How do we find out what our soul's purpose is, Luana?" one of the women asked.

"There are many ways, and I will explain some of them to you. One way to better understand what our life is about this time around is through studying our past lives. How many of you believe there might be truth in the concept of reincarnation?" All six of the women raised their hand. "Would you all like to investigate this topic within the group?"

It was decided by the entire group that Luana would share what she had studied about the spiritual concept of reincarnation. She gathered several books she had read on the subject and suggested to her group they each pick one book to read individually. In two weeks, each woman would report back to the group what was covered in their book, and then they would all discuss it. The women agreed to do this and chose one book to take home to read. At the end of the meeting, Luana asked the women if they would enjoy experiencing a group past life regression. They were fascinated, and Luana affirmed that she would facilitate a group regression in a few weeks. After the meeting ended, Luana reveled in the fact that her group of women was so like-minded. They had even begun to meet each other outside group meetings for lunches and outings. She had a sense that they would all stay good friends at the group's closure.

As Luana prepared for bed that night, her novel on the night table caught the corner of her eye. She quickly gathered it up and plopped onto her bed. Before she opened to the marked page, she strained to remember the details surrounding the last few chapters to capture where she had left the heroine within the book. She did remember that Destiny had visited her parents and that she was feeling freer to take a few risks with her life since being so rigid with her schedule of working and studying. However, Luana needed to reread a few pages from the previous chapter to catch up on exactly what Destiny was planning for her life.

Eighteen

There was a strange atmosphere in the pub, but Destiny chose to dismiss her initial feelings of trepidation. She ordered another Guinness and began to see Chester as a rather fascinating sort. He certainly talked on and on about himself, as though he expected Destiny would be thrilled to listen. Since this was only the second time she had met him, she hadn't gathered her opinions about him. The evening passed quickly and it was obvious the pair was getting tanked. After a few more rounds of Guinnesses, they went arm in arm to a corner table to continue the small talk that didn't seem to interest either of them. When the pub was closing, Destiny accepted Chester's offer to drive her home. She knew she'd drunk well over her personal limit, and felt she should not drive. Chester, on the other hand, seemed quite sober all of a sudden.

Arriving at Destiny's cottage, Chester held her up by one shoulder to walk her to the front door. He pulled her to him and planted a deep kiss on her mouth. Being somewhat fogged, Destiny lingered a bit too long and Chester almost dragged her through the door. He immediately fumbled with the buttons on her satin blouse, groping her breasts. Destiny was so inebriated, she hardly knew what was happening. She certainly did not recognize the blatant signals Chester had displayed. Once their bodies hit the couch, her eyes opened wide and she realized a strange man was slumped on top of her. Finally, she managed to say, "Chester! Get off me! I am not ready for this...please get up."

"Ah...What the bloody hell? I thought you were into it!" Chester rolled off the couch onto the floor.

"I guess I drank too much. I had no intention of having sex with you, Chester!" She sat in an upright position to smooth out her blouse.

"Well, I sure would have bet you were into me by the way you kept talking and asking me questions," Chester countered.

"I drank too much, and was just trying to be friendly. Maybe if we meet in the daytime, and really get to know each other…" Destiny left the sentence open for his interpretation.

"Splendid! Maybe we can meet tomorrow, then?" he boldly assumed, still sitting on the floor.

"*If* I show up at the pub tomorrow…but, if I don't, well, do *not* come looking for me. I don't want a stalker!" Destiny was sobering up fast and could now read Chester's intentions.

"Okay. I will see you at the pub tomorrow same time, then," Chester said firmly, as he rose from the floor. Then he grabbed Destiny's hand and used it to pat the front his trousers.

"Please leave now, Chester. If I show up, we'll talk more." Destiny freed her hand and pulled him to the door. After he left, she immediately locked the strong bolt. Her heart was pounding so fast the alcohol she had consumed had no chance to cloud her brain.

"How could I get myself in such a terrible situation?" she asked her cottage. She left the lights on, changed into her pajamas, and sat straight upright on her bed. The alcohol had since evaporated within her and she felt frozen inside. The only warmth she felt were the tears that slid down her face. She grabbed her journal and began to write:

> Journal—Aug. 1981: What the hell am I doing? I don't even like this chap! Why must I always choose such wankers that cheat their way into my heart? I am twenty-three years old, where is the fellow who is supposed to be my soulmate everyone is raving about? Soulmate, what a crock! From now on, I am going to lay off gents altogether.
>
> Aren't I supposed to have real love in my life? Is there such a thing as real love? I see through all the happy marriages that find dark halls to play illicit games of lust and deceit, it turns my stomach like a bitter lemon drink. Never again will I allow a bloke to enter my private seclusion.
>
> I must not drink. I think it is poison to my brain. I can't believe I allowed myself to get so wrapped up

with a chap like that. I don't even know his full name! I pray he stays away from me when I don't show up at the pub tomorrow. Maybe I won't go back, ever... *Oh, but what if Ian comes one day and I miss him! I will just have faith that if we are to meet again, it will happen.*

After that night, Destiny made sure to keep her door bolted. She had a feeling that Chester would not bother her, but decided to not risk being stupid either. For several weeks, she made sure there were no motorcars following her to and from work, and avoided the pub altogether. She spent her days off work sitting in the library, hiking in the woods, or reading a book. As the year came to an end, Destiny had studied several metaphysical and spiritual books, including one by Shakti Gawain titled *Creative Visualization*. She enjoyed the book's approach to creating one's desires, therefore one's reality, through a process the author termed visualization. She read from the little book that, "Physically, we are all energy and everything within and around us is made up of energy. We are all part of one great energy field." With all the visualizations Destiny had experienced throughout her life, she quickly connected to the little book.

Soon, Destiny learned how to use visualization to align with the principles of Universal laws to help her with her massage clients and in teaching her classes. The more she practiced the techniques she read about in the book, the more she felt confident in herself and what she desired for her life. At one point during the following year, she even called her parents and invited them to come for a visit. She felt a sense of confidence and pride when giving her father directions to her cottage. In the spring of 1982, Helen and Henry arrived in Swindon Village.

The cool fog hung lightly over Destiny's cottage at Wyman's Brook Bungalows. As her parents approached the flower-lined stone walk, they stopped briefly to look each other in the eyes with an inner knowing only they held between them. They shared that moment with pride for their headstrong daughter who had etched out a life for herself against great odds. Helen never told Destiny that she had shared her secret about the rape and pregnancy with her father. There were some secrets that needed to remain secret.

Knocking gingerly on the door, Henry glanced around at the ivy and delicate blooms surrounding the grounds. He pointed to one area of the garden just as Destiny opened the door. "Destiny, the grounds here are so colourful! I must make a note of some of these plants and incorporate them into our garden." Henry leaned forward to receive a hug from his daughter.

"Yes, I love the colour, it goes on and on throughout Swindon. I can't wait to take you for a walk in the woods," Destiny said with excitement, and invited her parents into her home.

"Please, sit over here on the couch, Mum. Father, I have some scones and cheese over here on the table. How was your drive?"

"Very smooth, no barriers or stops, a straight through shot. We plan to stay a few days, Destiny. Reservations were made at the Queen's Hotel in Cheltenham. We already popped in and left off baggage." He stood at the table and nibbled on the snacks Destiny had provided.

"Mum, would you like to see my room and the loo?" Destiny asked.

"Oh, yes, dear. You have decorated your little cottage brilliantly," Helen offered, as she followed her daughter into the bedroom.

They sat on the edge of the bed for a few minutes while Destiny shared details about her cottage. Helen stood to look through the white lace curtains covering the only window in the room, and commented, "Oh, what a lovely view you have, Destiny!"

"Yes, we must take a hike in the woods tomorrow, after you are rested from the drive. Mum, I wanted to let you know that I left one of my personal journals in the bureau drawer in my room. I forgot to ask you to bring it, could you post it please? There are some writings in it I really do not want Dad, or anyone, to read," she confided.

"Oh, why of course, Destiny. I would be happy to, dear," Helen assured her daughter.

Destiny felt that her personal journal would be put in the post. "Ta. Let me show you the back garden. I love sitting and reading there when I am home."

The three went outside and sat with the lush garden encircling their chairs, and chatted to catch up on the past several months. Destiny's parents invited her to come to visit them again in the summer. Helen shared their daily routines of gardening, shopping, club games, and dinners out with friends. Destiny admired her parents' easy mood together and witnessed their affection for one another as if for the first time. In that moment, she closed her eyes and vowed to never keep secrets with the man she might marry. With her eyes still shut, she experimented with visualization and envisioned herself sitting with her parents in the future and introducing them to…Jess! As clearly as she could visualize her mum and dad, Jess entered her vision, or was it a trance? Opening her eyes, Destiny shook her head to snap the image from her consciousness. She stood to retreat into the kitchen, saying, "Excuse me, I'll go get us something to drink."

What does this mean? Why would Jess show up in my mind so vividly? After her parents left, she settled down to write in her journal about this experience:

> Journal—April 1982: Am I opening myself up to future visions? I am convinced I did not make up that visualization; it just appeared in my mind. Oh, my god, Jess? Is Jess going to be in my future? I have all but forgotten him. How long has it been? Five years, or six? I think I need guidance with my visualizing! Maybe I could investigate more about it by seeing a psychic.
>
> Could I create Jess to be in my life again? Do I have that power? Do I really want him in my life? I don't know! He surely could have connected with me by now, if he wanted to have me in his life. Besides, what I have studied certainly indicates we cannot control another person's destiny, only our own. Are we predestined to meet again? I guess I could believe that. Maybe we are supposed to be together, like we felt so many years ago.
>
> Note: I must look into finding a psychic!

Summer's warmer days urged Destiny to make some changes. She decided to have her long hair trimmed and frosted. She wanted a more up-to-date look, and blonde highlights were all the rage. As she walked out of the hair salon, she admired her new do in the refection of a shop window and smiled with approval. *It's time for a change. It's time for a fresh start*, she thought. As she passed the library, her eyes widened as she spotted Ian coming down the steps. "Ian! Ian, is that you? It's Destiny, over here," she shouted.

As he came within speaking distance, Ian replied, "Yes, Destiny? It is so good to see you again. I am not sure I would have recognized you with that new do!"

"Oh, do you like it?"

"Oh, yes…now turn around, let me look at you." Ian held Destiny's shoulders while slowly spinning her around. "It is most becoming, indeed! I see you are turning a new leaf, as it were. Are there other changes in store for you, Destiny?"

"Oh, I don't know. I have been working hard and doing a lot of reading and studying. I guess I am in that library as much as at home." Destiny nodded toward the entrance of the building.

"Are you still interested in learning about creating your reality and the like?" Ian asked.

"Oh, yes. I have been reading so many books, some on visualization and some on metaphysical and Universal laws. Do you know of a good psychic in Cheltenham? I am very interested in getting a reading, or at least learning if I have some psychic abilities," Destiny shared with Ian, as they walked across the street to the centre square.

"Spot-on, Destiny. Let's sit over there, if you have the time," Ian said, and pointed to the park.

"Sure, I have all day free." She took Ian's arm and walked with him to a nearby bench; they sat side-by-side.

"I have been thinking of you, Destiny. I am not surprised we ran into each other today. I want to share something with you. Once each month at the library, I join others in a group who explore our extrasensory or psychic abilities and experiences. Sometimes the topic is dreams, sometimes it is meditation, intuition or visions. This may sound a bit weird to you, but I believe you keep popping up in my life because there are things I am suppose to share with you...maybe it's this group! There has got to be a reason we keep bumping into each other, right?"

"Well, that's a lovely assumption, Ian. I would love to check out your group and see what I might learn. Some of my visualizations have been very vivid, and it would be great to share them. Maybe I can even learn what they mean. Many of the things you have predicted for me have happened! Remember when you told me that *I would learn more than I would share* when I visited my parents last year? You were spot-on! It is all so exciting to think I might learn to envision my future."

"Well, I do have some psychic ability, or so I've been told. In our group, we share some of the insights we have...what we sense about each other, and such. If you want to come to the next meeting, I am sure it would be spot-on. Are you interested?"

"Oh, yes! Give me the date and time, and I will be there. The group meets up here in the library, then?"

"Yes. Have you been in the basement of the library, where the old reference books are stored?"

"No. I thought that was only for library personnel. Is that where your group meets?"

"Yes. Go down the back stairs to the basement, and find the door with the sign marked, "Metaphysical Group." I'll be there and will introduce you to the others in the group. I have actually spoken about you a few times because you keep popping up in my visualizations, and I tell the group about them. I have even had *dreams* about you, Destiny."

"Really? What kind of dreams?"

"Well, let's leave my dreams to be shared in the group next month when you are present. But I will say, I feel our souls have connected before." He stood up from the bench, and admitted, "I do need to get on, Destiny. It was so good to see you again. I look forward to seeing you in our group. Our next meeting is exactly one month from today at three o'clock."

Nineteen

Two weeks later in Luana's women's group, each member presented a brief talk about the book she had chosen to read. The subjects ranged from reincarnation to channeling spirit in the afterlife. The women were eager to explore the topics further, and several suggested that those who wanted to share more details might do so at the next meeting. Luana agreed with the group's plan and wrote down each woman's subject matter, so she could bring further information to the discussion. Metaphysics, the study of all things beyond the five senses, presents an abundance of intriguing information to explore, and Luana was well-equipped to handle most questions her group members might ask. She could also provide books to those who wanted more reading material. She had gained personal experience and acquired much insight into many of the aspects contained within the mysterious metaphysical world.

As Luana reminisced about all the topics she could present, she remembered she had promised to facilitate a group past life regression. She was a certified Clinical Hypnotherapist and used the modality many times in her counseling practice. She found hypnotherapy to be particularly useful in determining exactly when an issue had originated within the life of a patient. By using age regression techniques to allow her patient to regress back to an earlier time period in their life, would many times uncover subconscious memories of an event that initiated current troubling behaviors. Luana was also able to regress her patients to past lives to discover undefined explanations regarding unwarranted negative emotions, irregular actions, critical triggers, or persisting physical pain. She was looking forward to providing the women in the group the experience of venturing into one of their own past lives. As she sat at her computer to continue what she hoped to fit together to form a metaphysical novel, a memory of one patient from years ago tugged at her awareness. He was a gentleman of about sixty years old who was seeking relief from terrible pain that had plagued him for most of his life.

When the man came to Luana's office, his wife accompanied him. He described his pain as emanating from his left temple, and he was wearing an eye patch over this eye. Over the past several years, he had endured a few surgeries in hopes of ending the pain, but none had been successful. One of his friends had suggested he try hypnosis. The man was very religious and skeptical about attempting hypnosis, but agreed as a last resort. After Luana received all the necessary patient information and signed release forms, she explained to him how hypnosis works. She explained how she would be utilizing an age regression method to allow his subconscious mind to gather memories from his childhood. She suggested that a previous event as a child may reveal when he might have injured his head that was currently causing his pain.

Then she asked her patient to lie on his back on the office sofa, and close his eyes. Luana proceeded to gently relax him into a deep state of hypnosis, and then began to count him backward from his current age to an age when he was a young boy. She had done this type of age regression on hundreds of her patients, and each time they easily regressed to an earlier childhood age. Luana's patient explored a few childhood years during his regression, but no traumatic experiences were revealed that would cause his extreme pain.

Luana then instructed her patient, "Go to the time and event that caused you to have this current pain." In hindsight, she realized the exact words she used to instigate a *time period* were too general for his subconscious mind to interpret. Her patient immediately went back into a past life! He began to talk with a southern accent. In this drawl, he vividly described what he was experiencing. At this point in her career, Luana had facilitated few past life regressions and was quite taken aback, especially since she thought she had instructed her patient to regress to another of his childhood years. She allowed her patient to continue sharing the entire experience he was viewing in his mind. In detail, he related an event in the past life that caused an injury to his left temple. When Luana brought him out of his hypnosis, she explained to him what had transpired. He did not believe her. She decided to ask his wife if she would videotape the next session so they could watch it afterward. The patient's wife agreed, and the couple made an appointment to return the following week.

When Luana's patient entered her office for the second session, he commented that his pain had gotten better, and he was no longer wearing an eye patch. After she relaxed him into a deep trance, she invited his wife to enter the room and begin taping the session. The man again began to relate the exact past life event that evidently was causing the unbearable pain he was experiencing in this lifetime. While living as a man in the early 1800s in a mid-western state in the United States, he was accidentally shot with a gun in the left temple. He didn't die from the bullet wound, but instead lived a life heavily drugged on the pain medication of the era called Laudanum. After he completed explaining this past life event, Luana assured him the lifetime was now over and he did not need to carry the pain he had incurred from it. She told her patient that he'd learned all he needed to from the experience, and that he could now let the pain go completely. She proceeded to bring the man out of hypnosis, all the while assuring him he didn't need to hold onto the pain in his left temple any longer.

After her patient had fully regained his conscious awareness, he sat up to ask what had happened. Luana instructed his wife to play back the video for them to watch together. They were dumbfounded to what they were viewing, but could not challenge their own eyes. When they returned for a follow-up session, the man's pain had completely vanished! He told Luana his doctor could not account for why the pain had subsided. He also shared that they had decided to take a trip to the location where the past life had taken place to look for documentation of the lifetime, and perhaps even the shooting event.

Luana's writing muse arrived spontaneously and jogged her awareness back into reality. Shaking her head to the wonders of hypnosis, she realized how many of her patients' hypnotic sessions contained incredible experiences that she could write about. She hoped one day, when she was an old woman, her manuscript would transform into a complete book and be published. She felt the insights would help enlighten those who wished to learn more about hypnosis and the unseen world of mystics and mediums. She had no title for the manuscript, only pages filled with explorations of spiritual challenges that the reader could easily identify. There were no words like quantum physics, or such elevated language as existentialism to cloud the real nuts and bolts surrounding journeys of reincarnation, extrasensory perception, and other paranormal events that was being addressed. Only laymen's words would be included in her metaphysical literary concept. She imagined when the volume was complete, the information that poured from her conscious-ness would bring comfort to those who might be sitting rigid on the proverbial fence as to whether a soul really exists, or if humans can actually use their intuitive abilities to predict the future. Whatever her book offered its reader, Luana would be content knowing that she had taken the risk of revealing her spiritual beliefs to the world.

Luana closed her eyes to ruminate on the direction her manuscript would follow. As if magic, her subconscious mind fed the words to her conscious awareness as she typed:

> *Awake! Be the witness to your thoughts*. These wise words were spoken by Gautama Buddha. They are similar to the anonymous words etched on a plaque hanging on my kitchen wall: "To make your dreams come true…Wake Up!" Both of these quotes command that as human beings, we must become aware of our spiritual selves—the larger Self within that is connected to a Higher Power or Divine Being. Many call this spiritual aspect of our consciousness a soul.
>
> To define this quality notable only beyond words, many use terms like true Self, inner Self, the small voice within, or God-Self. Whatever name given to this unseen, yet many times felt dimension, we accept the gift of enlightenment when we become aware of its connection. Once enlightened, or awakened to the knowledge that we are a spark emanating from the Oneness of Infinity, we can learn to create our dreams and our reality.

Luana continued writing late into the night to allow the words to flow from her consciousness onto the keyboard as her fingers typed unrelentingly for hours. After several dozen pages had been added to her manuscript, she took a deep breath and lowered her hands from the lettered keys. "Sometimes I feel as if I am channeling these words!" she whispered to herself. It was well past her regular bedtime, but there was an inner persistence edging her to continue writing. Once again, she posed her fingers over the magical computer keys and listened to the words as they hummed their song. It was a mixture of automatic writing and her consciousness searching for truth that found its way onto her computer's screen that night. A combination of educational, experiential, and esoteric knowledge formed uncounted pages of spiritual wisdom for the manuscript that Luana, one day, would claim as her life's work.

As the weeks passed, Luana's women's group became more intimate and they all decided to continue their meetings indefinitely. The women were enjoying learning about the spiritual topics introduced each week. They also enjoyed ending each meeting sitting in a circle holding hands to send healing energy out to their family and friends, and then everyone on Earth. Luana would begin a slow chant and encourage the women to join in to center their group energy toward all in need. At the beginning of each meeting, the women had the opportunity to share recent dreams. Under Luana's guidance, they were getting quite proficient at dream interpretation.

At one meeting in late March, Emma shared a recent dream that was like many experienced in her childhood. She explained that she was originally from Europe, moving with her parents to the east coast of America when she was about ten years old. Emma said that she was an only child, raised mostly by a nanny, and had invented imaginary friends to keep her company. One of these friends she named Rachael, who came to visit her within her dreams. Rachael appeared to Emma as a beautiful young woman with golden brown hair and big brown eyes. Sometimes, Rachael would share secrets with her, or help her with studies from school. Emma detailed her current dream with the group, and then asked for feedback to help interpret it. In her dream, Rachael was wearing a white, almost see-through dress, and was hovering over her bed. Emma related that

Rachael's lips didn't move, but she could understand what was being said. Rachael told her, "Soon the truth will be revealed."

The women in the group were fascinated with Emma's dream and offered many different suggestions to what it might mean. Then Luana asked Emma, "Since you have had this other-worldly relationship with Rachael as a child, do you suppose she might be more than just an imaginary friend?"

"What do you mean, Luana?" asked Emma.

"Well, your dream, as you describe it, sounds more to me like a visitation from beyond this level of existence. Perhaps, when you were a child it was easy to consider all your *friends* in the same category, thinking Rachael was also from your imagination. However, I believe Rachael may be a spirit guide, or an angel."

"Oh, do you really think so, Luana? What a wonderful thought! I'll have to meditate on that possibility," Emma said softly. "She is the only friend I used to see in my dreams. I know I made up the others to have someone to play with when I was a young girl. It is strange to me that Rachael would return in my dreams now that I am an adult. Have any of you had dreams like this?"

None of the other women in the group had ever experienced anything similar. Luana gave Emma a book with information pertaining to guides and angels, hoping it might shed some light on Rachael's appearance in her dreams. At the end of the meeting, she asked Emma if she would be interested in undergoing a hypnosis session to try connecting with Rachael. "Perhaps some insight might be revealed from your subconscious mind about Rachael's presence. Have you ever been hypnotized?"

"No, but the idea sounds intriguing! It would be fantastic to understand why she came to me with this message, if possible."

"Let's schedule an appointment for you, Emma. When are you available?"

"What about next week, just before group?"

"Okay, that sounds perfect. Come about two hours before our group meets, and we'll give it a try!" Luana gave Emma a hug.

The following week, Emma arrived at Luana's house exactly two hours before the women's group was to begin. Luana had rearranged her office to accommodate a hypnosis session, including a reclining chair for Emma to lie back comfortably. She explained how the process of hypnosis would not harm her in any way, and that she would have complete control over her session. She reassured Emma that once she was completely relaxed, she would enter a hypnotic state of consciousness but could open her eyes at any moment to stop the session. Emma gave her permission to be hypnotized.

After Emma entered a hypnotic trance, Luana engaged age regression techniques to allow her to experience herself as a young child. She suggested to Emma that she recall a dream with Rachael present within it. Emma easily began to relate a dream she had in which Rachael had spoken to her. Luana proceeded to instruct Emma to ask Rachael why she had come to visit in her dreams. She continued by saying, "Rachael has something very important to tell you, Emma. Listen carefully. You will remember what Rachael tells you when you are awake."

Luana gave Emma a few positive suggestions before bringing her back to present time, and told her that she would feel rested and relaxed when she awoke. As Emma opened her eyes, she yawned and said, "Oh, Luana, I feel so relaxed! Did I fall asleep?"

"No, that's how being in a state of hypnosis feels. I regressed you back to your childhood and suggested that Rachael tell you why she is visiting you in your dreams. Do you remember what she told you?"

"Ummm…not really. Maybe if I meditate on her I will remember something. Oh, wait a minute! When I was little, Rachael visited me in a dream and told me that she was near me all the time, and that she is always watching over me! Is that it? Is that what I was supposed to remember?"

"No doubt that is part of her message, Emma. It sounds like she has been with you your entire life, and is a spiritual guide. Tonight when you sit in meditation, ask her to come to you again and share what the important information is that you are supposed to know."

During the group meeting that soon began, Emma shared with the other women about her hypnosis session and how it made her feel so relaxed. "I actually thought I had fallen asleep! Luana's voice was so relaxing. I just sat back and sank into a place something like when I am in a deep meditation. I'll definitely be here if Luana does a group past life regression for us!"

Luana explained that she would offer the group regression at a time when those who wanted to participate were available. She handed out a sign-up sheet and told the women there would be no problem if some of them decided not to participate. She shared with the women what hypnosis was, as she had done with Emma, and gave each of them a copy of a small purple book written in the 1980s by one of her hypnotherapy teachers, Charles Tebbetts, titled *Self Hypnosis and Other Mind-Expanding Techniques*. The book covered many metaphysical topics from meditation to ESP, or extra-sensory perception. Luana felt reading a bit more about how the conscious and subconscious mind works would help the women decide if they wanted to experience hypnosis.

"After you have read through this book, we will discuss your participating in a group past life regression. For those of you who want to experience it, we'll choose a date outside of our regular meetings," Luana explained.

She felt confident that all of the women would decide to participate in a group regression. A few had stated they felt a strong connection with another woman in the group, and hoped a past life would surface between them during the regression. She, herself, had experienced the same type of sensation when she'd first met Edward. They didn't have a joint regression to verify the cognizance, but she was positive their souls had been together before. She had felt this awareness with only two other people in her life, her mother and her brother. She acknowledged that the feeling included very close to reading each other's thoughts, and many times knowing how the other would feel or react in certain circumstances. Luana's mind now raced with excitement as she pictured some of the women identifying a past life with another from the group.

That night, she awoke with a jerk. She sat up in bed straining to recall the dream that startled her awake. Turning on a nightlight, she reached for her dream journal and wrote down a few sentences that would ignite her memory in the morning. She ended her notes with the words: "Destiny was the woman in this dream!" Early the next morning, Luana reread her notes to refresh her sensing about the telling dream. Then she rationalized to herself that the dream was only her subconscious mind urging her to finish reading her book.

Without getting dressed, she made her cup of hot lemon ginger tea and returned to her bedroom. She sat in a chair that was huddled in the corner of the room that she recently found in an antique store. She closed her eyes for a moment to refresh her memory about the young woman in the book, and who had entered her dream earlier that morning. She opened the novel to search for clues if her dream would, in fact, unfold within the captivating plot.

Twenty

Consciously Creating Circumstances, the book Destiny casually slipped into her bag during her last visit to her parents' library, fell onto the bed. She picked up the unassuming book to scan the outer slip cover that boasted it was *full of metaphysical dynamite*. Remembering the day when she'd spied the book, Destiny again felt an attraction to the title. The cover also promised its readers how they could *live a better and happier life*. It was written by a master teacher and leader in the esteemed Rosicrucian Philosophy. Destiny read the inside book jacket: "The theme of this book is that you have within yourself powerful but hidden natural powers which you can uncover, develop, and use for attaining happiness. That these inner powers exist has long been known; how to develop and use them has heretofore been known only to a few." In that moment, Destiny knew she must read the little book immediately.

Since it was Destiny's day off, she folded her legs beneath her to get comfortable, knowing she had plenty of time to read through the short book. It was a mere one hundred and twelve pages in length, and she figured it would take her less than two hours to read. She figured wrong—it took her that long to complete the first few chapters! The material was an in-depth study, with psychological and philosophical inferences she had not heard or read about in other books. Taking out her journal, Destiny wrote several notes to help her better comprehend the material. The teaching included not only how to create from one's subconscious energy, but also a detailed step-by-step process to achieve it. She continued reading and writing well into the night, taking breaks only to nibble a scone and use the loo. Finally, as she completed the book, she read her final note copied directly from the book:

"Remember always that you are a part of and a channel for all the Power in the Universe. That Power will manifest through you in just the degree that YOU permit...your own subjective mind is limited only by the arbitrary conditions of time, space, force and the other natural laws under which you as a human being are limited. But it has no further limitations."

Destiny was mesmerized by the words and guidance found in her newest book. As she finished reading the last pages, she felt as though nothing was impossible for her to accomplish, nothing was too big to explore. She checked the publication date on the title page and discovered the first printing was in 1935. *I wonder if Mum has read this book!* she thought as she shut out the lamp. *I wonder why this book was in their library? I must ask Mum the next time we chat.*

Drifting into a deep sleep, Destiny dreamed of oceans and sandy beaches with sea birds and clouds engulfed in blue skies. She was strolling once again on miles of shoreline, stopping to inspect tiny shells and sea creatures as they scurried from her footprints. She glanced in the distance and noticed a long wooden pier jutting out from the foamy waves and quietly fading into the ocean's hidden depths. Blackened by the constant pounding of salty sea, the pylons harbored crowds of crusty mussels clinging for safety. She sat for a moment to inhale the ocean breeze as it swirled through her hair while invisible salt kissed her cheeks. Destiny's dream continued as her subconscious mind swam in the sea of new knowledge and insight.

Upon awaking, Destiny sensed a new feeling of lightness. She moved through the following days and weeks with more joy and happiness. She greeted each day with the awareness that she had the power to create it by choosing positive thoughts, or *thought-forms,* as described in the book. This new awareness gave her a confidence that she had never experienced. Her clients and students became more receptive to her touch and instruction, and there was an emanating force that seemed to project from her body. On the night she was to meet Ian at the library for the metaphysical group, Destiny thought she gleaned a radiant light reflecting in her mirror. It was a soft turquoise beam that surrounded her head and shoulders. "Can this be my aura?" she asked the mirror. "I must tell Ian, maybe someone at the meeting can see auras and will read mine."

Arriving on time, Destiny found the marked door in the library basement. She spotted Ian walking toward her. "Ian, I am so glad you are here."

"Hello, Destiny. I want you to meet some of the regulars. This is Penny and Jon. They're some of the first people I met when I learned about the group meetings. Penny is a psychic here, and Jon studies at the university in the parapsychology department."

"Nice to meet you," Destiny said, and shook their hands.

"The group is about to start, let's sit over here," Ian suggested as he took her hand.

Destiny and Ian sat side-by-side, both ready to learn whatever would be taught that evening. The person lecturing that night was Jon. He shared some of the material being explored at the college regarding remote viewing. Destiny listened attentively, but did not comprehend most of the information. She wished she would have brought a notebook to jot down questions, but tried to stay on track with the conversation as best she could. Once the lecture was over, everyone formed smaller groups to discuss psychic or paranormal events they had experienced, or witnessed. Ian introduced Destiny to the others in their group, adding he had successfully predicted a few events about her life. Destiny nodded in agreement and everyone cheered Ian's abilities.

At one point, Destiny asked about auras and if anyone could see them. Penny replied, "Why, yes, Destiny. I can see a person's aura. The room needs to be fairly dim, but it is quite easy. Would you like me to read yours?"

"Oh, yes, please!" Destiny exclaimed.

"Come over here out of the light, and sit perfectly still," Penny instructed.

Destiny followed Penny's instructions and sat in a chair opposite her just a few feet away. Penny explained she would concentrate on Destiny's forehead for a few moments until the aura came into view. Everyone nearby was respectfully silent as the two women stared intently at each other. Within a few seconds, Penny said, "Destiny, I see a beautiful turquoise colour about your head and shoulders. Then above that it is a pure white that reaches up toward the ceiling."

"Oh, my god, Penny! I saw that colour tonight in my mirror as I was getting dressed to come here," Destiny said. "I can't believe I saw the same colour. I guess I can see auras too! Let me concentrate and see if I can see yours."

Destiny studied Penny's face, who sat still with her eyes closed. She focused her eyes, and then a muted haze of light made its appearance. The aura was a warm pink on one side of Penny's head, and a soft green on the other. Destiny told Penny what she was visualizing, and then waited to hear if others could confirm her reading.

Ian spoke first, "Yes, Destiny, I see those exact same colours around Penny."

Penny opened her eyes, and told Destiny, "Those are the colours my aura has been for several weeks. When you study the colours of one's aura, there may be several colours, or only one. There are specific ways to interpret an aura and to understand what each colour means by its composition and where it is located. As you practice seeing them, it will be easy for you to see your own and others' auras whenever you wish."

"Spot-on! Can you tell me what the colour of my aura means?" Destiny asked.

"Turquoise is a high vibrational colour for the approaching New Age. It signifies that you have great potential to become highly intuitive and even psychic. Keep studying metaphysics and your path will become known to you soon," Penny said mysteriously.

After the meeting, Ian walked Destiny to her motorcar where they sat and continued talking for several hours. He asked her to visualize his aura, and closed his eyes in meditation to become more open to Destiny's energy.

"I see a true blue emanating around your forehead and throat, Ian. And at the top of your head, I see a golden hue. Do you know if that is what your aura looks like?"

"I don't see auras as well as you and Penny, but I sure like the sound of those colours. In holistic healing, the colour blue signifies speaking and all communication. Since that colour is around my throat, it seems to reflect that interpretation. I am not sure what the colour gold means though. Do you know anything about the chakras?"

"In massage training, we were taught about chakra energy, but I don't remember anything about the colours of them. We'll have to check out a book and read up on them. I am so glad you invited me to your group. Will I see you again at the next one?"

"Yes. I intend to come each month as always, but I feel something big is going to enter my life soon. I am not sure what's in store for me, but I am remaining open to all new adventures!" Ian smiled at Destiny, and then winked.

"That's funny, Ian, because I have been feeling the same exact thing! How exciting that we can be so positive and unafraid of what life has to offer us. I am definitely ready for a new adventure!" Destiny smiled with a wink in return.

Destiny continued attending the metaphysical groups each month and learned new insights at every meeting. In the late spring, she asked Penny to schedule an appointment for her to receive a psychic reading. She thought Penny looked to be in her fifties, but it was difficult to know for sure. Penny had long black hair with streaks of grey trailing to the ends. It was pulled to one side, falling over Penny's left shoulder to caress an ample breast. She stood an even five feet two inches and spoke with a low raspy voice. Destiny discovered that Penney lived alone just outside Cheltenham. When she drove to the address, there stood a red brick bungalow with rusty shutters closing each window. As she entered, the first item to catch her attention was the large crystal ball centered on a round table covered with a purple cloth. Penny greeted Destiny quickly, and then instructed her to sit in one of the chairs that circled the table, each quilted in deep red upholstery. Immediately Penny took Destiny's hands and turned them one way and then the other, inspecting the lines resting unknowingly within her palms. Then Penny spread a deck of weathered cards in front of her. She asked Destiny to choose three cards by placing each one face up on the table in front of her. Destiny did as she was told, and then asked, "What do you see, Penny?"

Penny took a deep breath and began her reading. "Destiny, you are a special being with a healing guide watching over you. Your life has been filled with opportunities for growth and learning, and it will continue so. Your soul has chosen many lessons for this lifetime. You must be prepared for many more adventures. Destiny...do you plan to move?"

"No, I am not planning on moving anywhere."

"Be prepared, I see a new environment for you, near a warm sea. You will settle there and live many years with a man whose soul awaits you. I see you encircled in papers all about, like notes or pages of your writing. Destiny, you will write several books!"

"Splendid! I do love to write in my journals. Tell me more about the new place in which you see me living," Destiny begged.

"I only see the ocean, sand, and you as a middle-aged woman. Your life will be full, Destiny, if you allow yourself to uncover your abilities and create exactly what your heart desires. You must allow your past to guide your decisions; it will then bring you to this future I see. Your life is always within your abilities."

"I have been studying books on creating my reality most of my life. Is this what you mean by learning my abilities?"

"Yes, dear. You have recently discovered this gift. Learning how to create your reality is one gift you can continue to develop to help you choose positive decisions. Look inside yourself, meditate each day and ask for direction from your Divine Self. Books are guides for you, containing many lessons, but you must *use* that guidance. Learning new lessons requires *action*. Nothing is completed without it. Continue reading and implementing the metaphysical practices, Destiny, and you will learn that you are creating your future each day." Penny ended the session by gathering the cards from the table and tucking them securely into a black velvet box. She stood to hug Destiny and whispered in her ear, "Life can be difficult, but remember you hold the key to your own happiness. There may be a need for you to forgive yourself in order to move into your future."

As Destiny drove home, she repeated what Penny had told her. She wanted to write down important parts of the reading in her journal before it slipped from her memory. As she entered her cottage, she sat at the kitchen table and wrote everything she could remember. She took a deep breath and thought, *Should I believe everything Penny said?* Then out loud, she shared with her cottage, "Well, I certainly would like to live by the ocean one day. If I meet a soulmate to share it with me, that would be spot-on! I do trust Ian and he recommended Penny, so I am going to trust her and that I truly can create my own destiny."

She put her journal to one side to unwrap the package she had bought before going to get her reading from Penny. Inside was a small box, not more than three-by-four inches. She opened it and took out a black velvet pouch. Placing her hand inside the little bag, she fingered the smooth, cool stones at the bottom. Withdrawing three of the stones, she placed them on the table. Destiny studied each one for several seconds, then opened the accompanying guidebook titled, *The Book of Runes*.

Ian had suggested that Destiny buy the set of Runes because he had recently used them with a friend and found them to be fascinating. She read the first few pages of the book to better understand how the Rune stones could be used. It related that the symbols etched on each stone contained an ancient meaning, and that the Runes were an Oracle used for divination. She once again inspected the three stones she had chosen by passing her fingers slowly over the engraved demarcations. Matching each Rune symbol with its corresponding interpretation found in the book, the Runes were clear that Destiny must continue to work on her Self and allow Joy to enter her life. She also read that at a certain point in the future, she would be offered the path needed to complete her life lessons.

Destiny set the book next to her journal and gazed out the kitchen window. The garden was filled with lavender and sage blooms sweeping across lilies that lined the stone walk. She slowly stretched her body and walked outside to smell the fresh foliage. She scanned the woodsy yard and spotted several snails lingering beside a fallen yellow leaf, declaring autumn would arrive early. She drew in a breath and released the air through her mouth with a tone that resonated from deep within. Destiny declared her own transformative season would soon arrive.

Until early autumn, Destiny found herself absorbed in her writing. She filled her journal pages with poems and tidbits of notes and short stories that unendingly streamed through her mind. Needing new journals, she entered a book store in Cheltenham to find the right blank notebooks and a few pens. She decided on two books lined with silk covers, one blue and the other purple, and a jet black pen that suited her precise taste. As she stood in line to pay for her choices, she looked up and locked eyes with the young woman behind the counter. The woman's eyes began to tear, as she said, "Destiny! I can't believe it's you...it's me, Tina."

"Oh, my god, Tina! Is it really you?"

"Yes, it's me. I didn't think I would ever see you again. I hardly recognize you with that do! What are you doing in Cheltenham?"

"I moved to Swindon Village soon after...you know. I wondered if I might meet up with you one day. Do you have time to hang about to chat?"

"I shan't be able to leave for another hour on break. Can you meet up then?"

"Right, then. I'll be back and we can chat a bit. It will be lovely to hear how you are getting on."

Destiny left the store and walked to a bench to wait out the hour until Tina would be free to chat with her. Her mind filled with scenarios of what could have happened to Tina after she left Charter Manor. She instinctively placed her hand on her stomach, and then realizing her gesture, quickly released it. *Maybe it would be better if I pushed off and didn't meet up with her*, Destiny thought. She opened one of her new journals to record her thoughts:

> Journal—March 1983: I am to chat with Tina! After all these years, almost eight, it seems like a lifetime ago. I wonder what her life is about now. The connection is still there, I feel it. I shan't talk about that time back then. Why go there and dredge it up? No, I will focus on today and how we are getting on presently.
>
> She looks different somehow, still the petite thing, but even more fragile. Her hair is in a fashionable do

for her age. How old would she be now? Maybe twenty-one or twenty- two years old? What a few years can do to a person! Look at me, I certainly have changed. I finally feel like I am an independent woman. I hope Tina feels this way too. I wonder if she has found a fellow. I bet she is married with children by now!

It certainly is a fancy how our lives change with our experiences. What did that little book say? Something like, "We have the ability to change our lives as we see fit. If we choose to follow the same path we are walking upon, our lives will benefit in ordinary and known ways; however, if we make the choice to walk a different path, our lives can change in innumerable ways. As we look back at the years we have lived, it is easy to see where we have taken a new path and when we have stayed firm on an old one."

I see this shift happening in my life all the time! It seems as if I have a need to experience new beginnings. I like that about myself, never a dull moment!

Walking back to the store where Tina worked, Destiny reflected on the friendly fourteen year old girl she had met so long ago. Why would a horrific experience befall such an innocent girl? What did she go through when she returned to her parents' home? Destiny had so many questions, yet knew she didn't want to chat about the past, so tucked them away and smiled when she spied Tina walking toward her.

"Where shall we go?" Destiny asked Tina, and then gave her a genuine hug.

"How about we sit in the centre square, since I only have a short time to chat," Tina suggested.

"That would be lovely." The pair walked arm in arm toward the square.

They found an empty bench and sat side-by-side, both eager to hear the other's tale. Destiny started first by explaining that she had moved to Cheltenham because of the stories she had shared with her about its beauty. She continued to talk about her years in school, finding work at the spa, teaching and moving into her cottage in Swindon. When she stopped to take a breath, Destiny realized she had been doing all the talking, and asked Tina, "What about you? Are you married? Where do you live?"

"Oh, Destiny, I do miss our chats. As you were telling me all that you have accomplished in these short few years, my life seems to pale. After my baby was born, it did not live but a few minutes. I was grief-stricken and could not cope at all. My mum took me in, but my days were filled with emptiness and pain. I could not look my father straight in the face ever again and in less than a year, I moved into a small flat above a pub. Mum would come to check on me each day, but honestly Destiny, I wanted to die. I actually even took a bottle of pills once, but they just made me horribly sick."

Tina took a moment to compose herself and sat upright as she continued, "Destiny, my life has been filled with the struggle to overcome the loss of my baby. Still to this day, I shan't talk about it to anyone. Some days, it's all I can do to get myself home from work and eat supper. How have you gotten on so brilliantly?"

"I guess my determination to live a positive life has something to do with it. I have always been the type to strive toward being the best I can be, no matter what the Universe throws at me. Then I learned that I don't have to wait for experiences to *happen to* me. I can bring into my life what I desire and then react in ways I choose. Do you understand, Tina?" Destiny asked hesitantly.

"Well, it all sounds rather bold, Destiny. How did you get to be so smart?"

"It's not being smart, it is just learning how to realize my goals and desires, and then direct my energy toward achieving them. I am always reading books on these subjects. I can share some of them with you, if you wish," Destiny offered.

"Well, it all seems a bit too impossible for me to understand, but thanks for the offer. I better push off and get back to work now. If you ever want to hang about and chat again, you can find me here most every day. It was spot-on chatting with you again, Destiny. I do wish you the very best in your life." Tina stood to walk back to the store that had become her second home. She gave Destiny a hug and waved as she turned to leave.

"Tina, I hope to chat with you again, too." Destiny waved in return. She knew they would never meet up again. Their souls were to touch only at a time in their lives when each could support the other, and that time had vanished.

Twenty-One

Soul's Peace

Misty oceans of darkened sea
Held high above the Earth
Where, oh where, is home for me
Disclose where is my birth.
Glistening heavens so far away
With suns and stars abound
Which starship sends my ray
That lights each new path found.
I envision streamers strung
With secrets sailing near
Encased in clouds gently spun
Deafening voices I hear.
Open wide oh sea of Life
Release all mystery
Tell me of my lighted quest
Reveal my true soul's peace.

For months, Destiny found herself immersed in writing. She wrote poem after poem that entered her consciousness at all times of day and night. Her dreams brought elegant lines of rhyme and words paired to fill page after page in her journal. Writing had always been something she automatically allowed to flow through her mind, but now the words had an intensity of meaning and direction. She was determined to use her writing ability to help guide her toward her future. Sometimes, the words retreated into the past, strangling her younger days filled with fear and doubt. Then within the next pages, a sense of release appeared as her words searched for freedom. She wrote short stories laced with memories of her childhood, and she sometimes used automatic writing to allow her soul to splash onto the page, divulging truth and passion. Lines of poetic prose graced her journal with words that touched her ears as sweet peace hung its cloak over her shoulder. Sometimes, she didn't know what she was writing. She allowed words to tumble from her mind dripping from the cottage walls like midnight dew, sticky and unforgettable. She had no intention of sharing her writing, but continued nonetheless.

One short tale Destiny wrote spoke of how many people who claim to be metaphysical misuse their knowledge of the principles found within metaphysics.

Reflections

Have you ever noticed how some people claiming to believe in the metaphysical laws and principles seem to adjust those concepts to suit their own personal needs? I knew a woman who felt she was very enlightened in New Age thought, including the concept that we create our own reality. She experienced much pain in her life and made sure others knew about it. Often she would enlist the attention of near strangers to belabor her life trauma, but did not seem to talk about her part in creating the turbulent dramas. A bit later, I overheard her address the topic of another's challenged life and how they had created it!

When we use metaphysical concepts to rationalize, condemn, or criticize the lives of others, it reveals that we are not fully secure with the enlightening concepts. You might first ask yourself if you honestly believe you create, or co-create, your reality. Study your reactions closely, and you may be surprised. Justifying our beliefs by making them fit to the circumstances of the moment will not make them real. As we create our reality, we also have the power to create our beliefs in that reality. Since belief precedes experience, therefore reality, once this is accomplished you are well on your way to creating a positive future. In other words, do not fool yourself into believing anything that doesn't ring true for you.

At one time in my life, I needed to adjust my metaphysical beliefs regarding my world and how I was living it. Most likely, we all do this to some degree. When my life is running smoothly and everything is coming up roses, I tend to thank my guides, Higher Self, God/Goddess, or others, forgetting that I created it all! Then, when I find myself in a negative situation, perhaps experiencing my shadow side, I ask, "Why did this happen to me?" Instead, I have learned to ask, "Why did I create this mess?" I check the lessons I have've learned from the situation, and try to figure out how I allowed myself to entertain the experience. Then finally, I try not to allow it to happen a second time.

Increasingly, Destiny's free days and nights were filled with writing. She opened her creative imagination to flow freely through her pen, writing line after line of poetry and prose. She allowed her thoughts to collect and meet in the cracks of her cottage ceiling until the right placement revealed itself. Theories, conjectures, and assumptions all clustered together waiting for her to pluck when the subject appeared on the page. She became obsessed with writing, just as she sometimes felt obsessed with reading. Once a topic formed in her mind, it was as if she couldn't stop herself from writing about it. Sometimes, sparks of interest arose from her inner inquires that had been left unanswered from her past. One thought sat unresolved, heavy and leaden with questions: *What was my lesson in getting pregnant when I did?* This question would appear in most every paper she wrote. It would sneak onto a page with soft echoes of disappointment, or arrive in bold words not to be overlooked by lazy eyes. The query stood as a hidden composition, waiting to be noticed and dissected. One of her poems housed thoughts of youth:

Forgotten Youth

Windows forming in my mind
To view a different rhyme—
Days of fun and laughter roam
Beside companions fresh with pints
Of ripened foam atop a glass
Each night.
Where are those days of

Unrelenting joys that took
My youth so fast?
Where are those times of
Sheltered bliss that hides
My mind, alas?
Looking outward, the windows
Now fogged with
Smudges old—
Show me true my days
Gone by, show me why
Oh, why…

"When Karma surrenders to Dharma, we meet Destiny."
Destiny absorbed the significant words as they entered the silent
room filled with attentive people. Learning about Eastern
philosophy was a treat for her; she had only read a few books
on the subject. She felt herself drawn to its philosophical flow
of life, death, and rebirth as depicted by the speaker. The flyer
in the library introducing the lecture stated simply, "A Lesson
Found in Buddhism." The man speaking looked to be in his late
sixties, bearded, and was dressed casually in all white attire. He
held a book in his hand much of the time, referring to different
quotes and reading passages to backup his oration. After the
lecture concluded, Destiny proceeded to check out a few books
on the spiritual belief system that emerged so long ago. She
acknowledged there had been an unsolicited progression to her
learning about religions that presented a rhythm of life, death,
and rebirth. The pull was strong, and she became immersed in
learning all she could about Buddhism.

The year seemed to pass without incident, and Destiny
became a recognized teacher at the massage school. She still
worked at the spa occasionally, but her responsibilities to her
students at the school began to override her practical, hands-on
work at the spa. Minutes turned into hours, days into months,
all seeming to be illusions forgotten in the yesterdays of her life.
Lectures, meetings, and groups surrounding her leisure studies
of metaphysics and Eastern religions followed her from day to
night and day once again. Destiny now greeted each morning
with prayer, and a chanted mantra. Each of these Divine

offerings contained pathways of transformation to guide her toward the woman she desired to become.

Through the years, Destiny and Ian's friendship became very close. They would talk for hours about their individual studies and compared their notes after meetings. Their relationship took on a deep spiritual quality, but not a romantic one. Just before Destiny turned twenty-six in May of 1984, Ian explained that his birthday gift to her was a trip to The Brighton Buddhist Centre near London. The centre originated about ten years prior and the magnificent grounds were filled with multiple shades of green in every direction, forming paths and inlets to walk or sit and meditate. During this adventure, the pair sat for hours in meditation and met others from all over the world who had come to respite within the surrounding peace. When they returned to Cheltenham, Ian offered Destiny another surprise.

"Destiny, I have been offered a position in the States and I need to travel there to scout it out. I will be leaving at the beginning of next year. I know you have talked about traveling abroad; and, I wondered if you might like to accompany me? You could hang about the area for as long as you wish and return whenever you like, or travel back with me. What do you say?" Ian continued before she could answer, "I know this is a big decision. That is why I am presenting it to you so far in advance. You don't need to tell me your answer until you have completely thought through the proposal."

"Oh, Ian…what a holiday that would be! It certainly would be a great opportunity for me to see America a bit. The thought of traveling with you is a spot-on idea. When do I need to let you know my decision?"

"The trip will be in early spring of next year, so you have plenty of time. Oh, and please, the airfare and lodging will be taken care of," Ian assured.

"Brilliant! I was wondering if I could afford the trip. What part of the States do you need to travel?" Destiny silently hoped it would be near the Pacific Coast so she could see the beaches she had dreamed about so often.

"I need to go to California, and then circle back to New York. The whole trip will take about seven days. I realize you must be wondering about the accommodations, please know I will arrange separate rooms all the way." Ian smiled with his familiar wink.

"Oh, I knew you would handle that issue, Ian. We are friends, the best of friends. I have a friend who moved to California many years ago. I wonder if I could find him..." Destiny's voice trailed off as her mind entered that secret room where she had tucked her memories of Jess.

"Destiny? Hello? Where did you go?" Ian ventured to ask.

"Oh, I am sorry. I have've thought about my friend in a long time. I know he is still in my mind somewhere and I was trying to retrieve his memory. His name is Jess Drew. He moved to the States and was going to stay in touch with me, but he did not." Destiny lowered her head in defeat.

"Well, if he is in a directory of some sort over there, perhaps we could ring him up," Ian responded with encouragement in an attempt to lighten Destiny's mood.

"Oh, my god, that would be bang on! It has been so many years though, I doubt if he is even in the same area. Well, I will give you an answer by the end of the year. You will have plenty of time to schedule me into your plans, if I decide to accept your offer."

"Spot-on!" Ian exclaimed.

That night, Destiny lay in bed unable to sleep. Her thoughts traveled back to the year she had met Jess and all that they'd shared. Retrieving her memories was not difficult; he had always been close to her heart. She wrote out her fears and doubts, sharing with her journal her most secret feelings:

> Journal—May 1984: Oh, my god! The thought of seeing Jess again is both frightening and exhilarating at the same time! It's been seven years since he left, would he even want to see me? He might be married with kids by now! Maybe this isn't such a good idea after all. Wait a sec...it wasn't me that messed about not returning posts! I tried to mind our relationship; it was him that nudged it. Maybe he went dotty or something and cannot write or speak!
>
> Pull it together. If I did decide to go with Ian, I can't just pop in and say...What would I even say to Jess? "Hello Jess, this is the girl you met that almost ran you

down with a cycle, and then fell in love with you. Want to meet up for a pint?"

I could write him another letter and wait to see if he responds. After all, I've got six months to make up my mind if I want to go. The question is: Would I want to go with Ian even if I didn't get to find Jess?

For the next several months, Destiny could think only of Ian's offer to travel to the States. He mentioned that his first destination would be near Los Angeles, in the town of Irvine. As she had requested, Destiny's mum posted her the journal she'd left in her room, and the tiny paper with his address was still wedged between two pages. She easily found the town of Mill Valley on the map, and wondered if she could figure out how to get there from San Francisco. She bought a map of the United States with clear markings of California. She studied the distance from Los Angeles to the airport in San Francisco. By her calculations, it would take a second plane trip to get to where Jess had told her he would be living. Two weeks later, the post to Jess was returned. The envelope was unopened with bold lettering across the front: **No such person at this address.**

At the November meeting in the basement of the library, Destiny told Ian, "I think I will travel with you next year. The adventure would be good for me, don't you think?"

"Spot-on! Yes, most definitely you need to get about. I am planning on renting a motorcar so when I am away at my meetings, you can take trips about to wherever you wish. I hear there are lots of places to visit in Los Angeles. There will also be a few free days that we can hang about together. Oh, Destiny, it will be a bang on holiday!" Ian picked Destiny up, and twirled her in the air.

"Put me down, Ian, people will think we're dotty," Destiny whispered, and straightened out her blouse as he released her.

"Oh, right..." Ian mumbled. "Okay, then, I shall get your airfare ticket and give you a schedule for the trip. Will you be at the December meeting, then?"

"As far as I know. I have no big plans for the Christmas celebration or New Year's. For me, it is a time for more parties to avoid. I may go to visit Mum and Dad, not certain yet. What month do we leave?"

"We start out the middle of March. I am sorry you are so put off with the coming holidays, Destiny. Do you want me to pop over for a visit for a few days? I can stay at the inn where I always do when I am in Cheltenham, if you like," Ian offered, but Destiny started to shake her head negatively before he finished his question. "Well, right then...I'll see you at the next group meeting."

"Ta, Ian, see you then." Destiny waved and headed for her motorcar. As she was driving, she thought to herself, *Ian is such a great fellow. It's too bad I am not attracted to him in a romantic way. We have a lot in common with our studies and all. Maybe he will hit it off with an American girl after he moves.*

> Journal—May 1984: When we fall in love, where does the love come from? One moment it is nowhere, and the next it is all around us. Why does someone fall in love? Is it to belong in another's heart, or merely a means to an end that brings its own rewards? Have I ever been in love? I thought I was falling in love with Jess, wasn't I?
>
> Words, all words—or a reality I have not yet found. If Love does enter a relationship, how does one know? If Love enters my soul, I will wear it for all to see upon my face! I will feel Love's emotion as it lingers in my smiles. I will sense Love's presence as my body is touched, and feel its depth as we make Love. Yes, I will wear Love for all to see upon my face...upon my face.

Twenty-Two

Soon the holidays arrived and the New Year's celebrations seemed to pass quickly for Destiny. Her days seamlessly moved from one to the next until the holiday songs, parties, and fashions faded into remote memory. January seeped through a hole of her reality and drifted into obscurity. During the administration meeting at the massage college after the first of the year, it was announced there would be a new turnover, and Destiny was not happy about it. Her position would be divided between two instructors and this change would cut her income by one third. She knew her job at the spa was set, and if needed, she could take on more clients to fill the financial gap; she was not particularly concerned. However, there was an issue she was not fond of: She would be sharing her lessons with another co-teacher. She had worked hard to accumulate all her teaching materials and the thought of allowing another person to use them didn't sit well with her. By the beginning of February, yet another change was revealed: Destiny was asked to become Head Instructor. The new position was announced in an early morning meeting without prior warning.

That evening, Destiny found herself in juxtaposition between wanting to be top instructor, and not wanting to put in the extra hours the position required. If she accepted the honor, she sensed an overload of responsibilities with no time for herself to read, write, or travel. If she turned it down, her income would plummet. The college gave her two weeks to decide if she wanted to accept the new position. On top of this dilemma, the trip with Ian to America was less than two months away and she was worried it might need to be canceled if she became head instructor. *I need to meditate and clear my mind to allow all these possibilities to take a proper place in my life.*

Arranging her bed pillows to firmly meet her spine, Destiny sat in silence. The birds softly sung outside the window and the setting sun gifted a golden ray of light across the room. She sat for an entire hour, allowing her mind to bring a vision that would direct her decision. Finally opening her eyes to a darken room, she stared deeply into the corners of her conscious awareness, and whispered to her cottage, "I know my life is being directed...there is no need to worry. I trust that as I continue with my plans, my life will unfold as needed to attain my peaceful place, my goals, and my destiny."

Stretching her arms and legs, Destiny reached for the lamp to illuminate the room. She picked up her Runes, tucked her right hand deep into the velvet pouch and pulled out three tiles. The symbol engraved on each stone guided her to rely upon *her own intuition during times of change*. Returning to work the following week, Destiny told the administration board that she was honored to be chosen the head instructor, but she would not be taking the position. She followed her instinctual guidance that how she used her *time* was more important than climbing the proverbial professional ladder at this point in her life. Instead, she began teaching with a co-teacher, and offered her knowledge and teaching materials with compassion. She felt a sense of relief by staying true to herself and her intuition.

Luana's bookmark again made its way into the novel, securing a place for her to continue reading at a later time. She noted that her comforting book was coming to its end, and wondered briefly if she could finish reading it later that evening. The group members would be arriving soon, and she wanted to bring out the newest books to share with them. She fluffed up the pillows on the sofa and the larger floor pillows, so each woman could find their perfect spot in which to settle for the meeting. Stacking the books on the coffee table, she noticed a silver chain with a gold cross dangling from one end that was lying inside a book near the bottom of the pile. She instantly recognized the chain, and her mind traveled to the day when her father gave her the bookmark so many years ago. A few days before her twelfth birthday, he came into her room with two store-wrapped packages. Handing Luana the first present, he said, "Luana, I know how much you enjoy reading. Here is a book filled with short stories that you can read and reread many times through your life, and receive new lessons with each reading. Cherish it always."

Luana slowly untied the bright pink bow, and then opened the matching pink paper to reveal a small weathered hardbound book. The cream-colored cover had one green stem that exploded into golden blossoms like an umbrella that bent down over the title that was etched in gold letters, *Ships and Havens.* Turning the delicate yellowed inner pages, she read the publication date, 1897. "Oh, Daddy, what a treasure! Thank you so much!"

Her father then handed her the second gift held together with only a wide purple ribbon. He placed a velvet box in the palm of her hand without a word. Luana gently untied the treasure to reveal the matching purple box and unlocked the tiny clasp. The box held within it a silver chain. She held it high in the air to swing the golden cross, and then she hugged her father tight. "I know this will be a bookmark for my special books, Daddy. Thank you so much!"

Through most of Luana's life, she read that precious little book to gain wisdom from its wise words. It was also one of the books she used like a divining tool. She would open it to a random page to help answer pending questions or guide her through a difficult time, especially during her teenage years. Luana hadn't thought of the book in a long time. She believed it had been hidden in a packing box filled with other books. As she wiggled the old book from between two larger volumes, it opened to one page she remembered reading over and over. Marked with pencil brackets she had drawn years ago were the words:

> "What is our desired haven in the venturesome voyage of life? We are not at rest; we are on a journey. Our life is not a mere fact; it is a movement, a tendency, a steady, ceaseless progress towards an unseen goal. We are gaining something, or losing something, every day. Even when our position and our character seem to remain precisely the same, they are changing. For the mere advance of time is a change.
>
> But what is it, then, the haven towards which you are making? What is the goal that you desire and hope

to reach? There are three ways in which we may look at this question, depending upon the point of view from which we regard human existence. When we think of it as a work, the question is, "What do we desire to accomplish?" When we think of it as a growth, a development, a personal unfolding, the question is, "What do we desire to become?" When we think of it as an experience, a destiny, the question is, "What do we desire to become of us?"

Do not imagine for an instant that these questions can really be separated. They are interwoven. They cross each other from end to end of the web of life. The answer to one question determines the answer to the others. We cannot divide our work from ourselves, nor isolate our future from our qualities. A ship might as well try to sail north with her jib, and east with her foresail, and south with her mainsail, as a man to go one way in conduct, and another way in character, and another way in destiny."

Luana placed the antique book on her lap and closed her eyes. Instantly, the thought came to her to introduce the contents of this book to her group that day. She would read a passage at a time and have the women discuss its importance to their own lives. She placed the chain at the beginning of the book and removed the remaining books from the coffee table, replacing them with her newfound gem. Silently to herself, she repeated the words, "We are not at rest; we are on a journey." She thought, *I have always believed this…my life has moved in ways I had not expected, but each new experience has led me to explore the many journeys of my life.*

At the beginning of the group time, Luana helped the women focus their attention on their own journey to this point in their lives. She asked the women to write down these three questions: Can you trace your life's journey through the years? How did you arrive where you are today? Who or what were the most important people or events along your path that brought you to this point in your life? The women were instructed to wander through the yard for twenty minutes, or to sit in meditation and study their life's journey thus far. Upon returning, each one would have an opportunity to share their revelations. As the group members were individually recalling their life's meaningful experiences, Luana sat cross-legged on a floor pillow in participation to remember more of her past experiences that were important to her growth. After she closed her eyes, one memory instantly arrived at the forefront of her mind.

The memory began on a sunny winter day soon after she had turned forty-five years old. Luana was riding through the Napa Valley wine country on a day trip with her brother. They always managed to find a few days to get together to catch up with each other every few years. She noticed an abundant overgrowth of wild flowering mustard plants weaving in and out of the rows of grapevines on both sides of the road. The thin plants looked like little fairies dancing with their yellow wings fluttering in the cool breeze.

Her brother was driving and seemed somewhat out-of-his-body at the time, and commented how lovely the yellow color was, and then he added, "They must make a lot of peanut butter up here out of these plants."

Luana stared at her brother for several seconds, and then inquired with a puzzled face, "Peanut butter?"

"No, no, not peanut butter...what do they make from mustard seeds?" he stammered.

"Mustard!" Luana shouted, and then patted her brother on the head like a child. They both laughed until their sides ached.

Thinking back on that moment brought fond memories of her brother, and instantly she knew the episode would fit nicely into the manuscript she was writing. She now had tentatively titled her book in progress, *Edge of the Water*. Luana opened her eyes and grabbed a pen: New chapter, "Mustard Seeds and Peanut Butter."

The women were returning from their self-exploration, and Luana asked who wanted to share their experience first. Jo Ann related that her memories of her life became clear when she started deep breathing exercises about ten years ago. She explained it was easy for her to trace her life's journey through the many experiences she had, and felt she was exactly where she needed to be at this point in her life.

Mary Ann shared that the exercise was difficult for her, and she could not relate an event in her life that directed her to who she was presently. As she began to tell the group more about her life, however, she recognized how one experience had progressed to the next until several incidents seemed to have run together. She exclaimed, "Now I see what you mean, Luana! Each time something happened to me, I had a choice as to how I would react or respond to it, and that choice led me to who I am now! I need more time to really explore this concept. I'll come back with more information about my life next time."

Emma shared next, "I guess I am missing something here...my life seems so ordinary and bland. My memories of early years, before ten years of age, don't even register. Through my teens and early twenties, it all seems to run together with no important markers at all. Even my marriages were not the exciting, lustful type; they hardly made an impression on my life. I think I am still waiting for that important event to take place that will lead me to my true destiny."

Luana asked, "When you experienced your hypnosis session, and again when you dreamed of Rachael, did you feel *those* events were meaningful, Emma?"

"Well, yes. I guess I did feel they were special experiences. Is that what you mean?"

"Those two experiences definitely could be important events to your progression of figuring out who you are becoming, and why your life contains an important gift. Not very many people have actually experienced their spiritual guide like you did as a child, and perhaps still do. To clarify, significant life markers can be a literal type of awakening to a better understanding of who you are, and your life's journey as Emma Wells," Luana instructed. "Let me share with you a brief event that happened to me, which I believe might help you all understand how even trivial experiences can make huge impressions upon your life's journey."

Luana began to share her memory that surfaced only a few minutes earlier about driving through the wine country with her brother and seeing the wild mustard plants. She continued, "A few days after this trip with my brother, I remembered the tiny mustard seed my father gave me when I was about five years old. I went to my jewelry case to check if I had kept it, and there it was. The seed is encased in a glass ball with a ribbon of gold to cement the two halves that capture the essence of the sole mustard seed for all eternity. I drew in a deep breath remembering the words my father said as he watched me unwrap my gift. He told me, "If you have as much faith as this tiny mustard seed, Luana, you can do anything." I wore that charm on its gold chain for many years, making it a true talisman for my young life. This nearly antique relic still nourishes the wisdom of metaphysical thought from wise teachers. A philosophy of *faith* must command our human nature—a faith in ourselves. The wording inside the clear ball surrounding the seed reads: *If ye have faith as a grain of mustard seed, nothing shall be impossible unto you.*

Luana continued sharing words that flowed from her lips without effort:

> "What does it mean to have faith as a grain of mustard seed? Did you know a single grain of mustard actually produces thousands of flowering plants? The tiny seed entrusts itself to the winds of nature and time. Its capsule-like fruit has two chambers divided by a thin septum, which at maturity splits and divides to form two distinct parts. I feel the life of a mustard seed addresses our own innate claim for survival with its bonding and separation. Metaphysically, we understand we co-create our reality; but many times, we forget to sustain the faith needed to secure our beliefs. The mustard seed has that faith. It possesses faith that the winds of time will deposit it in fertile ground to be nourished, and trusts that it will divide and separate to renew the entire process over and over again. This type of faith in oneself spurs the action of moving forward, leaving the past, and separating from old patterns and un-supporting relationships. Having faith is only half of what is required to live successfully in our metaphysical reality. The *action* of moving toward a desired goal is the other half. This action is the peanut butter of life!
>
> As you all know, eating peanut butter is tricky business. It sticks to the roof of your mouth, it's

difficult to swallow, and it certainly prevents you from communicating, verbally expressing yourself. A move forward, the risk of action, is also tricky. Many times, we know it is time to move ahead and leave the past, but often the peanut butter of life gets stuck in our throats preventing us from speaking our truth and sharing our needs and desires. We find it difficult to swallow the possibility of losing the familiar patterns of the past. However difficult it is to consume, the peanut butter events of our life can nourish and sustain our continued growth.

I also think it is most interesting that mustard seeds and their blooming flowers are bright yellow in color. This third chakra color has been equated with fear, rejection, and even jealousy. However, yellow is also the shade attributed to intelligence, curiosity, inner strength, and the energy of the sun. Let's believe in the faith of the mustard seed and of ourselves in all its golden glory! Another tidbit to ponder about this amazing yellow seed is that two-thirds of all mustard plants are found in southwest and central Asia. Do these people possess *more* faith?

I am reminded of an image of my father and mother spreading Skippy's chucky peanut butter on just about everything before eating it! They believed their meal was nourishing to their bodies if it included peanut butter. Remember to have faith as a grain of mustard seed, and manifest a faith in yourself through positive action."

Luana stopped abruptly, realizing she had been almost lecturing to her group. She composed herself to sum up her inadvertent speech, "So, when considering which life experiences may be important on your journey to self-discovery, don't overlook the lighthearted events, as well as the traumatic ones."

Emma sighed, and said, "I understand now what you mean by experiences shaping our life's direction. Thanks for sharing some of your own journey with us. I guess if I really looked deep inside, I would find some events that have helped shape my life. This group has been so informative for me, thank you everyone." Emma glanced around the room and accepted the smiles of affirmation from the other women as she continued, "I will be more attentive when I have visits from Rachael, and will share my dreams and experiences with you all."

Twenty-Three

Luana sat in her reading chair, determined to finish the book that has stayed forever in her mind for the past several months. There were only a few chapters remaining of the novel that seemed to weave its intriguing tale into her heart. She allowed herself to take a moment to predict how Destiny's story might unfold. Perhaps she will fall in love with Ian while they travel together, or maybe one of his colleagues will fall in love with her! Luana knew how enticing a trip to a new country could encourage one's inhibitions to escape their prison and allow a sense of freedom to delve into unawakened territories of love and lust. She had experienced firsthand the fiery passion usually held at bay until a single moment in a new environment stirred its unbridled emergence. *Maybe Destiny and Ian will decide to work together, exploring and teaching classes in New Age metaphysical thought! Now, wouldn't that be rich?* Luana savored the vision.

As she remembered the book's time period, she gleaned that metaphysical thought was just becoming more widely explored. It was the 1980s, the same decade when her own budding curiosity rose to investigate the wonders of the New Age and all it had promised its followers. She had gone to hear lectures by Ram Dass, and encountered the secrets of Transcendental Meditation. Her consciousness studies education was well advanced and encompassed professors who were awakening the world's minds to new thought beyond words. Luana had experienced the vast knowledge of teachers such as Ken Wilbur, Frances Vaughn, Terry Cole-Whittaker, and Gary Zukav. She envisioned her joy of discovering a new way of thinking without the rigors of a constricted religious viewpoint to pry it apart or dissect its contents. She thoroughly enjoyed her experiential education that allowed her to explore her conscious and subconscious awareness until a suitable fit between truth and acceptance emerged independently. *I have to admit, my life has certainly unfolded in ways that have afforded me a unique way of living and loving myself, and my world. I am truly grateful. I hope Destiny finds herself among those who appreciate who she is becoming, and what she has endured thus far.*

In the book's unfolding plot, Luana realized how Destiny's character was enlisting many of the same metaphysical principles that she was currently teaching the women in her group. The heroine of the book had experienced several difficult events, as well as many enlightening incidents to help guide her on her life's journey. *What's really fascinating is that Destiny recognized this important element, and used her intuition to guide her choices in life. This book would be a nice teaching reference for my group,* she thought.

Turning the book over to glance at its back cover, Luana noticed the author's photograph. It was a thumbnail photo of a lovely woman with long brown hair kissed by the sun that highlighted copper hues catching the wind as she sat on a sandy beach. Barely visible in the background were a few pylons of a large wooden pier. Luana turned the book over to look again at its front cover. She admired the painting, or photograph, of the old pier jutting out from the shoreline that had caught her attention earlier when the book sat posed waiting to be plucked like a virgin. She had not noticed the author's name. Luana felt her body physically jerk and heard herself shriek as she read, Destiny Collins. Her mind quickly acknowledged that the book she thought was a well written fiction novel was in fact an autobiography! She checked the inside copyright page to learn the book was published in 2014.

Learning that *Finding Destiny* was a true story, Luana was even more in awe of the young heroine she had slowly learned to honor and admire. "I can't wait to find out what happens to Destiny!" Settling back into her reading chair, she carefully opened the book and removed the marker to eagerly learn the conclusion of Destiny's journey.

Destiny and Ian met outside after the February meeting in the library basement. They needed to discuss their plans for their trip abroad. It was decided that Ian would pick her up and they would drive together to Heathrow airport. Their travel plans included a brief stopover at the JFK airport in New York, and then on to Los Angeles in California. Ian noted they would be renting a motorcar in Los Angeles to drive the remainder of the trip to his destination in the city of Irvine. Destiny had meticulously marked all the destinations on the map with her black marker. She was grateful that Ian's business appointments would keep him busy much of the time, so she could investigate some of both New York and Los Angeles. She had a mindset to thoroughly enjoy the holiday, whether with Ian, or alone. One sight she was hoping to visit was the Statue of Liberty, and of course, the Pacific Ocean was on the top of her list. She felt as though she had strolled the sunny California beaches many times in her dreams and meditations, and to actually feel the warm breeze on her face and the wet sand between her toes would be magical.

The pair headed out with positive energy directed toward their time together as friends. Destiny felt Ian might be harboring a secret crush on her, but as the trip progressed it was clear his only intentions toward her were ones of admiration. During one of the many long talks they shared while in flight, Ian confided that he admired her independent nature. He also divulged some of his lonely childhood, which had ultimately directed him to explore his paranormal abilities. Destiny listened attentively and could easily relate to his experiences. She began to realize how her own childhood, and the traumatic event as a teen, had edged her to seek a more personally spiritual life. She shared some of her own intuitive nuances, and quickly received Ian's positive feedback about her unique psychic abilities.

"We all have that sixth sense about us," Ian commented, "however, not everyone wants to acknowledge it. Sometimes the thought of being different, or even dotty, gets in the way of a person seeking a better understanding of their extrasensory perception. I am glad you had the courage to investigate and explore these areas of yourself, Destiny."

"In the end, I think everyone who is supposed to acknowledge the idea of a natural flow of energy will do so. In that way, some who study the theory become teachers while others become students. I guess I am becoming a teacher."

"Indeed, I believe you are. I would not be surprised if one day you took on the task of writing what you have learned about metaphysics." Ian winked his familiar wink.

Once they landed, the pair secured a rental car and Ian expertly drove the rather hectic and confusing motorway to the hotel he had reserved. His interviews and subsequent meetings were to begin the following day. They were both exhausted from the long flights and their highway excursion, and agreed to retire early. Destiny knew Ian would be busy the following day and evening, and was excited to begin exploring on her own. In her room, she laid out her maps and made plans to drive the next day to a beach called, Newport.

Managing the American freeway was the hardest part of Destiny's first day in California. Everyone drove so fast, and to her, on the opposite side of the roadway! She finally arrived at an old overpass bridge with a green sign stating that on the opposite side of the bridge she would be entering Newport Beach. She drove slowly through the rows of quaint beach cottages for several miles, and then approached a thoroughfare resembling a roundabout that veered off to the right. She followed the cars in front of her to a parking area and chose an empty space. She watched others put coins in a meter and fumbled in her pocketbook for a few American coins that fit the slot. The meter marked the time allowed. She turned around and looked straight up to the sky to witness the brightest sunshine she had ever seen. The warm rays penetrated her face until she had to look away for fear her skin would burn.

Taking her time, Destiny slowly walked through the motor park to the footpath, or sidewalk as the signage noted. It was a concrete walkway that went as far as she could see in both directions. On the right, she saw that the sidewalk was bordered by shops and stores, across the motor park was the sandy beach. As she looked to the left, she viewed beach cottages all along the sidewalk as far as she could see. Destiny watched as children raced and rode cycles weaving through adults and dogs on leashes that were darting in and out of shops. Gents and ladies were dressed in bathing suits or shorts, and wore sunglasses and hats that covered their faces.

Destiny slowly walked along the storefronts and spied a row of straw hats hanging on a rack in the front window. She knew her fair skin would burn if she didn't cover her face, and bought a wide-brimmed hat with a purple scarf tied around it. She walked past surf shops, beachwear stores, and all types of food establishments. Choosing a café where she could sit outside, she ordered a basket of fish 'n chips and a Coke. She had never seen such massive beaches with sand that stretched for miles with no visible end. She asked the waitress, "I am new here and I don't know the rules. Can I walk down to the shoreline?"

"Yes, of course! Where are you from?" asked the young girl who noticed Destiny's accent.

"I am from England and am just visiting."

"Well, welcome to southern California. You'll want to go walk out on the pier while you're here. It's that way," the waitress said with a big smile, pointing in the opposite direction than Destiny had been walking.

"Oh, thank you." Destiny returned a warm smile.

After eating her lunch, Destiny began walking toward the pier. As she squinted beneath her giant hat, she spied the blackened pylons standing at the edge of the water. The columns rose as custodians from deep within the wet sand to ensure the safety of the pier's platform. Multiple black wooden ties crisscrossed the pier's pylons to form dark shadows on the sand below. Destiny had an urge to draw a sketch of the backdrop, and then realized the familiar image had been etched in her mind since childhood. It was difficult for her to comprehend how the pier in front of her was precisely as her visions had reproduced it repeatedly throughout her life.

She began to walk along one side of the wide pier, and stopped often to take in the beauty of the vista in all directions. Both sides of the pier were lined with fishermen day-fishing with an array of buckets, poles, and fishing tools spread across their area. The smell of fish filled the air as they pulled their lines over the railing to display the flailing catch. Onlookers signaled their approval at the sight of the scaly fish being plunged into buckets filled with seawater to await their turn to be sold at the fish market held daily on the beach below. Destiny's senses were filled with sights and sounds that fed her creativity as poetic words swirled in her mind. She made several mental notes to write down the gamut of emotions she felt as each new experience hastened to greet her. There were children running from their parents trying to climb the rails to peer over the top and witness the crashing waves below. Seagulls circled each fisherman's catch with one eye searching for its next target, and then swooped down to find only remnants of bait. Their screeching sounds echoed through the sky, landing on the deaf ears of beachcombers probing the grains of sand for unknown treasures, and crusty old men wrapped in blankets to protect themselves from the cold winds at the pier's end. It was all Destiny had envisioned, and more. She walked to the very end of the lengthy platform to become hypnotized by the ocean's expanse, and then raised her arms in the air and felt the surge of the sea wash through her soul.

After several minutes of communion with the ocean, Destiny walked back to the moist sand beneath the pier where the pylons began their march to carry the hefty platform to meet the depths of the sea. She removed her shoes to feel the tepid water caress her feet. Echoes of children's voices and crashing waves formed in the tunnel-like curvature between the sand and the pylons, bouncing off each other and then returning into nothingness. Destiny began to walk along shallow waves filled with foam that lingered at the edge of the dry sand sculpting imaginary waves of their own. Soon, she allowed the turquoise water to kiss her legs below the hemline of her thin skirt. After walking for what felt like several miles, Destiny found a pristine untouched area of sand and sat comfortably in her cross-legged fashion. She closed her eyes to the glistening waves rolling endlessly in front of her. She closed her eyes to the glare of a sun initiating patterns of heat waves over the expansive sand. Sitting in deep meditation, Destiny allowed her inner-self to calm her outer, and thought only of how grateful she felt for this day. She knew she would return to experience and explore much more of this enticing paradise.

Ian and Destiny briefly met for a bite to eat in the hotel dining room that night. They were both exhilarated and tired, but each was able to share their day's excitement. Ian was most impressed with the people he met, and who would become his colleagues if he was offered the teaching position. Destiny also related her excitement of finding the exact beach she had envisioned throughout her life which she felt were true precognitive episodes. She explained to Ian about the pull she had to return to the same area the next day. "Ian, I hope it will be all right that I roam about the beach again tomorrow. I feel such a strong pull to explore it all."

"Yes, right then. This is your time to have an adventure, go enjoy yourself! I will be entrenched in meetings again until evening. On our last day here, I will have more time to see the sights."

"Brillant! I will be off to the beach, and this time I am taking a swimming suit. I cannot get over how warm the water is this time of year. Ian, it is most lovely, you must come to see it," she shared, with a new gleam in her eyes.

"I see a side of you I have not seen before, Destiny. I am happy you are enjoying the sights." He gave Destiny a light hug, and said his bed was calling his name.

"Ta, then, Ian. Sleep well."

When she returned to her room, Destiny needed to write the mental notes she had tucked on a creative shelf at the back of her mind. She opened her journal and began to write about her day trip, as well as hopes for tomorrow. She wanted to drive past the pier, to go further on the divided motorway to investigate the entire area. Writing well into the night, she unleashed a passion to begin accepting herself as she was, and to make new goals for her life. A tentative thought even entered her mind about one day moving to California to live near the ocean. There were such familiar undertones of excitement and freedom surrounding the beach, like it was her destiny to find it.

Morning came quickly; Destiny had not gone to sleep until past midnight. She wanted to get an early start to drive to the beach city again. She ate a light meal and headed out toward Newport. When she arrived at the motor park where she had visited the day before, she decided to drive past it to investigate more of the surrounding area. Again, she noticed hundreds of little beach cottages lining both sides of the roadway. She also noticed multiple rental signs posted about many of the cottages, all within walking distance to the beach. At one point, Destiny pulled over to check her map and discovered another body of water opposite the ocean. It was noted on the map to be a marina and bay. She followed the map that denoted she would soon arrive in a place called Balboa. Markings on the map indicated another pier. She decided to go see the second pier as well, and continued her tour. Following the signs, she turned into a motor park and again put the coins in the meter. She could already see the beginning of the pier. It was not as long as the one she'd walked on yesterday, but had its own uniqueness about it.

After walking the length of the pier and refreshing her energy with a cool drink, Destiny asked a young woman sitting near her, "Are you from this area?"

"No, not really, but I come here all the time. Those are my two kids over there in the sand…they love to play in the sand. So, I bring them here a few times a week. I also love to just sit in the sun. Somehow, the ocean air feels so healing, don't you agree?" the woman asked.

"Yes, most definitely. I am truly fascinated by this area. Is there anything else other than the two piers that you would suggest a tourist might like to visit?"

"Oh, I love your accent! Are you from London?"

"I am visiting from England, but I do not live in London. I guess many people equate England with London. I live near Cheltenham. I am sure you don't know where that is, but thank you for the compliment."

"I have always wanted to travel there…anyway, if you haven't been to the Balboa Fun Zone across the street, you might like it. My kids always have to visit there to get a hot-dog-on-a-stick and a chocolate-covered frozen banana. It's just across the street, over there." The woman pointed past Destiny to show the direction.

"Well, thanks, then. I do appreciate your kindness and all. Have a lovely day. I think I will walk over to see what the park is about."

Destiny stood up and began to walk away when the woman said, "Maybe we could meet here and talk, if you ever come for another visit?"

"That would be lovely," Destiny shouted back to her unknown admirer.

Destiny found the narrow walkway along the bay. The calm dark water was filled with boats of all sizes tied to small docks. There were parents sitting in outdoor cafés watching their children examine the many boat rides being offered. Adults and children also lined the footpath as they ate pink cotton candy; ice cream bars; dogs-on-a-stick thick with mustard; and drank large sodas in paper cups. To Destiny, the diversity of people and food both excited her senses and made her anxious at the same time.

Wandering into an area of crashing bumper-cars, a spinning Ferris wheel, and other rides, Destiny quickly found an exit. There was a large building that had been adapted into a restaurant that was located just past the Island Ferry that carried vehicles to the opposite side of the bay. Destiny thought the café looked like a perfect place to dine. After being directed to the veranda on the second floor, she sank into a comfortable chair that hosted an amazing view of the bay. Lining the docks were hundreds of sparkling white boats with their blue sails waving, and motor boats low in the water sporting large engines. At that moment, Destiny enjoyed being a tourist who was gazing at the scene from an outside perspective. She had no intention of partaking in the activities below her luncheon perch.

Twenty-Four

On Destiny's second day in California, she couldn't be more content. After her leisurely luncheon at the amusement park in Balboa, she drove back to the Newport Pier to lie on the beach in the sunshine. Her swimwear was waiting beneath a light overdress, ready to bare her pale skin to the rays of the day. She spread out the beach towel she had purchased in a shop along the boardwalk and lay down to daydream. The woven beach hat covered her closed eyes, as she allowed the sounds around her to float through her being. She heard the chatter of young children as they built sandcastles near the water's edge, and the seabirds vying for their share of the seaweed washed to shore. She allowed herself to ignore the muffled adult voices and honed in on the repetitious white noise of the rumbling ocean waves. The warm sun melted her resistance to relax as it slowly sailed across the blue skies.

Free from her normal English restrictions, Destiny covered her legs with her dress and fell asleep while lying defenseless on the sand. She dreamed of vague images fleeing across a seascape of deep purple, landing on an island. The images turned into an unknown couple holding hands as they explored the isolated landmass, and then stood together to watch the sunset of the evening sky from their beach cottage. At that moment, she opened her eyes to realize she had slept for hours. The sun was sinking, dipping its lower perimeter into the rim of the horizon. She gathered her hand basket and slipped her dress back over her swimsuit. Standing to face the ocean, she silently thanked it for a perfect day. Her skin felt slightly pink, but not burned.

When Destiny arrived at the hotel, she was excited to share her full day with Ian. He arrived a bit late to meet her in the lobby, and apologized, "Destiny, have you been waiting long? I was detained at the last meeting. I am sorry for being tardy."

"No worries. I have been reflecting on my perfect day. It was wonderful, Ian. I want to tell you all about it!" Destiny exclaimed with a new excitement in her voice.

"It must of have been a smashing day! What did you find to occupy yourself to bring such joy to your face?"

"Well, I discovered another pier, a wonderful parade of boats, and people eating all sorts of off-putting food. Then on the shoreline, I experienced such peace that I have only dreamt about. You must come with me tomorrow to experience it all," she told Ian, displaying a wide smile.

"Oh, but if only I could...I must meet yet more professors tomorrow. I know it is our last day here, and I promised I would see the sights, but I cannot. Please do not be upset with me."

"Well, I am a bit disappointed, but totally understand. After all, this is a business trip for you. Perhaps we may have more time together in New York, then?"

"I do hope so. What would you like to do there?"

"I would like to visit the Statue of Liberty. How many days will we have to see the sights there?"

"It might be two days. I don't know exactly what I need to do, or who I am to meet. I better not promise anything to you at this time. I will do my best to accompany you to see the liberty statue. We leave early on the day after tomorrow for the airport in Los Angeles. I do hope you can find a bit more to entertain you for one more day here. Feel free to take the motorcar again, Destiny."

"I most likely will return to the beach, it seems like a second home to me already."

"Right, splendid. I was asked to join a group meeting in the lounge this evening for drinks, would you like to accompany me?"

"Brilliant! Let me go change my dress and I will meet you back here in twenty minutes."

"Spot-on, then. See you in a bit." Ian winked at her.

Entering the lounge, Ian recognized the men from the college and introduced them to Destiny. They were just beginning to exchange a few words when the band began to play. The music was loud, but familiar. It was a popular song and one of Destiny's favorites, "Joy to the World." One of the men asked her to dance and off they went to join others on the dance floor. That night Destiny sank into her bed with a smile on her face and her mind filled with memories she knew would remain for a long while.

As Destiny was brushing her blonde-streaked hair, she admired the shoulder-length style her short bob had grown into over the past few years. Her hair now framed her face with highlights that accented her cheekbones, reflecting a new maturity. Studying herself in the hotel's dim light, she caught a glimpse of the younger teen she once had been. Out loud, she asked the illusory teen reflection, "Have you healed from your ordeal, dear one? Have you released the negativity harbored so deep? I want you to know, you will recover and revel in the fact that you made the best choices you could at the time. Do not be sad, for your life will be filled with new adventures that will help fade your injurious years and guide you to who I am today." For a few seconds, Destiny continued to look at her face in the mirror until her present refection was staring back at her. An aura of golden light shone around her head. She felt content with her appearance as a twenty-seven year old woman who had experienced more in the past ten years than many women did in their entire lifetime.

Destiny packed her bag with the beach towel, her journal, and a paperback book to read that she had purchased at the airport. The tiny yellow book was titled, *As a Man Thinketh*. There was barely time for her to inspect the book at the time, but she automatically opened it to a single page to read: "Dream lofty dreams, and as you dream, so shall you become. Your Vision is the promise of what you shall one day be; your Ideal is the prophecy of what you shall at last unveil." The words quickly resonated with Destiny and she knew she must buy the book, thinking she would read it on the flight back to England.

After she finished packing, this time she easily drove the few miles to the bridge to enter the magical land of Newport Beach. She knew exactly which motor park was the closest to spread out her things on the soft sand. Once again, she would feel the warmth of the sun and relinquish herself to its powers. As

Destiny was walking by the shops to the beach, she glanced down an alleyway and saw a row of cycles fanned out in a line, ready to rent. *What a wonderful idea!* she thought. *I could ride the length of the footpath and view many of the beach cottages.* The thought of riding a cycle free in the breeze stuck firm in her mind. It would give her the opportunity to see more of the beach and the cottages. She had noticed the day before that most of the homes had large picture windows facing out toward the beach. Many of the cottages wore seashell chimes like jewelry adorning porches that boasted bountiful flowering plants, most of which she did not recognize.

She first decided to walk along the edge of the waves in the direction away from the pier. She darted back and forth as the water approached her feet and then retreated to tease her to come near once again. The day was perfect. The cool March breeze softened the heat from the sun's penetrating rays, allowing her to bare her head and feel the wind in her hair. After her walk, she sat on her towel laid out in the sand. She visualized what she wanted to manifest for her future. She envisioned a beach cottage filled with seashells filling woven baskets lying about, and cut flowers from a thriving garden in every room. She saw blue and white dishes settled on a shelf in a quaint kitchen aglow with sunlight streaming through small paned windows. There was a plush white rug in the middle of the front room and two chairs made of rattan with cushions covered in sand-coloured fabric. She imagined looking out the front window to see the ocean in all its grandeur, and a pier in the far background. Destiny opened her eyes and sighed with a release of emotion she had not realized had been held inside.

Deciding to rent a cycle, she walked to the shop and purchased a two hour rental. She took only her bag filled with necessary items and a light sweater in case the weather turned cooler. The cycle was much like the one she had bought at home and it felt comfortable to manage, even though riding on the opposite side of the walkway took some getting used to. Passing by the many homes facing the boardwalk, Destiny rode slowly to gaze through the front windows. After riding for several miles, she turned the cycle around to ride back toward the pier. At one point, sand blew onto the sidewalk and the wheels of her cycle locked. She lost control and was barely able to land on her feet as the cycle came to an abrupt stop. It was then that she looked up to see the cottage she had earlier envisioned. Startled, she looked around to see if anyone had observed her awkward display, but there was no one. She looked again at the cottage and noticed a rental sign in the window. For no apparent reason, she made a mental note to memorize the address.

On the final mile of her ride, the line of stores and cafés appeared and she slowed her cycle to weave in and out of the pedestrians who were also making their way through the crowds. Then, all of a sudden, her cycle seemed to have a mind of its own and the front wheel veered to the left, striking a fellow walking ahead of her! "Hey there! Watch out!" Destiny shouted in a warning tone, but the fellow could not move out of the way in time. The front tire hit his left leg, knocking him to the ground.

Destiny jumped off her cycle and dashed to the kneeling chap. "Are you all right? I am so sorry... Jess? Oh, my god! Jess Drew, is that you?" It took her a few seconds to recognize him behind the scruffy beard and sun-bleached hair.

"Oh, my god! I can't believe you ran me down again! Destiny, what in the world are you doing here?" Jess exclaimed, as he awkwardly tried to get up.

"I...well, I...I can't believe you are here!" Destiny babbled. "Let's go find a place to sit."

"Yes, yes, of course. Let's walk your cycle to the sand over there, so we can have a chat. You look amazing! You must have tons of questions...but I have tons of answers." Jess directed Destiny's bike to a sandy area with a bench for them to sit on. "How unbelievable to meet you here! May I give you a hug, Destiny?" Jess gestured with his arms outstretched.

"Ummm...I guess I need one about now," she said, waiting for the hug that was way past due.

"I have missed you terribly, Destiny," he whispered in her ear. Then he released his hug to hold her at arm's length, all the while studying her eyes for a sign of emotional reciprocation.

"Oh, Jess, whatever happened to you? I tried to keep in touch with you, but never received your return post. Eventually, I assumed you were not serious about me and just stopped expecting to hear from you. Recently, I even wrote one last letter to the address you had given me, in hopes I might visit you while I was in the States. It was returned unopened. What happened to you?" Destiny was almost in tears by the time her last words left her lips.

Jess tenderly touched her lips with his fingers, and said, "Dear Destiny, I am so very sorry I couldn't respond to your posts. I apologize for not ringing you up..." he hesitated a moment, and then continued, "My heart has always been with you, Destiny, please believe me. I will tell you all about what happened to me, please listen. Our meeting today certainly confirms my belief that we are meant to be together. You have never left my heart or awareness."

Jess began to relate his traumatic story of the past several years, which included a car accident that had left him in a coma for several months even before arriving in Mill Valley. He had never received Destiny's posts. Because he had no relatives in the States, his employer arranged for his doctors to move him to a rehabilitation facility for when, or if, he regained consciousness. He was in a coma for several months before his long recovery from the accident. When he awoke from the coma, he was told his right leg had been amputated. He also had many minor injuries from which to recover. If that wasn't enough, for an entire year he could not remember who he was, or the incident that caused his memory loss.

The months and years passed in a fog of rehabilitation, including physical and psychological therapy, and a myriad of medical appointments. By that time, as his memory slowly returned, Jess rationalized that Destiny had most likely continued on with her life and decided not to contact her. Miraculously, his employment had paid for his medical care and was still waiting for him to return after his release. He felt acutely self-conscious of his disabilities and really didn't want to burden the company that had stood by him; however, they reassured him they would allow him to live wherever he wished if he returned to his position. He wasn't exactly sure why he ended up at the beach in southern California, except a strong pull to experience the warm sun to help him heal.

Destiny sat quiet, almost rigid, unable to completely comprehend that it was really Jess sitting in front of her explaining why he had not reached out to her. His story was almost unbelievable, except she knew he would never be untruthful. The visual fact that she could see his artificial leg protruding from beneath his baggy and brightly printed beach trousers also confirmed his story. When Jess finished his heart-wrenching narrative, she could only wipe her tears from her cheeks with one hand, and his with the other. She sat silent for several minutes to digest all Jess had related; and, Jess could only study her face and kiss her hand as it passed over his salty lips.

Can this be happening? Or, is this another vision brought on by a heatstroke from riding so long in the sun? How could Jess be here at this exact moment in time, and how could we meet exactly as we had so many years earlier? This can't be real! Destiny was not sure if she mouthed her mind-rummage aloud, or posed the questions silently to herself. Shaking her head to clear her dazed mind, she purposefully said, "Jess, I am truly sorry you had to go through those terrible experiences. I cannot even relate to the pain, fear, confusion, and self-doubt you must have felt. I will say this—I have always felt in my heart that you would return to me." She reached to hold his head between her hands, and kissed his lips igniting the passion they had kept exclusively for each other. "I'm a bit fogged right now. I need to return my cycle to the rental shop. Then, let's go sit in the sand where my things are, so we can sort through all this." Destiny pointed in the direction of the alleyway. Jess agreed and followed her to drop off the cycle, and then to her beach towel that was waiting for her return. They sat side-by-side, facing the ocean's waves as they held each other's hands, and traced back through each year that had slipped from their budding love affair.

Destiny ended her own catch-up story by telling Jess about Ian and how she had accompanied him on his business trip. She related how the beach seemed to draw her to this exact spot that had been so familiar in her visions and dreams. She ended her tale with numerous questions. Her final question was, "When will you be returning to England?"

"To tell you the truth, I love it here! I have a little beach cottage much like the one in Swindon that suits me splendidly. You must come to see it, Destiny! Can you come now?" Jess had more excitement in his voice than Destiny ever remembered.

"Yes! I would love to visit your cottage...I dare say, however, I am disappointed you will not be coming home soon." Destiny twisted her mouth in a frown.

"Well, you could move here! You'd love it here, as I do. The sun is warm and the beach life is so lovely. Think about it, Destiny, truly *think* about it," Jess urged.

"That would be a massive consideration...let's see where we might go from here first." Destiny winked, and threw her arms around Jess' neck, almost knocking him over again as they sat in the sand.

They walked a few miles to a beach cottage along a side avenue not facing the shoreline. It had a white picket fence surrounding a lovely garden filled with flowers of all different colors. The cottage's wooden panels were painted to match the fence. It was a quaint little beach home with modest furnishings. As Destiny entered the main room, a clock on the wall alerted her it was almost time to meet Ian at the hotel. She wanted to stay with Jess for the evening, and thought she might call the hotel to leave Ian a message. Jess took her hand and showed her each room of his cottage, and then they sat on a soft beige couch to stare into each other's eyes.

"Jess," Destiny began, "I want to stay the evening. May I use your telephone to ring up Ian to leave him a message?"

"Oh, Destiny! I am so happy to hear you want to continue our reunion, and hopefully, our relationship. Of course, you can ring him up. The phone is in the kitchen." Jess motioned with his arm toward the kitchen. Then he added, "If Ian wants to come join us, it would be brilliant!"

"I was actually thinking that we could be alone to see where our feelings are with each other. Is that all right with you?"

"Splendid! I wish you could stay the entire night!"

"I am afraid that is impossible, for Ian and I leave for the airport early in the morning. We have had such a short time together, Jess, would you consider flying to England for a longer visit?" She asked, not actually knowing at this point if Jess was as serious as she about continuing their relationship.

"Destiny, I will follow you anywhere. I don't want to lose you again." Once again, Jess cupped Destiny's face in his hands and parted her lips with his own.

Twenty-five

It was late and Luana couldn't keep her eyes open to read a minute longer. She had misjudged the number of remaining pages in her book, and reluctantly laid it down on the night table. Even though her reading was not finished, she felt an inner sense of calm that Destiny and Jess had found each other again. Discovering that the story was true teased her curiosity and encouraged her belief in the concept of soulmates. The concept of souls meeting in several lifetimes to experience one another through different bodies became a new thought for her. When she'd met Edward, she certainly felt a deep connection from beyond her current life. Their relationship together had spanned two decades of nothing but love and compassion that prompted the idea of soulmates meeting in several lifetimes.

As Luana lay in bed awaiting sleep's gentle nudge, she retraced the time she and Edward shared about their previous marriages. There was no ridicule or jealous innuendoes to disrupt the storytelling, only compassion for each other's loss of love. Edward explained he had fallen in love with one of his professors when attending graduate school. The relationship rose from young passion and unquenchable lust. Her name was Margaret and she taught classes in relationship counseling. Edward found himself in love with her the moment she raised her head to view the classroom of new students. He sat near the front row and could easily read her body language as she studied her notes. Hanging on each word she spoke, Edward became fascinated by her and soon let her know. Margaret admitted to him after they married that she, too, fell hopelessly in lust the very first day they met.

Their marriage was filled with many of the same elements as Luana and James' relationship that seemed to rely on passion, but was soon shadowed by reality's turbulent call. After seven years, Margaret told Edward that she had fallen in love with another of her students. Edward was crushed, but knew he could not hold her back and accepted the painful proposal to separate. Luana's heart broke when Edward shared this story with her. It reawakened her own heartache when she and James ended their marriage.

When Edward finished relating the details of his first marriage to Luana, he strongly added, "But, Luana, I know deep within me that our love will last as long as we both give it the compassion it requires. I feel that our souls have lived together before, do you?"

"Oh, yes! The moment our hands touched as you handed me my glass of wine that first time we met, I felt a familiar spark between us as if it had been reignited. One day we should have a joint past life regression to confirm our feelings."

"That won't be necessary, my dear. I already know we have lived other lifetimes together. I dreamed once that I would meet my soulmate and you are her. I even believe if we each ask our subconscious to have a dream about a lifetime in which our souls have lived together, we will have the same dream. Let's do this one night." He moved close to Luana and gently smoothed her hair, and then placed his hand over her heart, and said, "I bet we could even sync our heartbeats!"

"Now that would be amazing, but going a bit far, don't you think? I know I feel as close to you as any one of my family members, and also know I have lived at least one other lifetime with both my brother and Mother. I love the idea of trying to set up a dream synchronization though! Wouldn't that be fantastic if we really did have the same dream? Even if it wasn't about a lifetime together, it would be positively amazing if there was something in common about them," Luana said, with excitement in her eyes.

"Let's do it tonight!" Edward exclaimed. That night just before they turned out the lights, they held each other close and asked their subconscious minds to give them a dream of the same past life when their souls had been together.

Luana and Edward had studied much of the same topics in graduate school, which included all metaphysical subjects such as cosmology, duality theory, quantum physics, dream analysis, and all paranormal phenomena. They both were attuned to their own bodymind connection, as well as their spiritual viewpoints. The 1980s, when they had attended graduate and post-graduate studies, brought a new approach to the counseling arena. Instruction included learning how to delve into the transpersonal aspects of a patient. The counseling courses addressed investigating the total patient—mind, body, *and* spiritual components. This inventive theory introduced the grassroots of a new branch of psychology called Transpersonal Psychology, which was difficult for many therapists to accept. However, for Luana and Edward the new concept of communicating with a patient about his/her spiritual beliefs, and religious viewpoints, was a welcomed dynamic to their counseling techniques.

On the morning after they had asked to receive a dream of a past life together, Luana opened her eyes first and reached for her dream journal to write out the one that had awakened her. Quietly she lay on her side, facing away from Edward, to capture each scene from her dream. Just as she had completed her journaling, Edward opened his eyes and whispered, "Did you have a dream about a desert cabin, or somewhere rather barren, in or around the 1700s?"

"Oh, my god! I was just writing it out so I would remember to tell you every detail. Why don't you write out your dream before you forget it, and then we can compare them," Luana instructed.

"Oh, yes, that'd be good. Then we won't try to make each other's dream fit our own," Edward agreed.

Edward began to write his dream that lay at the edge of his awareness. Luana sat up in the bed with a pillow at the small of her back, eagerly waiting to hear Edward's dream. She thought again of the dream her subconscious had gifted her in the early morning hours. In the dream, there was a young woman standing in a makeshift classroom with six children. The cabin was a single open space with wooden chairs and a few tables. The children were sitting to face the woman who couldn't have been more than eighteen years old herself. She was telling the children to rest their heads on the table in front of them, and each child did so. The young teacher took out a book from the cupboard behind her and placed it in her lap. She sat still for several minutes, and then told the children to listen to her read from the book. There was one little girl about eight years old with golden hair and deep blue eyes who was wearing a pair of trousers that were way too big for her. There were straps attached to the pants that went up over her shoulders to keep them from falling off. Luana felt she was experiencing the dream-story from this little girl's perspective. When she realized this fact, she felt strongly that she was, indeed, the girl in the dream.

"Okay, I have written out my dream! Who should go first?" Edward asked.

"You tell me your dream first, and then I'll read you what I have written about mine."

"Okay, here goes…The room was dim, barely enough sun light entering through two tiny windows. I knew I was a young boy in the dream, because I was watching the events through his eyes. He was about twelve years old and had reddish blond hair and blue eyes. The room seemed to be made of tree logs, because there were still a few limbs that jutted from between some of them. There was nothing placed between the logs like cement or mud, or anything. I got a sense the time period was in the 1700s, or maybe 1800s. Anyway, the boy is listening to a young woman read from a book she is holding in her lap. The book looks like an old storybook you see in museums today. I can't hear all the words she is reading though, I am now feeling that maybe I, the boy, can't hear well. There isn't much more to the dream before I woke up. Now, tell me yours."

"I have to say, this does sound very similar to my dream!" She began to read the details of her dream from her journal.

"We must have been those kids, don't you think? I wonder if they are from the same family, or just live in the same area. Well, I am convinced we had at least that one lifetime together, aren't you?"

"It certainly seems like it. We could go under hypnosis to see if we come up with more details about that time period, and the lives of those children. But, Edward, I don't need to know anything more to believe our souls have chosen to be together in other lifetimes. I am content to have you here with me in this one." Luana placed her arms around Edward's chest to spoon their bodies. They lay still for several minutes, absorbing each other's love and energy. Turning to face Luana, Edward wrapped her in his arms, kissed her neck and then her lips to ignite an early morning passion.

Ian and Destiny enjoyed visiting a few tourist sights around the New York area the last few days of their holiday. The short stay Destiny had with Jess left an unforgettable impression on them both. She was eager to return home to prepare for his visit to Cheltenham in two weeks. Ian was also looking forward to meeting Jess, mostly to affirm a strong intuition he had about their future. When she arrived home, she cleaned her little cottage until it sparkled. The flowers and plants in the garden were weeded and trimmed, and she bought shelving to organize her books by stacking them properly in rows. She was happy when the college told her she could cut back her hours during his visit as well.

Jess rang up Destiny almost every day to hear her voice and reassure her that he was truly coming to be with her. He said his flight ticket was purchased, his bags were packed, and his heart was filled with love for her. She was also filled with love, and happy they would finally have some intimate time together. She rang up her parents to inform them of the new chap in her life, and that she might bring him round for a visit soon. Her only concern was the thought of discussing with Jess her past pregnancy. It consumed her days even though she tried to push the issue to the back of her conscious awareness. The thought of actually telling anyone, other than her mum, that she had given birth to a child she did not keep had never entered her mind. *Will Jess be outraged that I gave my baby up for adoption? Will he just walk away and never want to see me again?* So many unanswered questions floated in Destiny's mind.

One day, while grappling with her dilemma, she felt a strong desire to walk through the woods behind her cottage. The fog was thick and she could only see each tree about four feet in front of her as she made her way to the old tree log. In the damp air, she stood upon it brave and strong, and then shouted to the invisible sky, "Must I tell my sordid story to Jess? Why can't that part of my life just be forgotten forever? Tell me what to do..." Only the silent fog heard her plea—there was no audible answer. Destiny stood firm to her spiritual ideals, and found she already knew what she must do.

The day Jess arrived she raced to open the cottage door wide and opened her arms to receive his hugs. Her kisses were hard and longing and he returned the same. They had agreed over the phone that he could stay with her for his two week visit and sleep on the couch. Their plans and expectations were instinctual, and the first few days passed quickly. They talked for hours, walked in the woods, and made each other meals in the cottage kitchen. Then, Destiny offered to give Jess one of her special body massages, which he eagerly accepted. The hour melted into two as their bodies filled with passion and ended under Destiny's lavender scented sheets. Their lovemaking took the couple to heights of ecstasy neither had experienced before, and their bond promised to last forever. Destiny had never been so at peace.

As the time neared for Jess to return to California, they both felt a tearing pain within their hearts. Jess begged, "Come to live in California with me, Destiny...marry me!"

"Oh, my god! Jess...yes! I want to marry you and live with you wherever you live." She jumped into his waiting arms with such vigor they both landed on the floor!

"Why is it you are always knocking me down? You must promise not to do that in the future," Jess laughed. "We shall be married on the beach, near the pier you love so dearly. The seagulls will squeal above us as we walk into the sunset. It will be perfect!"

"I am so excited, Jess. Could this really be our future? I have so many questions! How will I ever leave my jobs? What will I do living at the beach in a country foreign to me? I need to start creating a vision of my...of our future. It needs to be spread before me, with all the details laid out. How can I just up and move to America?"

"We need to think this out a bit, that's all. We can search for the right future to create together. We have all the time we want now!" he said, managing to calm Destiny's fears.

"Yes, we shall be so happy! We do have all the time we need to create our perfect reality, there is no reason to rush. I want you to meet my parents; and, I want to meet your sister too. Let's take a breath here...all this cannot happen overnight. But,

I can't wait to start my new life with you, Jess." Destiny reached up for a finalizing kiss and received it, and more.

Jess had his bags repacked and was waiting at the door when he shouted, "Hurry, sweetie. I must leave in half an hour to make my flight."

"I am coming, Jess," she yelled from the bedroom. She was mulling over her decision to tell him about her past at the last moment before he left, or wait and tell him on his next trip in a few months, or never tell him. If it was to happen, she wanted to get it over with, but her stomach churned in rebellion. In the end, she could not bring herself to say the words that were caught in her throat.

After asking the love of his life to marry him, Jess flew back to the States. He was jubilant that Destiny had accepted his proposal and knew their plans would fit together easily. He kept the vision of their love as he settled back into his home in Newport Beach. Talking to Destiny each day over the telephone also helped keep his dream alive. He felt secure that they would create their life together in a positive fashion. He felt secure that Destiny could work at whatever she decided once they were married. Whether she chose to continue her teaching and massage work, or to start a new profession altogether, he would be content and supportive. He was so happy to have her back in his life, he didn't care what Destiny's future plans were, as long as he was a part of them.

Soon after Jess left for California, Destiny became sick with worry. She knew she must reveal her past pregnancy, but was afraid Jess would never want to see her again. She regressed from her place of spiritual strength, to hover near depression. It was Ian who recognized Destiny's mental state, and arrived unannounced on her doorstep. "Destiny, may I come in to speak to you?"

"Ian, how nice of you to come for a chat. Although, I don't feel up to discussing metaphysics or such tonight. Maybe another time..." Destiny almost closed the door in his face.

"Destiny...*hear* me now. I need to come in and speak to you," he insisted, and placed his foot to the doorstop so it would not close.

"Oh, well, then…come in. What is so important? Are you all right?"

"I am fine, it is *you* I am worried about, Destiny. I know you too well to not recognize something is amiss. Remember, we have shared an intuitional connection for a long time now. I know you are not yourself. Tell me what is wrong, perhaps I can help," Ian said in soft tones, and then sat down on the couch motioning for Destiny to do the same. "Now, what is it?"

"Oh, Ian…I don't know where to begin," she moaned.

"At the beginning, Destiny…always start at the beginning."

Destiny shared her agonizing past with Ian that night, and cried on his waiting shoulder. He offered his sympathetic understanding, and she felt a sense of relief. Ian insisted that if Jess loved her as he proclaimed, he would feel only deep compassion for what she had experienced. At that moment, Destiny knew she would share her story with Jess the next time they were together.

"Oh, I am so happy for them!" shouted Luana. "My dream about Destiny and Jess has come to pass." Tears began to form in Luana's eyes as she envisioned the couple walking off into a sunset framed by a sandy shoreline as she had dreamed. Now that she knew the story was an autobiography, the book delighted Luana's romantic nature even more. It was late, but she could not wait another day to read the book's conclusion. She walked to her bathroom to wash the makeup from her face, hoping the cool water would help keep her awake. Before reopening the book, she hesitated a moment to run a movie in her mind of what she hoped would unfold for Destiny. That way, she theorized, even if the storyline ended differently, she could always imagine the ending as she desired. Her mind-movie included Destiny sharing her past with Jess. Of course, he being the upright chap he was, he would take her into his arms in consolation and compassion. The movie-image in her mind ended with the lovers standing in the sand encircled by seabirds and the hues of a majestic sunset.

Luana couldn't help but began, once again, to reminisce about her life with Edward through their years together. After their marriage, Edward's counseling practice continued to thrive. They decided to keep both of their beach homes, which allowed them to work in their separate locations without having their patients seek new counsel. They would schedule several days to be at one home and then several at the next. They always had their evenings and days off together. Edward was about ten years Luana's senior, and this arrangement worked for almost ten years of marriage, until Edward turned sixty-five and was about to retire. At this time, they agreed that their finances would not be able to accommodate the two homes after Edward's retirement, so he moved to Laguna to live with Luana. Their love flourished as she continued to take several days off a week to stroll the beaches with her devoted Edward. When Edward had his stroke, he was left with some minor disabilities and Luana was glad he had already sold his home in Torrance. It would have been much more stressful for her to manage it all alone. Luana felt their life together had been more blissful than she could have imagined. Edward passed away just before his seventy-fifth birthday in 2011.

Second-thinking her decision to plow through to the end of her book, Luana closed its cover. *How can I read the end of this tale without first knowing it will end happily? I have invested way too much emotion in this book for it not to end on a positive note!* Then she said out loud, "Perhaps I should wait before finishing it, or not finish it at all! What if this woman's life ends in another painful play of circumstances? How would I be able to sleep knowing Destiny might, even now, be going through a less than content and happy life? I could try to find her and ask her. I wonder if she still lives in Cheltenham? Maybe she actually moved to Newport Beach, which is just a few miles from here! Oh, I hate to think what she would be going through if her dear Jess were not still at her side."

Luana tucked the book between two others in a row of dozens frozen in place on the bookshelf. She was not ready to read the final chapter. She was not able to allow herself to feel Destiny's pain if she did, in fact, live the rest of her life alone and abandoned by her only true love. Luana's sleep was tortured for several nights with visions of babies left crying in long dark halls that led to nowhere, and tidal waves lapping over fishing piers demolishing small villages. She dreamed of

Destiny and Jess laughing as they walked the boardwalk hand in hand, and then of Destiny standing on her old tree log screaming to the sky that she no longer wanted to live. Luana awoke in the morning rubbing her swollen eyelids and dragged herself to the kitchen to brew her ginger tea with lemon. Her women's group was to meet later that day, and she must prepare her materials. She wanted to introduce a new book to her group that she knew they all would enjoy, and that might help them sort through their lives and view it more positively. It was titled, *As a Man Thinketh*.

Twenty-six

"Recently, my dreams have been all over the place," Luana told the women in her group. "I guess it's because I have been reading a book for the past several months which I have allowed to enter my very being. There is such a similarity between the main character and myself that I think I have become attached to the storyline in a bizarre type of admiration transference! I am sharing this with you today because I want each of you to think back through your dreams over the past few weeks to consider if you have influenced them in some way. There may even be an actual experience you have had, or are having currently, that has seeped into your subconscious to spark a particular dream. I am quite positive my dream state has been stimulated and swayed by the story in my book, which I cannot seem to get out of my mind!"

"Well, I have done that exact same thing!" Jo Ann shared. I got so tangled up in a novel once that it almost felt like I was the heroine!"

"I can relate to how one could do that, Jo Ann. Is anyone else having an extraordinarily active dream life and would like to share it with the group?"

"Lately, my dreams have centered on my childhood, or what I know of it," Emma exclaimed. "Or, my guide Rachael enters a dream to tell me something. When you hypnotized me, Luana, I remember you told me to listen for a message that Rachael might share with me. Well, a few nights ago, I had a dream that Rachael told me I had been adopted as a young child. The dream was so vivid I almost called my mother to inquire if it was actually true!"

"Emma, because we have discussed your close connection with Rachael, I suggest you do just that! You have mentioned you don't have much of a memory of yourself earlier than five or six years old. I'd think you might be curious to follow through with your dream's instruction, even if only to get more details from your mother about your childhood. Do you think it would terribly upset your parents to inquire about it?"

"Oh, I don't know…maybe. I imagine Mother might think I was crazy to come up with such a silly question, but doubt she would be emotionally affected. If I have that same dream again, I'll call her to ask more questions. I'll be sure to let you all know what she says, if I do call."

"Well, all right then. Let's get to this little book I have for each of you," Luana said, as she passed out the small yellow books. She asked Emma to begin reading the first page.

Emma read aloud:

> The aphorism "As a man thinketh in his heart so is he," not only embraces the whole of a man's being, but is so comprehensive as to reach out to every condition and circumstance of his life. A man is literally what he thinks, his character being the complete sum of all his thoughts…

Emma stopped reading to exclaim, "Why does this book only refer to *men*? Where are the women? It seems a lot of books were written this way in the past, it's unsettling. I understand what the author is trying to convey, even though it is in a rather old fashioned way. It means that we create our future by what our thoughts have been and are today. Is that correct, Luana?"

"Exactly! As we get deeper into this tiny gem of a book, we'll explore the metaphysical laws handed down for many generations by well-educated people all over the world. This book was written in 1921, and I've had the fortunate opportunity to study it early in my life. Later in the book, the author continues his lecture about thoughts creating our reality by writing: *Good thoughts and actions can never produce bad results; bad thoughts and actions can never produce good results.* Let's discuss this theory." They continued studying the book until the two hours had quickly passed.

After clearing the living room of tea cups and snacks, and leftover books and pens, Luana sat on her sofa in deep thought. *I can clearly see how my thoughts and actions throughout my life have formed who I am today. If I truly believe what I know and teach, I should be able to accept whatever Destiny has created for her life as valid and as it should be.* "I must finish reading my book!" Luana said out loud. She walked to her bedroom trying to remember between which two volumes she had hid her precious book. *Why is it so difficult for me to remember something I did only this morning?* she admonished herself. She finally spied the prized book's spine snuggled next to her hard copy of *Seat of the Soul*. She tossed it onto her bed and jumped beside it to devour its last few chapters. Luana was now ready to discover how Destiny's thoughts, actions, and reactions had directed her life, and helped mold her into the woman she was today, a notable author.

Destiny became bored and disillusioned at work due to the current teaching arrangements. She felt she could not enlist her creative and unique massage methods when there was another teacher presenting her techniques. She felt a bit self-conscious, and began doubting her teaching abilities. This new development at work resulted in her plummeting self-esteem. She started to feel defeated between the ominous decision to talk to Jess about her past, and this new issue surrounding her teaching ability. Ian's words echoed in her mind...*if Jess truly loves you, he will feel only compassion for you.* Destiny held tight to that thought and tried desperately to believe in Ian's insight. Jess had made plans to fly over sometime during the end of June, and related that he was eager to meet her parents during this trip. He also wanted to finalize the plans for Destiny to move into his beach cottage before summer's end. He insisted she needed to experience California in all its glory during the summer months. Destiny agreed, and once again prepared for his arrival. She notified the college and the spa of her intentions that she would be moving. Lastly, she rang up her mum to let them know she would be bringing Jess to meet them.

Destiny wanted her heart to be filled with as much joy and love as she had experienced during Jess' initial visit, but a dark cloud hovered above her. Nonetheless, she made a commitment to herself that she would share her complete story with him during this visit, even though the weight of it was almost more than she could tolerate. She decided to ring up her mum to discuss her concerns.

"Mum, it's me. Do you have time to chat?"

"Destiny, of course, dear. I can always make time to chat with you. What is bothering you? There is a strange tone to your voice. Are you ill?"

"No, Mum. I am not ill. As you know, Jess will be arriving soon and I so want you to meet him. However, that's not the reason I rang you up. It's that...well, I have not shared with him about my pregnancy. I am beside myself with grief that he will be so upset, he will never want to see me again!" Destiny's shaky voice turned to sobs.

"Oh, my dear! You are too hard on yourself. If he loves you as he proclaims, he will stay by your side. Love overcomes a great deal, Destiny, as you and I can attest. You must tell him now, or he may find out in another manner and then you would be heart stricken."

"I know you are right, it's just so hard for me to talk about it. I haven't even told Father yet. I know I am stronger than my past experiences, and that I must forge on with it...mustn't I?"

"Yes, my dear, but I must admit to you at this time, I shared your experience with your father. I broke my promise to you, Destiny. But please know, he was so very sorry for your having to go through it all alone. He even remarked that he had the same sorrowful feelings that he had had for me when I shared my past incident with him. Please know we both love and support you, no matter your past. Your past has become a part of us. It will also become a part of Jess as he opens himself to receive it with compassion. He will love you no less, Destiny. Feel that inside yourself now..."

"All right, then, Mum. I am glad Father knows. I will brave it all! *As a tree stands, I am strong.*" Destiny repeated the words for the umpteenth time, since finding her cherished book of poetry so long ago.

The arrangements for Jess' visit were set, and Destiny finally felt a sense of relief. The plans were confirmed that Jess would meet her parents during this trip, and the couple would declare their engagement and their plans to live in California. Destiny wanted Jess in her life no matter where they lived, and was excited to move to California as soon as she could get her employment situation finalized. Everyone at the spa was happy and excited for her when she shared her plans. However, when she told the college administration board, excitement was not the reaction. They did agree to give Destiny the highest recommendations, if she chose to continue teaching in America.

Ian volunteered to retrieve Jess from the airport because he wanted a bit of alone time to chat with him. During the return drive, the two fellows discovered they had more in common than either of them realized and discussed metaphysics the entire time. By the time they approached the Wyman's Brook cottages, they both agreed their souls had incarnated to experience previous lifetimes together!

"Jess, I can tell you truly love Destiny. I wish you both much happiness. There is a good chance I may be moving to the States also, and will be sure to look you up if I do," Ian announced, as he stepped from his motorcar.

"Spot-on! The three of us would have a bloody time. What is your trade then?"

"I was offered a professorship at the university in Irvine. It is located rather near the beach where you live."

"Brillant!" Jess exclaimed.

Arriving at Destiny's front door, the fellows were shaking hands when she opened it. "I see you two have taken on with each other. I knew you chaps would chum it up once the time was allotted." Destiny kissed Jess on the cheek while patting Ian on the back. "Ian, can you stay for supper?"

"Lovely, I would love to. Shall I lay the table for you?"

The evening supper was shared between the three with a lighthearted discussion surrounding the theories of the big bang and evolution. Ian invited Jess to attend the upcoming metaphysical group, and Destiny further explained what the group entailed. She said this meeting might be her last before her move. Jess was fascinated and accepted the invitation. As Ian left, he whispered in Destiny's ear, "I totally approve." He smiled and winked his blue-eyed wink. She took this as his way of encouraging her to tell Jess everything about her past, and there would be no worries.

During his prior visit, Jess had slipped into Destiny's bed knowing he would be welcomed. This visit was no different and he followed her directly to her bedroom after Ian left. "What a brilliant chap he is, I rather like him. We seem to have much in common." Jess began to unpack his bags.

"I am happy to see you getting on with him. Jess, come over here to sit with me. I have something I must tell you." Destiny patted the bed covers for him to join her.

"What is it, love?" Jess asked, with a puzzled look.

"I should have told you long before now about the complete incident surrounding my rape as a teen. I have had a rather difficult time sharing the entire experience with anyone. Please do not interrupt me, or I shan't get through it." Destiny took a deep breath, and then focused her eyes directly into his. "As I had shared many years ago with you, when I was seventeen I was raped. I was a virgin. I will not go through the details again. I rather hope you have forgotten all that you envisioned when I first shared about it. My story does not end there. I became pregnant." At this point, Destiny's eyes filled with tears. This had not happened when telling her mum, or Ian. She began to cry uncontrollably and flopped face down into the pillows

Jess wanted to comfort her, but remained sitting upright thinking he should not interrupt her story. He reached over and gently stroked her back, allowing her to continue as she desired. Destiny raised her head slightly to whisper between her tears, "Jess, I gave my baby up for adoption."

The cottage bedroom waited in silence for Jess to respond. He lay silently beside her until her sobs subsided. He cupped her head in his hands and she opened her eyes to see tears trailing down his cheeks. Destiny whispered, "I am so sorry I did not share this with you before, but was too ashamed. I didn't even know I was feeling this much emotion until now. I really thought I had made the best decision for the baby. Now, I can only pray it was the right one. Please do not hate me, Jess..."

"Hate you? I could never hate you, dear Destiny. I feel only empathy for you, as if I have also experienced your pain. You could never tell me anything that would make me hate you. We still have much to share with each other. I am honored you were able to tell me your secret, and share with me how you have become who you are today. I love you dearly..." Jess wrapped his arms around Destiny, and they remained entwined until morning.

Destiny awoke first. She slipped out of bed and into the lavatory. She studied her face in the gold-framed mirror hanging over the facet. There were no marks of shame, no signs of the humiliation she had felt the night before. In fact, her face radiated an element she had never seen before. It was the glow of self-forgiveness, and an inner acceptance of her emotions. She had finally released her feelings of regret for giving up her child. The revelation entered her very being as she sat on the edge of the water closet. *All these years I have resisted my thoughts of regret, silently keeping myself burdened with what I assumed was an unforgiving past. How could I not recognize this?* She softly mused, "This must be what Penny meant when she told me: "Life can be difficult, but remember you hold the key to your own happiness. There may be a need for you to forgive yourself in order to move into your future."

Beginning that day, Destiny and Jess made a pact to be totally honest with each other. Their relationship bloomed as they shared their innermost feelings with openness and compassion. Jess released his own pent-up emotions surrounding his accident and how it had affected him. He told Destiny that he still harbored anger over losing his leg, and would work on letting it go. Destiny was able to help steady Jess' emotions as she listened to his heartfelt story. She developed even more love and admiration for him.

Toward the end of Jess' two week visit, they traveled to visit Destiny's parents where the four celebrated the young couple's engagement. Jess and Henry hit it off and talked business the entire stay, while Destiny and her mum secluded themselves to discuss the details of how she'd met Jess many years ago. Helen was amazed at the story of running into Jess a second time in America. She was also very impressed with the couple's determination to keep their relationship alive. Destiny's parents were thrilled when they heard the news of the upcoming wedding, and eagerly accepted the invitation to travel to California to be present at the ceremony. Later that evening, Destiny shared with her mum, "I am so happy, Mum! Jess is a splendid chap and I love him dearly. I was able to tell him about the rape and my baby's adoption…he completely stood by me. I could not ask for a better person to spend the rest of my life with!"

"I am happy for you, Destiny. I sense a different emotion surrounding your past. The fact that you said the word *baby* makes me think you have worked though some feelings about your decision. Am I correct?"

"Mum, while I was telling Jess about being pregnant and all, I became aware of feelings which I buried so deep even I had not realized them. I know it cannot be changed, the documents are signed an all; but if there were a way for me to find the child, I would at least visit to know it was happy and had loving parents. Oh, I do pray a lovely couple is cherishing the child!" Destiny whispered, as tears formed in her eyes.

"Dear Destiny…my heart breaks for you. I trust you will know how to proceed as your emotions become more clear," Helen whispered back, tightly hugging her daughter.

The visit ended with firm approval all around between Jess, Destiny, and her parents. The four hugged and waved as the young couple left the Collins' manor. On their return trip to Swindon Village, Destiny asked Jess to pull off the thoroughfare when they entered Worcester. "Pull off a bit, Jess. I need to show you something. I feel a strong urge to visit the place where I stayed and gave birth to my baby. I am not sure why, maybe because I finally feel free from the emotional burden of it all, since I shared my experience with you. Do you suppose they would let me know if the baby was a girl or a boy?"

"Are you sure you want to do this, Destiny? It could be very upsetting for you," Jess warned.

"No, I'm not really sure at toll. There's just something telling me to stop off and visit the place again. The way is to the west through the roundabout somewhere. I don't really know the direction, but I'll remember the way as it gets close. Drive ahead that way. She pointed in the direction she was intuiting. "There! Over that way, it should be right there!" Destiny shouted to Jess.

However, when their motorcar came to a stop, the building that hung in her memory like an old oil painting was not there. Only an empty lot surrounded with wire fencing stared back at her. Destiny jumped out to read the post on the fence around the property. It read: "The Charter Manor for Women has been demolished for reasons of instability and rotting."

Destiny returned to the motorcar and whispered, "I doubt if the records could be verified anyway, I didn't use my real name on the documents. I guess it is fitting that I never find out."

"Destiny, we must trust our spiritual beliefs and trust that if you are to learn about the child, it will be revealed."

As Luana finished reading the last page of the book she had treasured for so long, she had not realized how shallow her breathing had been and involuntarily took in one long breath. She felt a sense of relief as she closed the back cover, but also a strange sadness. Luana had learned that sometimes when we finish a creative project or attain a sought-after achievement, a certain amount of time needs to elapse before we can accept its completion. She immediately felt a sense of longing that the story had not satisfied her quest for a happy ending. Setting it beside her on the bed, she sighed and mumbled, "Oh, I don't want the book to end! It is such a magnificent account...so telling of one's spiritual journey. I wish the author would have shared more current information with her readers. Did she ever find her child? Did she and Jess stay together? I have way too many questions to be satisfied with this ending!" Realizing there may be an Afterword in the back of the book, she quickly picked it up and fanned the pages to reach the end. There she found a final entry:

Author's Note

I have written this book to share my story with others who have experienced an imperfect past and may require a bit of encouragement to shed pent up emotions, or the pangs of regret. Many of the metaphysical concepts explored within the book have guided me through my life with insight and compassion. This book is also a means for me to seek public assistance in locating the child I gave birth to on July 12, 1976 in the city of Worcester, Worcestershire, England. I am hoping someone may read my story and pass the book on to those who might know of more information than I was able to obtain.

My life has been uniquely happy through the years, albeit, the loss of sharing it with my child. I didn't include my later years within the pages here, in hopes of writing a second book to *Finding Destiny,* one in which I have found my child. However, I will share that Jess and I married on the California beach where our souls met a second time to reunite our love. Under a magnificent sunset in the summer of 1985, we shared our vows and have lived a magical life together for almost thirty years. We still maintain our beach cottage and stroll the sandy shoreline with gratitude in our hearts for the synchronicities that brought us together not once, but twice.

I have become the author of several fiction novels, mostly written while sitting near the ocean's endless waves. At fifty-six years old, the only regret I have as this book goes to press is that I have not known my only child. I don't know the child's gender, or who adopted him or her. I pray they provided well for the child as I had intended. There has been an empty space in my heart since that day in 1985 when I admitted to myself, and my dear Jess, that I had regrets for giving my baby up for adoption. My admission was not an easy one, but necessary for me to begin my self-forgiveness process.

After discovering that the Charter Manor for Women had been torn down to the ground, I inquired where I might obtain birth records for the babies born there, but to no avail. My hope is that one day a dear reader will know of someone whose life may fit in tandem with my own as I have shared between these pages. I have faith that if I am to meet my child, he or she will be directed to search for me. I trust in the Divine Oneness that if we are to meet in this lifetime, it will transpire.

As you have read herein, I firmly believe in the magical metaphysics of our Universe. I feel that each of us contains strength unrealized until our consciousness awakens to encompass a greater Intelligence than our own. This Higher Consciousness moves within us to harbor our fears, shelter our pain, and direct our lives toward the lessons our souls have chosen. We must trust our sacred intuition to lead us to the life that reveals our destiny.

Contact information:

Destiny Collins Drew
#7 Twenty-Seventh Avenue
Newport Beach, CA 92663

Twenty-seven

Luana again set the book beside her, and then retrieved it to reread the last few paragraphs from the author's notes. She was happy to learn of Destiny's successful marriage to Jess, and the fact that she may continue to write her heartfelt life's story in a second follow-up book. After a few minutes in silent reflection, she had a vision and started shouting, "Oh, my god! Could Emma be Destiny's child?" Her mind began skipping through different paragraphs within the book, and matching up some of the conversations she had had with Emma. Then she made a conscious effort to sit quietly, allowing her mind to reconstruct the book's storyline. She closed her eyes and focused on clues that would affirm her intuition. After meditating for several minutes, her suspicions couldn't be traced to any definite conclusion. Then, it hit her. She opened her eyes wide and asked her question aloud, "What is Emma's birth date? If this date matches the birth date of Destiny's baby, that might cinch my intuitive hunch. I have known intuitively that there has been a reason I have been so infatuated with Destiny's life, even to the point of dreaming and writing about her. I thought the synchronicities between our lives was the reason, because I recognized many of my own struggles within her life's journey. Now, I am feeling that *I* may be the link to joining Destiny with her daughter!"

Luana soon realized that she would have Emma's date of birth on the astrology chart she had made for her at the beginning of the women's group months earlier. She rushed to her office to find the folder that contained the group member's charts. "Here it is!" Scanning the chart, she shouted, "Oh my god! Emma's birthday is the same date!" Her heart raced as she held the chart to her breasts. "I just know she is Destiny's daughter."

Early the following day, Luana called Emma. There was no answer, so she left a message for her to return the call. She waited anxiously, until she heard her phone ring late that afternoon. "Hello?"

"Hi, Luana, this is Emma. What's up? Are you all right?"

"Oh, yes, I am fine. I wanted to discuss something with you and wondered if you could stop by either this evening or sometime tomorrow?"

"Yes, of course. Would early evening be okay?" Emma asked.

"Yes, that'll be great. Stop by about five o'clock."

"Okay, see you then."

Luana was so anxious she wanted to confirm Emma's birth date with her as soon as she opened the door. Instead, she felt it would be better if she slowly explained her unsubstantiated intuition before assuming it was accurate. She began by saying, "Emma, I know you've been concerned about your dreams and what Rachael related to you about being adopted as a child. Also, I realize the fact that you can't remember your early childhood years has been unsettling for you. Well, I have got to share with you a book I just finished reading."

Luana showed Emma the book and explained some of the details of the author's journey. Then she concluded, "I think you might be Destiny's child! I've received a strong intuitional feeling about this, Emma. It came after I completed reading the book last evening. Look here on the last page written by the author, it states that she gave birth to her child on July 12, 1976. Isn't that your birthday, Emma?"

"Oh, my god! That *is* my birthday! At least the date I have always been told it was. I have never seen my birth certificate. Oh, Luana, could this really be true? How could I find out? Should I call my mother now and not wait for another Rachael dream? Why did the author give her baby away? Oh, my god! I have so many questions!"

"Let's take this one step at a time. I would suggest that first you call your mother and ask her to tell you honestly if you were adopted, and if so, was it while they still lived in England. If her answer is yes, we could proceed to find the author of the book, Destiny. She just might be your birth mother! I would also ask your mother if she has your original birth records. I'll be here supporting you all the way, Emma."

"Yes, that's the best way, I think. Oh, Luana, I must call her right away! Can I use your phone to call Mother right now? I don't think it's too late back in Maine to catch her before going to bed. I need to know this minute what her answer is."

"Of course, Emma. There's a phone in the kitchen you can use," Luana said, and pointed the way.

"Oh, Luana, I want you to be beside me. Please come to listen in."

"Okay, sure." Luana followed Emma into the kitchen.

Emma was able to reach her mother before she went to bed, and briefly explained why she was going to ask her the question which needed to be answered. "Mom, please do not get upset; but tell me truthfully, did you and Dad adopt me as a young child while you were still living in England? The reason I am asking is if I was adopted there is a chance my birth mother may be living near me, right here in California. It would mean a great deal to me if I could meet her to find out. You know I love you, Mother. This has nothing to do with you or Dad, or how you raised me."

"What dear? What are you saying? Did you ask if you were adopted?" Emma's mother whispered in confusion.

"Yes, mother. It's okay if I was…I just need to know now. You know I love you, and you will always be my real mother. But, it is important for me to know the truth. If I was adopted as a child in England, there is a chance this woman is the one that gave birth to me and I might be able to meet her. I feel I just have to know the truth," Emma said gently, as her eyes began to fill with tears.

"Yes, dear, I dare say. I should have told you long ago, but the opportunity never found my voice. I fancy you will always be my daughter, Emma. You know I do love you as if I had given birth to you. Are you well where you are living, dear? I do miss you. Do you need anything, dear?" Emma's mother continued asking her daughter questions with no further reference to the topic of adoption. It was as if there was nothing more for her to share on the subject.

Emma didn't want to upset her mother, and realized she could ask more questions at a later time. She thanked her mother for telling her the truth, and told her she was doing well and that she missed them both. Hanging up the phone, Emma turned to Luana and said, "I must read that book!"

A few days later, after the women's group ended, Emma stayed to talk with Luana about the book. "Oh, my god, Luana! I loved reading this book! I tried to get a sense if I could be Destiny's daughter, but the reach was too far. I guess it's because I am so close to my parents and cherish what we have experienced together through the years. My heart went out to the young heroine for all she endured. I certainly learned a great deal about the spiritual concept of manifestation! If Destiny really is my birth mother, it certainly would be lovely to meet her; she seems like a wonderful person. I even looked her up online to read about her other books. Many of them sound really interesting. There were also other photographs of her, and I believe there is some resemblance between us. I could not find a telephone listing for her name, however."

"I am happy you found the book intriguing, Emma. I absolutely savored it for several months. As for contacting Destiny, I know the exact location of the address she provided at the back of the book. I would be happy to drive you there one day, if you wish to meet her in person to discuss the possibility of your being her daughter."

"That would be great! I have to remember that she wants to connect with her child, so I wouldn't really be intruding. Also, I need to realize the fact that I may not be her daughter, and not to be too disappointed. My birthday may be only a coincidence of dates. Whatever the outcome, I would be willing to investigate it." Emma smiled, as she added, "As you have taught us so well: *Dreams are the seedlings of realities*. I know now that I can't ignore my dreams. Rachael came to me while deep in a dream to tell me I was adopted and that certainly became a reality! Perhaps the fact of you reading and sharing this book with me is also a synchronistic event I should not ignore. I feel a need to unravel the truth behind my adoption, even if it works out that Destiny is not my mother. One day, I will return to England myself to search for any possible records of my birth."

"I could not have said it better, Emma. When would be a good day for us go visit Destiny?"

"Saturday seems like the day to me. I have it off, and have the entire weekend free. Does that work for you?"

"Perfect. Why don't I meet you at your house, since you live so close to Newport Beach? I will be happy to drive you to the address that was given in the book."

"Perfect indeed," repeated Emma. "I can't believe this is really happening!"

Saturday afternoon arrived quickly for Emma. During the last few days, she kept rereading different chapters of the book, trying to visualize Destiny and her life's journey. She even put herself in Destiny's situation to ascertain what she would have done if she had been raped at seventeen and become pregnant. In the end, Emma realized Destiny's journey was not her own, and she shouldn't try to guess what her reactions would be to someone else's life experience. She felt only compassion for Destiny, even though it was difficult for her to relate to her painful experience entirely. She thought, *I guess the only true similarity I possess with Destiny is that we both experienced a difficult childhood. I am so happy that she found the love of her life and hope it lasts forever between her and Jess. I have given up on that dream.*

On Saturday morning, Emma dressed in a lightweight sundress and sandals. The sun was already exceptionally warm for a spring day that seventh of May in 2015. Luana was to arrive at noon. Emma glanced into her large mirror standing on a wooden pedestal in her bedroom and saw the woman she expected. Her blonde-streaked hair had become even lighter the past few years while living at the beach. She was always proud of her tall stature and stood with her back and shoulders straight to outwardly state the fact. She accepted her nearly thirty-nine years without being overly upset about her romantic losses. She knew she had gained that stiff-upper-lip mentality from her mother's English heritage. Adjusting her hemline, she turned to gaze again upon the book that may change her life's journey from this day forward. Studying the cover artwork, she smiled as she recognized the beach scene as the famous Newport Beach Pier at sunset. She so enjoyed walking to the end of that pier to watch the seagulls circle high above her to search the deep sea below for signs of life.

Her new adventure living in California had brought her an independence she had never experienced. She loved her teaching job and coming home to the quaint beach community she chose to move to on a whim while visiting California's coastline during summer break. She easily found a teaching position in a nearby private school. When she moved into her little house, Emma didn't know of the town's high reputation for hosting influential people and noted celebrities. She would always remember how embarrassed she became when seated next to a table where a famous movie star was eating his dinner in one of the fine dining establishments in Balboa.

Luana arrived right at noon and rang the doorbell of Emma's yellow stucco house wedged between two larger homes. She glanced around to inspect the three chimes made of shells hanging over the porch landing, and thought, *A person has to really love living at the beach to do so. Emma certainly seems to enjoy where she has settled.* She rang the doorbell and listened to Emma's footsteps rush down a hallway and into the entry.

"Come in, Luana," Emma said, and opened the door wide. "You are right on time as usual. I have to say, I am a bit nervous at the thought of arriving unannounced on the doorstep of someone I don't know. What will I say?"

"I can only imagine what you are feeling, Emma. Just be yourself and perhaps begin by telling Destiny how you have just finished reading her book. You might add a bit about your Rachael dream as well, and how you have recently discovered you were adopted. I will be right there to support you. If Destiny is anything like the woman she portrays in her book, I am sure she will be more than happy to talk with you," Luana said assuredly.

Luana drove Emma directly to 27th Avenue in Newport. She parked a few doors away from the address of the beach house mentioned in the book. Over the years, the modest little cottage described in the book had certainly been upgraded to a much more stylish modern home. Although, it did still have the white picket fence and dozens of seashell wind chimes hanging from the porch. Emma knocked on the front door and a handsome man with a graying beard appeared. He smiled, and then asked, "What can I do for you two young ladies?"

"Well, my name is Emma Wells. I am looking for the author, Destiny Collins, who wrote this book," Emma announced, and held the book to display its cover. "Is this the correct address where she lives?"

"Yes, yes, Destiny lives here. However, she is not home at the moment. She is out walking by the ocean, a daily ritual to be sure. I am her husband, Jess Drew. Does she know you are coming to visit then?"

"No, I am afraid not. We didn't have a number to call ahead, it's not listed. Perhaps we could wait in the car to see if she returns soon?"

"Why don't you walk on the beach a bit? No doubt you'll run right into her, especially if you stay close to the water. She usually walks to the pier in the dry sand or along the walkway, and then returns close to the shore. It's about time for her to be returning home. If you miss each other, return here and I'll set you up with tea until she arrives."

"Oh, that is a splendid idea," Emma agreed, and turned to Luana to ask, "Are you up for a stroll on the beach, Luana?"

"I am always ready to walk in the sand...let's do it!"

The women said their good-byes to Jess without explaining their mission, and walked to the oceanfront. They took in the beauty of the waves and felt the warm sun on their faces. For the short time Emma had lived in Balboa, she assumed the same fascination with the Pacific Ocean as Destiny had written about so eloquently. As they approached the warm water, Emma allowed the small waves to caress her legs without questioning if her dress would become drenched. She ran back and forth from the salty water as a child exploring the sea for the first time.

Luana, on the other hand, was focused entirely on searching for Destiny. She intuitively knew she would recognize the author if they passed by her, and began to examine the face of each woman coming toward them. It didn't take long, Luana recognized a woman approaching who looked exactly like the portrait photo on the back cover of the book.

"Emma, I think the woman approaching us is Destiny!" Luana leaned over to whisper in Emma's ear.

Emma raised her head from studying a large spiral shell peeking through the wet sand to see a woman with shoulder length brown hair bleached by the sun. She was wearing a pair of white wide-legged pants and a blousy turquoise gauze shirt. The woman had a large sunhat in her left hand and was looking down at her feet sinking beneath the moist sand as gentle waves eased over them. When they approached, Luana softly said, "Hello there...we don't want to disturb you, but we are looking for an author named Destiny Collins. Could that be you?"

"Why yes, I am Destiny...Destiny Collins. Can I help you?" she said, and raised her head locking eyes with Emma.

"Hello, Destiny. My name is Emma Wells and I...well, I just finished reading your book, *Finding Destiny*. And, I...well, I think I may be your daughter!" Emma blurted out with no warning.

"Oh, my god! I didn't actually believe anyone would respond to my message in the back of the book. I must say, I am overwhelmed. We must discuss this, shan't we? Emma is it?" Destiny motioned for the women to sit beside her in the dry sand.

With the ocean as their backdrop, the three women introduced themselves and began asking question after question between them. Instantly, Luana intuitively recognized that she was sitting beside a mother and her daughter. She listened to their conversation as they discovered each other's lives, and how they might confirm her suspicion that Emma was Destiny's daughter. Emma began to explain to Destiny how Luana had read the book and made the connection between them, and then loaned her the book to read. Destiny shared her appreciation to Luana for following her intuition. The three women talked about their love of books and their love of the issues surrounding metaphysics. They shared with each other how many of the spiritual concepts they all studied had influenced their lives.

At one point, Luana interjected, "Destiny, I do believe you have finally found your daughter. I am so happy for you both. I know you will continue to unravel the truth to this miracle. There was certainly an element of mystery to our timely connections. I believe we were destined to meet for many reason, and will be discovering many paths together. I am wondering if you both would like to be alone for a time. Emma, since you live so close, I am sure you can manage to get home if I were to leave now?" Luana rose from her sandy seat.

"Oh, Luana, thank you for your incredible intuition and in helping me find Destiny, who I now believe is my birth mother! Yes, I can take a cab or ride the bus home later," Emma said, as she rose to meet Luana in a long hug.

"You will do no such thing, Emma. Jess and I will drive you home after you have dinner with us!" Destiny insisted, and also stood to engulf both women in a group hug. She turned to face Luana, and said, "Luana, thank you again for your insight and incredible intuition. I'll get your number from Emma and will be ringing you up soon so we can chat. I will give Emma our number, so please feel free to contact me also."

Luana left the beach filled with an array of positive emotions, and secure that her intuitive abilities were still intact. She once again acknowledged how the Universe brings the right experiences at the exact moment needed to ensure our soul's journey. As she made her way through the warm sand, she watched the rolling waves race one across the other as the incoming tide forced them to explore the dry sandy beach. Then she approached the rhythmic waters and allowed herself the joy of feeling its splash upon her feet and ankles. She soon lost herself quickly in the timeless bliss of eternal motion that is called the sea.

While approaching the avenue where she had parked her car, Luana stopped to study the white beach cottage where Destiny and Jess had made their home together. A spark of excitement arose as the idea came to her to knock again upon the door to speak to Jess Drew. She had no hesitation in her gait as her pace quicken to the pathway. Knocking loudly on the front door, Luana waited patiently with a confidence she could feel inside. Jess opened the door to greet Luana a second time, "Hello again, I didn't catch your name but you were with Emma. Did you two find Destiny?"

"Hello Jess, my name is Luana. Yes, we had no problem recognizing Destiny as she walked toward us on the beach. Emma and she are still chatting, and I felt an impulse to stop on my way back to my car. I have to tell you, Jess, I found myself so involved in Destiny's book that I felt a part of it! Also, I am so very happy for you and Destiny to have found each other again. I know the feeling of finding one's soulmate...and couldn't be happier for you both."

"Brilliant! Thank you, Luana. Sometimes, I cannot believe it myself. Would you like to come in for a cup of tea? I would like to hear why you were so intent on finding Destiny."

"Well, one day I will take you up on your offer, but today, I must be getting home. I don't drive as well at night anymore and the sun is fast on his journey to see the other side of our planet. Oh, and the reason Emma and myself were interested in finding Destiny is I have a hunch that Emma may be her daughter." Luana looked Jess straight in the eyes.

"Oh, my god! That is spot-on! I cannot wait to learn more of this!"

"I will let the two girls tell you the story when they return. I am so glad you are pleased, Jess. It makes for such a great ending to Destiny's book and your lives together, don't you think?"

"I would say so, Luana. There is much more to Destiny's journey, however. I hope one day she will decide to write about it," Jess teased Luana.

"Oh, happy day! Another book would be grand!" Luana shouted. She offered her hand for Jess to shake good-bye, but he surrounded her in a warm hug instead. Luana knew this was just the beginning of their friendship.

As Emma and Destiny sat mesmerized while watching Luana continue down the beach, Destiny whispered, "Luana is a special person, Emma. I am blessed to have met her today." Then facing Emma, she continued, "Jess told me many years ago that if I was supposed to meet my child, it would happen. And now, I feel strongly that you are my daughter, Emma."

"I certainly can see the resemblance between us, and of course the fact that my birthday is the same day that you gave birth to your baby is terribly synchronistic. The difficult thing for me to understand is if I was left in an orphanage to be adopted, why can't I remember those several years of my younger childhood? Evidently, you never had your baby with you, even for a few years, is that correct?"

"Yes, that's correct. I decided I shouldn't even look upon my baby's face. I was in such a fearful and negative disposition back then, and so terribly young. At the time, I truly thought I was doing what was best for my baby. I had no way to raise it; and truthfully Emma, I was put off that it was conceived during an assault by someone I didn't even know. I didn't admit it to myself then, but I was so ashamed of being raped. I later realized that the manner in which a baby is conceived should not be a factor in a woman's decision whether to raise it or not. A baby has nothing to do with how its mother became pregnant, and it certainly should not be blamed in any manner. It is unfortunate this all happened when I was a mere seventeen. Oh, Emma, if I am your birth mother, I'm so very sorry I wasn't present in your life to care for you as a child." Destiny began to cry.

"Oh, please don't cry, Destiny. If I am your daughter, know that I have no anger toward you. My later childhood was a loving one to be sure. I had a dream in which I was told I was adopted, and my mother didn't share this truth with me until I asked her over the telephone just recently. I didn't even know I was adopted until a few days ago! Mother didn't seem to understand what it would mean to me to know I had been adopted. But, she and Father have been wonderful parents to me, and they are aging. I wouldn't want them to know I was upset with them for not telling me sooner. It's just so strange that I can't remember anything younger than about five or six years old. I believe this was before I was adopted, but will need to confirm the age with my mother. Perhaps it is for the best that I don't remember. Maybe I was taken to some terrible place and was treated poorly, so my mind blocked it all out. Well, we don't need to entertain negative thoughts like that, do we? If Luana were still here, she would say something like, 'Now girls, let's only deal with what we know, the past cannot be changed. Let us look toward creating a positive future.' Luana has been such a comforting mentor to me, Destiny. I can't wait for you two to become close friends!"

"Yes, I can envision the three of us walking on the shore talking and laughing, much like sisters. Let's see, Luana must be about ten years my senior and I am fifty-seven, so that would work for us to be sisters. But, I know you are eighteen years younger than me so that makes you thirty-nine. I guess it would be impossible for all of us to be sisters; but, I just know we will all get on well together. We must plan on a gathering soon to continue our new forming friendships. Emma, since you read my book that details much of my early life's path, you know more about me than I do about you. I have many questions to ask you. But, right now, is there anything more you wish to ask me in private?"

"I want to know everything about you! I think it's fantastic that you are also into metaphysics. I loved reading about how your life changed through the years because of your studying books on the subject, and going to groups. I am just learning about the principles of metaphysical thought by attending the group Luana started last fall. I find it all so interesting; she even put me under hypnosis once! I know we have the rest of our lives to learn about each other, but I do have a few more questions that I'm curious about. In your book, you wrote that you tried to find your child. Were you able to find any records at all in Worcester? Oh, and you mentioned you didn't have any other children. Would you feel comfortable telling me why?"

"Well, my dear Emma, Jess and I decided not to have any children together. He felt his disabilities would be restrictive to being able to raise them properly. And I must admit, when I was younger I didn't feel spot-on about having a child to raise, when I had one I did not keep. Looking back on that decision now, I can see the terrible flaws in the rationalization. But, alas! It was our decision at the time. As for actually finding any birth records or such, all my efforts have met a dead end. One reason my search was unsuccessful could very well be because I did not use my real name when signing the adoption documents. Have you had any children, Emma?" asked Destiny, changing the subject.

"No, I haven't. Both of my marriages were not emotionally strong enough to bring a child into them. However, I am okay with not having children of my own. I work with children every day and feel they are all mine." Emma smiled broadly.

"Oh, Emma, that's wonderful! The sun is setting and it will be dark soon; we better get back, or Jess will ring up the Bobbies!"

During a telephone conversation the following day, Emma shared with Luana that she and Destiny stayed on the beach chatting until the sun slipped into the ocean. She told her that she accepted Destiny's dinner invitation, and they talked well into the night comparing notes of their lives. Emma shared that they both acknowledged how they stuffed many emotions deep inside, and only recently learned how to share them or let them go. She related how Destiny asked about her two marriages and any present romantic relationships. Emma said that she asked Destiny how she knew Jess was her true soulmate, and that she also asked her to tell about her parents in England, who were no doubt her own grandparents.

At the end of the phone conversation, Emma reminded Luana that Destiny's birthday had been yesterday, May 7th. She related that Destiny told her that meeting on her birthday was the best gift she could have received. Emma said she talked to Destiny more about herself than she had to anyone ever before. After she concluded telling Luana everything that had happened the previous night, Luana said, "How fortunate you both are to have found each other. I am so proud of you, Emma, and that you trusted your intuition to seek out the truth about your birth."

Luana asked Emma to keep her informed of any progress in documenting that she was, indeed, Destiny's daughter. She also mentioned that if she could help in any manner to be sure to ask. Luana stated in a predicting tone, "I believe there is much more for you and Destiny to discover."

That evening, Luana settled deep in her reading chair and closed her eyes to visualize how Emma and Destiny's relationship would unfold. She was not surprised when a vision entered her mind of Destiny introducing a dinner date to Emma—his name was Ian.

About the Author

Barbara Sinor, PhD, is a retired psychotherapist living in northern California. *Finding Destiny* is Sinor's long awaited first fiction novel. Her other books are highly endorsed in the non-fiction genres of addiction recovery, childhood abuse/incest, adult children of alcoholics, and other self-help and inspirational topics.

Dr. Sinor encourages your comments and can be contacted through her website: DrSinor.com. Sinor's other writing appears in the quarterly *Recovering the Self: A Journal of Hope and Healing*, as well as other magazines, newsletters, and blogs. She currently facilitates women's groups, designs and makes jewelry, and is working on the sequel to *Finding Destiny*.

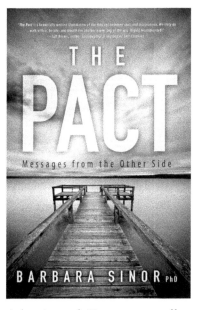

The Pact: Messages from the Other Side takes the reader on an adventure through time while weaving tales of love and determination. A vow between the author and her husband finds us tracing the steps of present and past lifetimes devoted to uncovering the mysterious cycles of life, birth, death, and rebirth.

The author shares the stories of some of her past lives and the insight she gained by channeling her departed husband's words. She shares lifetimes spent in Atlantis and Egypt, as well as, many other time periods. Barbara's stories resonate with readers because of their integrity, detail, documentation, and the sincerity with which they are expressed. Join the author as she searches with her departed husband to reveal their souls' explorations through time and space. *The Pact* is a fascinating mixture of contemporary memoir and past lifetime narratives reconstructed to allow the reader a glimpse into the metaphysics of life.

~ ~ ~

"Every once in awhile you read a book that takes you beyond the edge of the known and into the timeless realm of the soul. *The Pact: Messages from the Other Side* is one of those special books. It takes the reader on a spiritual journey through life after life. Dr. Sinor and her departed husband's personal life pact unfolds as a spiritual memoir that uplifts and inspires, uniting past, present, and future."

—Joan Borysenko, Ph.D.,
New York Times best-selling author

ISBN 978-1-61599-214-0

Marvelous Spirit Press

CPSIA information can be obtained
at www.ICGtesting.com
Printed in the USA
LVHW021102090520
654944LV00004B/292

9 781615 992997